'I've never given you an order,' said Tom, 'not since you were a lad.

'But I'm giving you one now. Go to Melbourne. Look things over for the firm. Take it easy, enjoy yourself, have some fun.'

'Drink, gamble, brawl and find a woman or two while I'm at it. Is that what you're suggesting, Father?'

Thomas's voice was as offensive as he could make it, and his expression was an angry glare. 'Would you prefer me to go the way my grandfather Fred Waring went? A fine piece of advice for an old man to give his grown-up son!'

D0182582

Dear Reader

Some years ago I did a great deal of research on the lives of those men and women who, for a variety of reasons, lived on the frontiers. Re-reading recently about life in Australia in the early nineteenth century, it struck me that an interesting story about them was only waiting to be told. Having written HESTER WARING'S MARRIAGE, it was a short step to wonder what happened to the children and grand-children.

Hence *The Dilhorne Dynasty*, each book of which deals with a member of the family who sets out to conquer the new world in which he finds himself. The Dilhornes, men and women, are at home wherever they settle, be it Australia, England, as in this book, or the United States of America, and because of their zest for life become involved in interesting adventures.

Paula Marshall

Recent titles by the same author:

A STRANGE LIKENESS*
HESTER WARING'S MARRIAGE*
THE QUIET MAN
MISS JESMOND'S HEIR

* The Dilhorne Dynasty

AN INNOCENT MASQUERADE

Paula Marshall

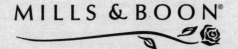

MILLS & BOON®

DID YOU PURCHASE THIS BOOK WITHOUT A COVER?

If you did, you should be aware it is **stolen property** as it was reported
unsold and destroyed by a retailer. Neither the author nor the publisher
has received any payment for this book.

*All the characters in this book have no existence outside the imagination
of the author, and have no relation whatsoever to anyone bearing the
same name or names. They are not even distantly inspired by any
individual known or unknown to the author, and all the incidents are
pure invention.*

*All Rights Reserved including the right of reproduction in whole or in
part in any form. This edition is published by arrangement with
Harlequin Enterprises II B.V. The text of this publication or any part
thereof may not be reproduced or transmitted in any form or by any
means, electronic or mechanical, including photocopying, recording,
storage in an information retrieval system, or otherwise, without the
written permission of the publisher.*

*This book is sold subject to the condition that it shall not, by way of
trade or otherwise, be lent, resold, hired out or otherwise circulated
without the prior consent of the publisher in any form of binding or
cover other than that in which it is published and without a similar
condition including this condition being imposed on the subsequent
purchaser.*

*MILLS & BOON and MILLS & BOON with the Rose Device
are registered trademarks of the publisher.*

*First published in Great Britain 2000
Harlequin Mills & Boon Limited,
Eton House, 18-24 Paradise Road, Richmond, Surrey TW9 1SR*

© Paula Marshall 2000

ISBN 0 263 82326 1

*Set in Times Roman 10½ on 11½ pt.
04-1100-82395*

*Printed and bound in Spain
by Litografía Rosés S.A., Barcelona*

Prologue

Villa Dilhorne, Sydney, 1851

Thomas Dilhorne, that proud and serious man once known as Young Tom, but now, by his own wish, always referred to as Thomas, walked into the nursery at Villa Dilhorne, his parents' home. Thomas's mother, Hester, had just finished feeding his infant son, Lachlan. When he sat by her, she handed the empty dish to the boy's nurse and the little boy to his father.

Thomas sat the lively child awkwardly on his knee, fearful that his careful and elegant clothing might be stained. Hester watched him, pain in her eyes, as Thomas carefully lifted Lachlan to his shoulder, kissing him gently on the way, his cold face never relaxing.

Hester loved her eldest son, but sometimes his sobriety, his almost total lack of humour compared with his father and his younger twin, Alan, troubled her. He had always been a serious, earnest child who rarely showed open affection, and as a man he was the same. In intellect very like his father, in appearance and temperament he bore him no resemblance.

The only person who had ever shattered Thomas's calm

severity a little had been his wife, Bethia. Hester sighed again when the coldly handsome face opposite relaxed into the faintest of smiles while the little boy stroked his father's cheek—and then lost it when Thomas saw his mother watching him.

He stood up. 'I must go,' he said, handing the child back to Hester. 'I have a busy day ahead of me. Master Lachlan will have to wait until the evening for further play.'

His mother smiled at him—a trifle ruefully this time—saying, 'Don't forget that we have a dinner party tonight', but she thought with dismay, Play, he calls that play! Two minutes and then he hands his son back to me like a parcel.

Thomas turned briefly at the door, to see Lachlan crawling towards him. His smile half-appeared, but was soon lost. He turned again and walked, straight-backed, through the door and into the world of work: the only world he now cared to inhabit.

Eleven years ago Thomas had married his childhood sweetheart, Bethia Kerr. Her father had been his father's best friend and the marriage had been a happy one. Bethia was a loving and gentle girl for whom Thomas was the centre of the universe. She had a gift for home-making and their beautiful villa in the newest part of Sydney was full of love, friends and happiness. The only thing it was not full of was children.

At first this had not mattered but, as time went by, Thomas and Bethia became increasingly disappointed that their happiness was not crowned with a family. At length they became reconciled to their lack, although every time that they heard of an addition to Alan's a small shadow crossed Bethia's face.

Suddenly, after years of marriage, the miracle happened. Seated at dinner one evening she told Thomas that their dreams had come true: she was increasing. For once Thomas's iron control broke and they had wept in one another's arms. Bethia's pregnancy was an easy one; even the birth had not been difficult, and she was able to hand Thomas their long-awaited son herself.

Alas, within twenty-four hours she was showing signs of fever; two days later she was dead. Hester sometimes thought that her son had died with his wife. Always reserved, he became impenetrable. Any affection which he had felt for anyone had descended into the grave with Bethia. He had never wept for her, and on the day of her funeral he had stood, cold and rigid, among the crying mourners. He was the only person present to show no emotion, to shed no tear.

Both his parents thought that only the fact that Lachlan was his last link with Bethia was why he tolerated him at all. Passing time appeared to make little difference to him—other than to drive him further into himself. He closed his own home and moved into Villa Dilhorne for Lachlan's sake, but he might as well have been a stranger or a lodger for all the emotion he showed, or the family life he shared.

'I'm afraid for him,' Hester said to Tom later that afternoon.

'I know,' said Tom sorrowfully, 'but there's little we can do but hope. I've tried to interest him in other than work, but…' and he shrugged his shoulders regretfully.

'He doesn't really love Lachlan either,' said Hester. 'He's just… Indifferent is the only word which fits him.'

'Yes, indifferent describes him well. I know it was a terrible blow for him to lose Bethia, who really brought him out of his shell—but now he's back in it with a vengeance! I've tried to encourage him to be easier with himself, but when I do he looks at me as though I were a stranger.'

They were silent for a little until Tom said, hope in his voice, 'Everything here reminds him of the past, so perhaps a change of scene might help. He sees Bethia around every corner. I could send him to Melbourne. Since the gold rush, it has turned into a major centre. He can look into our interests there, invest in the new railway and find out where else we can expand. We don't want Dilhorne's to be left behind. He's still a superb businessman; it's all he seems to care for—which isn't enough.'

'Yes,' agreed Hester, her face sad. She had already lost one son to distant England and did not like to see the other disappear, even if only inside Australia, but Thomas's needs came first. Hard though it was, it was time that he broke with the past. Bethia was gone, and grieving would not bring her back.

Thomas was seated alone at table the next morning when his father came in. Tom sat down in front of the giant Japanese screen which ran the entire length of the room. A rampaging tiger charged across it in full view of Thomas.

Tom poured himself tea. 'I'm getting old,' he said abruptly.

'Never,' said his son, affection for once in his voice.

'I'm in my early seventies, I reckon,' continued Tom, who was not sure of his exact age. 'I don't want to gallivant about these days. With this gold strike in Victoria and the new railway being projected, as well increased trade in shipping, one of us should go to Melbourne and, with Jack away in Macao, I think it ought to be you.'

'No,' said Thomas firmly. 'I don't want to leave Sydney.'

'A proper old woman you're becoming,' said his father. 'Set in your ways. Do you good to go to Melbourne.'

'I don't need to be done good to,' returned Thomas coldly. 'I'm sick of you and Mother nannying me about. I'm a grown man. Leave me to my own ways or I'll go back to my old home with Lachlan.'

'Nannying, is it?' said his father in his irritatingly equable manner. 'Seems to me that a grown man who doesn't want to adventure out a bit needs nannying.'

Thomas looked at his father with acute distaste, inwardly defying him. *Why can't he leave me alone? This is the second time that he has suggested sending me away. Can't he understand that I shall lose Bethia all over again if I lose the places where we were happy together...places where I can remember her beautiful bluey-green eyes?* He remained mute with something that was almost like rage.

'I've never given you an order,' said Tom, 'not since you were a lad. But I'm giving you one now. You need a holiday or a change of air. Go to Melbourne. Look things over for the firm. Take it easy, enjoy yourself, have some fun. See life a bit—why not, you've never really spread your wings? Let yourself go.'

'Drink, gamble, brawl and find a woman or two while I'm at it. Is that what you're suggesting, Father?'

Thomas's voice was as offensive as he could make it, and his expression was an angry glare. 'Roister about, like you and Alan did? Horseplay and similar folly. It's not how I wish to live, and you should know that by now. Or would you prefer me to go the way my grandfather Fred Waring went? A fine example he was before drink, whores and play did for him...'

His father said, a trifle wearily, 'Oh, yes, I know you, and what I know doesn't make me happy.'

His son interrupted him. 'I'm not interested in your happiness, Father. Have you told Mother that you think that I should go off and live the life of a debauchee? A fine piece of advice for an old man to give his grown-up son!'

Tom leaned back in his chair, the running tiger's head visible behind him. They both shared the same expression of intense irony and predatory determination.

'You're a self-righteous sanctimonious prig such as I

never thought to have for a son, aren't you? A damned arrogant swine who thinks only of himself, never of those about him who love and care for him.

'Poor Lachlan might as well not have a father for all the notice you take of him. It's in your mind, not mine, that pleasure is associated with debauchery. You must have a fine old sewer swilling about inside you to make you come out with that.'

There was no way that you could put down or annoy his father. He should have known that. He could insult his son with such calmness that the red rage inside Thomas, the rage which he had never known he possessed until Bethia had died, almost burst its bounds.

His usually calm face was twisted and purple. He rose, flinging his napkin down.

'So, that's what you think of me. I might have known. It's not enough for me to live a decent life but you have to twit me with it. Yes, I'll go to Melbourne, do my duty, and work for the firm just to get away from you. I shan't tell Mother of your preposterous suggestions and I'm not about to see life as you so charmingly put it. I've seen it all in Sydney and it doesn't attract. I'd as lief crawl around in the gutter.'

He stalked to the door, where he turned to confront his father again. Tom had not moved. His expression was as pleasant and cool as though they had been exchanging polite words over afternoon tea.

'Your duty? Oh, yes, your duty. By all means,' said his father drily, his expression still unchanged. 'I can see that that is what everything has shrunk down to. Yes, I'll be in the counting house later and talk to you then.'

'Of business—and nothing else,' Thomas flung at him. The heavy door shut behind him with a tremendous crash.

Temper, temper, thought Tom mildly. Not really perfect, are we, for all our protestations.

* * *

All that day, while preparations were being made for his journey to Melbourne, Thomas was glacially correct to his father, to such a degree that even the clerks commented on it.

His manner remained the same that evening. Before he retired to bed his mother, who had been told of his coming departure, kissed him, saying, 'You will be careful, Thomas. I understand that Melbourne is a dangerous place these days.'

'You may depend upon it, Mother. Your advice is always sound, unlike Father's, which I shall not be taking,' and he flung out of the room, banging the door behind him for the second time that day.

'Now what was all that about?' asked Hester after he had gone.

'I merely suggested to him this morning that he enjoy himself a little in Melbourne while he is there and he behaved as though I had told him to go straight to the devil.'

'Oh, dear! That was bad of him—but you know what he's like these days.'

'Yes, I do know what Thomas is like,' said her husband grimly. 'He's a man of strong passions who is not aware of it. One of these days he is going to find out. He can't sit on himself for ever. What will happen then, God knows. I sometimes fear for him. The trouble is, he's the image of your father—as he was before drink destroyed him. He may be fearful of behaving like him if he's not careful, consequently he's denying all human appetites. He eats his food as though he resents it, and a friendly word from anyone in the counting house earns a severe put-down—if he deigns to notice it, that is.

'At the moment he hates everybody, particularly me because I'm trying to help him, and he resents that most of all. If Bethia hadn't died, things might have been different…as it is…' He shrugged his shoulders sadly.

Hester gave a little moan of despair and, to comfort her, Tom said, 'Try not to worry. He might even enjoy visiting Melbourne. Away from his memories things might yet go well.'

But he did not believe what he was saying, and knew that Hester did not believe him either.

Chapter One

'It's big, Pa,' said Kirstie Moore faintly, shaking her ash-blonde head. 'Melbourne is even bigger than I thought that it would be. Are you sure we're doing the right thing?'

'Ballarat'll be smaller when we get there, my love,' said Sam Moore robustly, 'and you know that we couldn't stay at the farm. I explained all that before we set out.'

Kirstie nodded an unhappy agreement. She considered saying something along the lines of 'better the devil you know than the devil you don't,' but refrained. Once Pa got an idea into his head it tended to stay there.

She remembered the morning, nearly a month ago, when their neighbour, Bart Jackson, had come visiting and her father had told him that he could see a way out of the cripplingly narrow and poverty-stricken life which was all that living on their barren farms was giving to them. They and their children deserved better than existing on the edge of starvation in a place where young Kirstie would never find a suitable husband.

'We can sell our land, go to the gold field and make our fortunes,' he said vigorously. 'Jarvis, the banker from Melbourne, is only too willing to buy us out and sell them to some Melbourne bigwig with more money than sense. We can use the proceeds to outfit ourselves for the diggings. Come on, Bart, there's nothing left for us here. What's to lose?'

Bart, who had always followed Sam's lead, thought that this was splendid advice, and they shook hands on it. After he had gone Sam walked into the kitchen to tell his eldest daughter this exciting news. 'What do you think of going to the gold fields, eh, Big Sister? Ballarat, perhaps? They says there's riches there for the taking.'

Kirstie, who had been known to her family and friends as Big Sister ever since her mother's death in giving birth to little Rod, believed at first that her father must be joking.

'I thought you was off to milk the cows, Pa, not daydreaming.'

'No, Big Sister,' he told her. 'No more milking cows for me, I hope. I'm tired of working like an ox for nothing. We'll sell up, and be off to the diggings as soon as possible.'

'The diggings, Pa?' Kirstie nearly dropped Rod, whom she had been spoon-feeding, in her excitement and horror at hearing this unlikely news. 'What shall we live on there?'

'This,' he said, waving a hand at the few poor sticks of furniture in the room. 'Together with the money for the farm it'll give us enough for a stake, as well as for a couple of drays, digging equipment and a little something for food until we strike lucky. There'll be young men there, perhaps a husband for you, as well—there'll never be one here. Besides, others have made their fortune at the diggings— why shouldn't we?'

Kirstie's blue-green eyes flashed at him. 'And others have lost everything—and I don't want a husband, I've the family to look after and that's enough for me.'

'But it won't always be, Big Sister.'

'And we shall be leaving Mother's grave behind us.'

'Kirsteen,' he said, using her real name for once. 'She

left us nigh on two years ago and staying here won't bring her back. She had a hard life, daughter. I'd like a better one for you. You'll live like a princess if we strike it rich.'

'If…if…if…' she said fiercely. Big Sister was always fierce and kind and hardworking. 'It'll be hard for the little ones in the diggings.'

'You're wrong there. The little ones will like it most of all. They'll be free to run around, you see.'

Kirstie wailed in exasperation. She knew that it was no use trying to talk to him, he had already made his mind up before he had so much as said a word to her.

'Don't take on so, Big Sister,' Sam said humbly. 'I know it's hard. Harder to stay, perhaps. The kids are wild to go.'

'The kids don't know any better. You do.'

Sam Moore gave a heavy sigh and sat his big body down on a battered chair.

'Oh, Big Sister, can't you see? It's my last chance to have any sort of life. The farm killed your mother and it will kill you. You're already getting her worn look and you're still so young. Please say that you understand and will make the best of it. You've never failed me yet, however hard the road.'

This humble appeal moved her as his enthusiasm had not.

'Dear Pa, if that's how you feel, I'll try to do my duty by you—but I wish that you'd spoken to me first.'

'And now you know why I didn't. Oh, Kirstie, I want to hear you laugh again—there's not been much that's jolly here lately, has there—?'

She was about to answer him when the door opened and Patrick ran in.

'Oh, Pa, is it true what Davie Jackson is saying? That we're all going to the diggings to get rich? Oh, huzzah, I say.'

After that she could offer no more opposition, however

desperate she thought Pa's plan was. The notion that simply going to the diggings would secure her a husband was laughable, but she could not tell him so. Why should a suitor there be any better than poor oafish Ralph Branson whose offer of marriage she had recently turned down? It just showed how desperate Pa was that he could offer her such a prospect.

Besides, she didn't want to become a wife, since being a wife meant that you were simply a man's drudge both in and out of bed. No, she would prefer to stay Big Sister and, later on, perhaps, the kind unmarried aunt who had no responsibilities to any man.

In the meantime, she would cease to criticise Pa and offer him all her loving support in this unlikely venture.

So here they were, Pa, Kirstie, Aileen, twelve, Pat, ten, Herbie, four, and Rod, two, bang in the middle of Melbourne with all their possessions loaded on to two drays, drawn by bullocks. Pa was driving one dray and Kirstie the other, with the Jacksons' dray drawn up behind them.

Oddly enough, when they had started out it had been Pat who had burst out crying at the prospect of losing the only home he had ever known. In his young mind you could go to the diggings and still stay at home. To quieten him, and the little ones who had begun to roar with him, Kirstie gave Pat their scarlet and gold parrot to look after. When that wasn't enough she sang them songs from back home in England, songs which Ma had used to sing.

'That's my good girl,' Pa had told her quietly. 'I knew that you'd not let me down.'

When they had reached Melbourne they had found it full of people like themselves, all making for the diggings. There was nowhere to stay or to sleep except in and around the drays whilst they bought further provisions, tents and equipment. The little ones ran wild, dodging in and out among the many tramps who were lying in the street, dead drunk and clutching empty bottles: ruined before they had even reached the diggings.

Two of them were lying where the Moore party was parked in front of The Criterion, Melbourne's most expensive hotel. One was large with thick dark hair and a long beard and the other was red-headed and small. Both were ragged and smelled evil.

Kirstie sniffed her disgust at the sight of them, while Pa and Bart talked busily with those who seemed to know what ought to be done at the diggings if a fortune were to be made.

'Just the two of you won't get anywhere,' said one burly digger. They were all burly, rough and good-natured, as well as free with their violent language, blinding and bloodying in front of Kirstie as though she were not there. 'You need to form a small syndicate. A big chap would be best.'

The trouble with taking on a big chap, Sam thought, was that he might see the Moore family, tenderfeet all, as a suitable party for pillaging. Someone less powerful might be safer.

On the morning that they were ready to leave they had still not discovered any extra mates.

'We'll try to find someone when we get there,' said Pa hopefully—he was always full of hope.

They were just hoisting their last load of provisions into Kirstie's dray when a middle-sized Englishman, looking vaguely ill, came up to them. He was respectably dressed in clerk's clothing and said diffidently, in a low cultured voice, 'They told me at the store that you're off to Ballarat and needed a chum to make up your team. My name is Farquhar, George Farquhar. They call me Geordie here.'

Sam looked sharply at him. He scarcely seemed the sort of chum they needed, but then the stranger said, 'I can not only drive the dray, I'm good with horses as well. I don't drink or gamble and I'm stronger than I look. I also have a little spare cash to put in the pot if you'd care to take me on.'

That did it. Bart asked shrewdly, 'How much spare cash?'

The man said, 'Enough. I'll not show you here, too public. If you want a reference, I've been working at an apothecary's for the last three months. I'm steady,' he added, 'and they told me that you were steady, too.'

Sam looked him bluntly up and down, and, as usual, made a sudden decision on the spur of the moment.

'Well, Geordie Farquhar,' he said, 'I like the look of you and I'm inclined to take a chance with you. Money in the pot—and join us in the hard work. Just do what you can. Let's shake on it,' and he put out his work-calloused hand. Bart followed suit, and the three of them solemnly sealed their bargain.

Geordie proved helpful almost immediately. He persuaded them to stay an extra day and sell one of the drays and buy a horse and wagon—'It will be more useful than a bullock when we get to the diggings,' he told them.

'Except that we can't eat it,' Pa said practically.

'Oh, horse isn't bad,' Geordie told them. 'I've eaten horse rather than starve.'

The next morning, when an adventurous young Davie fell out of a tree on one of their earliest stops and broke his arm, Geordie set it for him carefully and patiently.

'I used to be a doctor,' he said brusquely when Bart thanked him. 'It might be helpful in the diggings.'

Back at the farm neither Kirstie nor Sam had thought that when they finally left Melbourne for Ballarat they would be part of a vast exodus of folk walking and riding to the gold fields. With two bullock-drawn drays and the horse and wagon they were among the more affluent of the travellers—although, as Kirstie commented, that wasn't saying much. They were mostly big, heavily whiskered men, many with pistols thrust into their belts. Some were already drunk, early in the morning though it was.

Pat, indeed, always lively and curious, gave a loud squeal when they passed a scarecrow of a man driving a rackety cart pulled by a spavined horse.

'Look, Big Sister, look, it's the two tramps from outside The Criterion. Fancy seeing them here!'

So they were. The little red-headed one was sitting up and looking around him while the big, dark one was lying on his back, eyes closed, a bottle in his hand, dead to the world already.

Kirstie sniffed her disgust at them. 'Hush, Pat. They might hear you.'

'Oh, Corny and The Wreck won't mind. They're used to people noticing them. Corny says they get more money that way. He's the little one.'

'There'll be more money for them in the diggings, perhaps,' commented Pa. 'And you're not to talk to them, Pat.'

'Oh, I don't talk to them. Besides, only Corny talks. The Wreck never says anything. Just looks.'

'And smells!' sniffed Kirstie.

'One thing, though,' said Geordie later, 'at least they weren't trying to cadge a free ride.'

He, Bart and Pa had been compelled to beat off with their whips great hairy ruffians trying to climb in beside them. One bold fellow, stinking of grog, jumped up and thrust his whiskered face at Pa, demanding that he sell him a ride. Pa threw him off, and left him behind in the dirt, hurling curses after them.

Some people were pushing wheelbarrows, full of their possessions, and their little children, some not as old as Herbie, even, were walking behind them. Public houses, inns and sly grog shops, so called because they were not legally licensed, lined the road. One lean-to shed had a sign, 'Last sly grog shop before the diggings,' which was a lie since a few miles further along was another with an even bigger sign saying, 'This really is the last sly grog shop before the diggings.'

Geordie, who had a dry wit which kept them entertained, suggested that ten miles after the last one they came to they ought to set up their own grog shop and make a fortune—except that someone else would be sure to build another a few hundred yards further on! He didn't drink, though, refusing a swig from the rotgut passed round after they had eaten their grub, and he never asked to stop at a grog shop.

He soon grasped that Sam Moore and Big Sister were the driving forces of the expedition. Sam was quiet and determined and made the decisions. Big Sister did all the donkey work. She rounded up the children, kept watch over them. scolded them, and bandaged their cut knees, in between doing the many chores which came her way. It was Big Sister who washed the clothes, lit the fire, cooked the food, banged a spoon on a tin plate and shouted 'Grub's up', a sound which began on the journey and which was to echo round the diggings in the months to come.

And on the road she entertained them by singing, in her small true voice, the songs which Ma had taught her to sing—their last link with long-gone England.

Kirstie knew that the diggings were going to be a man's heaven and a woman's hell as soon as they reached the ruined landscape which was Ballarat. The diggings were called the diggings because that was exactly what they were. There were hundreds of great deep holes, many filled with water, with soil flung up around them, and left there in heaps. Besides that, there were more people than they had ever seen before, even in Melbourne, crammed though it had been. They swarmed round the muddy holes and the canvas buildings like wasps around a honey pot.

Whatever there had once been of rural beauty before the gold rush began had long since disappeared. The settlement pullulated with life and noise, particularly noise, something which none of the party had expected, and to which none of them was accustomed—but which, like everyone else, they came to accept and ignore.

Symbolically, perhaps, the first people Kirstie saw as soon as they arrived were The Wreck and Corny lying in the muddy road where their driver had turned them out when he had found that they had little to pay him with. Somehow they had managed to beg enough to share a bottle and a pie between them, and were busy sleeping their impromptu banquet off.

Worst of all, Kirstie could plainly see that living in the diggings was going to be one long, improvised and dreadful picnic. Any hope that she might resume the orderly life she had been used to on the farm disappeared in the face of the cheerfully impromptu nature of gold-field society.

The men would love it, she thought bitterly, trust them. No need to be good-mannered, to sit down decently to eat. Male entertainment of every kind was laid on in abundance, for there was no getting away from the alleys where the grog shops, brothels, gaming halls, and bars flaunted their wares to the world.

There were even boxing booths, she discovered, and shortly after they arrived a small improvised theatre called The Palace started up—as though any palace could be constructed out of tent poles and canvas! There were few women in the diggings and Kirstie soon discovered that little was provided for them in this masculine paradise.

But exploring Ballarat was for the future. For the present it was time to settle in, to discover how to make one's claim and work it, and how to sell the gold—if they ever found any, that was.

Unkempt men, quite unlike the husband whom Pa had promised her, their soil-encrusted clothes reeking of sweat, came over to speak to the new chums, to advise them where the stores were, who was honest and who wasn't. They stared jealously at the drays and bullocks, at Geordie's horse and wagon, and the equipment which the men began to unload while Geordie helped Kirstie to light a fire outside, and set up a tripod and cooking pot over it. Meals would have to be eaten in the open.

'Really need all this, do you?' asked one ginger-haired digger. He was pointing at the trunks and blankets Sam was lifting out. 'Give you good money for this,' he offered, putting a hand on a storm lamp.

Sam pushed the eager hand away. 'Nothing to sell, mate. We need all we've brought for ourselves.'

'Seems a lot to me,' said Ginger, whose real name was George Tate. 'If you've ever a mind to sell anything, I'm in the market for what you don't want.'

The firing of a gun in the middle of removing Ginger's sticky fingers from Kirstie's cooking pots surprised them all. Kirstie dropped the frying pan she was holding and the younger children began to cry. Emmie Jackson, already depressed by their primitive living conditions, howled with them.

'That's nowt,' said Ginger phlegmatically. 'All digging has to stop when the gun goes off. It's time to light the fire, eat your grub, and…' he paused a minute to wink at the men '…that's when the evening's fun really begins.'

'For the men, I suppose,' returned Kirstie smartly, for only men, she thought, would want to live in this dreadful way—and enjoy it, too. No woman of sense would ever want to settle down in such dirt, confusion and mess, even to find gold.

Just to show that she meant business, she struck Ginger's hand smartly with her iron ladle when it strayed again among the pots lying on the ground. 'Give you good money for it, gal,' he said cheerfully—it seemed to be his favourite phrase.

'Don't want money for it, good or bad,' she snapped back. 'We shall need all we've got in this Godforsaken hole.'

Grinning at her, he wandered off—only to be succeeded by another set of diggers who, like squirrels, Geordie said, descended to try to wrench their stores from them. He made it his business to protect Kirstie so that she could prepare their supper. The children had long since run off to begin a disorganised game of tag in and out of the filthy maze of holes and the alleys which stood in for streets. It didn't improve her temper to see The Wreck shamble by, still clutching his bottle, Corny trotting along behind him.

Somehow Pa managed to round everyone up at last, after Big Sister had shouted, 'Grub's up,' and they ate their meal with all the relish of the genuinely hungry.

'Work tomorrow,' he said, after he had finished eating. 'Fancy a stroll, eh, Bart, Geordie?' Kirstie, gathering up dirty pots, an apathetic Emmie Jackson helping her, watched them go.

Pitched among the tents and the huts of the diggers were all the masculine delights which Kirstie had disapprovingly noted, and the three men found themselves part of the seething life which roared and reeled around them. They stopped at a sly grog shop, drank and moved on. The lure of a dance-hall was rejected. Fat Lil's Place, with Fat Lil outside in satin and feathers—the girls were all inside— was reserved for another night. Money best spent elsewhere at the minute, thought Sam regretfully, but Hyde's Place, as the Golden Ace gambling den was known, beckoned them in, not to play, but to watch.

Further down the alley was a music hall where the trio enjoyed themselves after moving on from Hyde's. After that they reeled home singing, waking up Big Sister when they stumbled around before falling into their improvised bedding.

Sam and Bart had already agreed that life was never like this on the farm!

The diggers in Melbourne who had told them that two of them were not enough to make a successful syndicate had not been deceiving them. Even adding Geordie was not enough, so the Moore party, as Geordie had nicknamed them, decided after a couple of weeks' fruitless work that they really needed a new chum—preferably one big and strong. Sam suggested that they try to hire someone—safer than trying to find a partner since they could control him.

'Well, now,' Bart said, 'that's a good idea, but who is going to hire themselves out when they can stake their own claim, eh?'

'You can't mean a layabout, Pa,' said Kirstie disapprovingly. 'He wouldn't work, not after the first pay day.'

'Never know 'til you try,' said Sam mildly. But even he quailed at the sight of some of the rogues and ruffians who worked until they earned a little money for drink and then lay about the alleys. Kirstie was probably right.

'What about The Wreck?' asked Geordie, while drinking tea one breakfast. 'God knows he's big enough.'

'The Wreck?' said Sam dubiously. 'You can't seriously mean The Wreck, Geordie.'

'Yes, I mean the big fellow Corny Van Damm brought here. Corny was the brains of the pair of them. I've been watching him. Ever since the police frightened Corny away he's been a lost soul. In and out of the nick, every penny thrown to him going on drink. But…'

Geordie stopped. How could he tell them that something

about The Wreck roused his pity and his interest? The occasional worried and questioning look in his eye, perhaps.
Whatever it was, Geordie had an impulse to save him.

'The Wreck!' exclaimed Bart derisively. 'What use
would he be? He's big enough, I grant you. But…'

'I know a few tricks to control drinking,' said Geordie.
'I could try them on The Wreck. Nothing would be lost if
I failed. We could throw him out again.' He shrugged. It
would be interesting to test whether he'd lost his touch.

'Geordie's right,' said Sam. 'We could take him in. Sober him up. Pay him by the week. Get rid of him if he
won't give up the drink.'

Bart rose. 'Last time I saw him he was lying outside
Hyde's Place. Yesterday afternoon, that was. There's a
patch of shade there he seems to like.'

'He was in a bad way,' said Sam. 'Likely the police have
picked him up. I'll go over to the nick. They'd be glad to
get rid of him to us.'

Kirstie put her oar in. 'I think you're all mad,' she said
tartly. 'Talking about taking on The Wreck. Only fit to trip
over, is The Wreck.'

'Now, Big Sister don't be hard,' said Geordie gently. 'A
bit of pity wouldn't come amiss.'

'Bit of pity!' scoffed Kirstie. 'I know who'll end up looking after him, cooking for him, and washing his clothes for
him—and it won't be you lot.'

'Don't think The Wreck's much bothered about having
his clothes washed, Big Sister,' was Bart's response to this.

'Ugh,' she snorted, 'and I object to that, too.' But nothing she said would move them, as she well knew. They
were entranced by the prospect of a new, large and strong
chum, even if he were at the moment a dead-drunk liability.
They all trusted to Geordie's magic powers to restore him
to rude health and strength.

That afternoon Sam harnessed the one remaining dray—

they had sold the other to raise money for more equipment—and took Kirstie shopping. While they were out they would look for The Wreck.

'Taken off to the nick, half an hour ago,' they were told by one of Hyde's strong-arm men, so once shopping was over they set off for it.

In the compound at the front of the nick an officer was glumly watching The Wreck, who was reclining happily against its front wall: he was too disgustingly filthy to be put inside, the officer told them.

Sam knew the officer. He made a point, unlike some, of always being well in with the law.

'In trouble again, is he, Mac?'

Mac scratched his head. 'God knows what we are going to do with him, Sam,' he said. 'Locking him up is no answer. He just goes straight out and…' He shook his head despairingly.

'What if I took him off your hands, Mac? Geordie reckons he can dry him out, and then set him to work.'

'That'll be the day,' said Mac drily. 'Miracle worker is he, Geordie?'

'Bit of,' said Sam. 'Done some good things for us, has Geordie.'

The officer looked at The Wreck, who smiled happily at them all.

'Can't lose,' he said, much as Geordie had done earlier. 'You'll be doing us a favour, Sam, by taking him off our hands for a little, even if you don't cure him. I doubt very much whether you'll be able to sober him up.'

'Depends on whether he's a hardened drunk,' said Sam, inspecting the sodden figure who now gave him the smile previously offered to Mac.

The Wreck said with great dignity, opening one red eye, 'I can't be drunk, because I never drink.' He closed the eye again and began to snore. The officer groaned and helped

Sam to haul him to his feet. Kirstie, sitting in the dray, was stiff with disapproval.

'You can't want him, Pa,' she called to her father. 'What use will he be?'

'He's a big fellow,' said her father. 'We'll dry him out and put him to work. We need him, girl.'

'I know that we need someone—but him? Can't you find anyone more suitable?'

'No one wants to work for anyone else now, girl. We're lucky to get him.'

So saying, Sam helped Mac to walk The Wreck to the dray, his feet dragging behind him. Between them they managed to hoist him into it. He was so dirty that Kirstie drew her skirts away from him, making disgusted noises which seemed to wake him up a little.

He opened his bloodshot eyes and stared at her.

'Where am I?' he asked.

'Where I don't want you to be,' she flung at him. When he tried to sit up she pushed him down again. 'Lie still. I don't want you near me. He's disgusting, Pa. I think that this is a big mistake.'

'Think what you want, my girl,' said her father equably. 'He's coming with us, and if he proves useless we'll throw him out.'

'I'm not disgusting,' said The Wreck reproachfully. 'Fred's tired, that's all. Fred needs to sleep.'

'Then sleep,' she threw at him. 'Your breath is as nasty as your person, and that's a feat in itself.'

'Unkind,' moaned The Wreck. 'Women should be gentle.'

'Gentle!' Kirstie's voice would have cut steel. 'And men should be decent. When you're decent I'll be gentle, not before.'

He ignored this and, rolling over, said placidly, 'I'll sleep now,' and immediately began to snore.

'Fred?' said Sam to Mac, now that their passenger was settled. 'Is that all the name he has?'

'Waring,' said Mac, glad to see the back of Fred—for the time being at least. 'Fred Waring, at least that's who he says he is. Not too sure about that sometimes. Doesn't even know where he is or what he's doing. Except drink.'

Kirstie drew her skirts still further away from Fred and looked to the front, offering Mac her opinion of the police for letting him go so easily.

Sam picked up the reins and began the journey back to their claim.

Geordie Farquhar was up to his waist in the hole he had started to dig the previous evening, just before the gun went. He was using his pickaxe, not with the same strength and vigour as Bart and Sam—Bart cleared nearly twice as much mud as Geordie in any one session—but there was no doubting his determination.

He was already far more muscular than the soft man he had been before arriving at the diggings. When Sam returned with the dray he put down the pick and hauled himself out of the hole, wincing at his blistered hands. Even Sam and Bart had trouble with their hands and they were far more used to manual labour than he was. Geordie had been proud of his beautiful hands once—but once was long gone.

He walked over to the dray. Big Sister jumped out, stiff with distaste. She said scornfully to him in passing, 'A fine creature we've brought you, Geordie Farquhar, lying there in his muck. The dray will need fumigating.'

'Give over, do, Big Sister,' said Sam in his mild way. 'Come and help me with the new chum, Geordie.'

Bart put his head out of his hole. 'Got him, did you, Sam?'

'Aye, and blimey, he's a big 'un. He'll do when we've sobered him off.'

The three men looked at Fred lying in the bottom of the dray. He was now fully conscious and smiled up at them sweetly—but showed no signs of wanting to get up.

'Big Sister was right,' said Geordie. 'We're dirty. *He*'s disgusting.'

'Get him down to the creek,' said Bart practically. 'Clean him up there. Sober him up a bit.'

'Right,' said Sam, 'but he'll need clean clothes. His are too dirty even for the diggings. He'll need boots, too. His are useless, but where shall we find clothes or boots for him? We're all too small for us to give him any of ours.'

'Andy Watt,' offered Geordie briskly.

'That's right,' said Sam.

Andy Watt had been a big digger and a neighbour on their last claim. When the rains set in Andy had got drunk, fallen into one of the flooded holes, and drowned. Geordie had thoughtfully 'saved' Andy's clothes and possessions and stored them away in his wagon.

'Might come in useful some day,' he had said. Geordie was a proper squirrel, they all agreed.

Geordie went to his wagon to collect the clothes, boots, soap and a towel. Sam and Bart hauled a protesting Fred out of the dray and walked him on his jelly legs down to the creek. Big Sister, still stiff with disapproval, watched them go.

Fred had a happy look on his face. He had no idea what his new friends were going to do to him when they reached the creek. If he had, he would not have looked so contented.

Geordie Farquhar, loaded with his possessions, gave Big Sister a wink when he passed her.

'What use do you think he'll be?' she shouted at him.

'Never know, Big Sister, until we try, do we?'

Bart and Sam had now thrust the protesting Fred into the

creek. You could scarcely call it cleaning him. The water was milky, if not to say murky, from the many washings in it of the muck and quartz in which the gold was embedded. But it performed the dual purpose of cleaning the encrusted Fred of much of his grime and half-sobering him into the bargain. Every time he tried to climb out, Sam and Bart shoved him back in again.

The noise and the excitement not only brought all the children down to see the fun, but attracted a small crowd of men and women as well. Finally Sam and Bart let him climb on to the bank—and then threw him back in again for one last soak. The watching crowd cheered lustily when, shouting and spluttering, he hit the water, which rose in a vast fountain drenching the spectators!

This time when he surfaced Sam and Bart dragged him out and began stripping him of his sodden clothing now that it was fit to touch. The women in the crowd screeched and covered their eyes when they pulled his trousers from a loudly protesting Fred. Geordie threw him the scrubby towel not only for very decency but so that he might dry himself.

Fred was now shivering so violently from reaction that Geordie had to help him to dress. Fortunately Andy Watt's clothing fitted him well enough. Even the boots seemed to be the right size. Once he was fully dressed and standing more or less erect, all three were agreed that he was indeed a right big 'un, and if he could work at all would be a useful mate.

Fun over, the crowd dispersed and Sam's party returned to base where Big Sister's withering stare seared them all.

'A right picnic you made of that. You should have charged for watching. We could have made enough to pay for next week's grub.'

She had to allow, though, that The Wreck was much improved after the trio's ministrations. His long hair was beginning to dry in rioting waves and curls. His beard needed a trim as well. Fred blinked at Big Sister when he saw her watching him and gave her a slow smile, revealing excellent white teeth. The smile was the first—but not the last—he was to favour her with.

'I'm Fred,' he said cheerfully. 'Who are you?'

'That's Big Sister,' shrilled Pat, who had watched the forced bath with great appreciation. It was better than a play, being real life not pretence.

Fred smiled again. Something about the young woman who was so cross with him appealed to his fuddled brain. Perhaps it was her bluey-green eyes which reminded him of someone, but exactly who, he couldn't remember. He wanted her to talk to him so he said eagerly, 'Hello, Big Sister. Say hello to Fred.'

He was so impossibly childlike that rather than attack him Kirstie swung on Pa, Bart and Geordie, who were all enjoying Fred's innocent unawareness of Big Sister's anger with him.

'Think it funny, do you?' she raged at them. 'Am I expected to cook and wash for him as well?'

'So long as he's part of the gang,' Sam told her.

'And how long will that be, Sam Moore?' That showed him how cross she was. She only called her father by his full name when she had been tried beyond endurance. The Wreck, Fred, whatever his name was, stood for everything which Kirstie disliked so about her new life. How could they arrive with such a useless creature and expect her to be enthusiastic about him? So far as she was concerned, he was more extra work for her while they would get little back in the way of work from him.

And all her father could say was, 'We'll see, girl, we'll see.'

'You mean, I'll see!'

'I'm hungry,' announced Fred, blithely unaware of what

a bone of contention he had become. 'Fred hasn't had anything to eat today.'

He had sat down on the ground at the beginning of the argument between Kirstie and Sam and it was now passing back and forth over his head.

'Yes, he ought to be fed,' said Sam. 'Do him good. Set him up for work tomorrow.'

Big Sister whirled on them all, shaking a rebuking finger, either at Fred or the other men, it didn't matter which. They were all as bad as one another.

'You see! You see!' she exclaimed. 'The first thing he wants is food—and I'm to cook it for him, I suppose.'

'You will?' said Fred hopefully. 'That's kind of you, Big Sister.'

The three men collapsed into laughter, whether at Fred's sublime innocence or Kirstie's anger they could not have said.

She shot into the hut and shot out again carrying two cold lamb chops and a damper—the diggings' primitive version of bread—on a tin plate.

'Will that do?' she demanded, thrusting it at him.

'Nice,' said Fred, beginning to demolish the food where he sat.

Kirstie stared down at him, watching him cheerfully chewing his way through the grub. For the first time her face softened a little.

'Are you sure that he's not simple?' she demanded of Geordie, who had been watching Fred with a trained eye ever since he had helped to haul him out of the dray. 'He seems simple.'

'No, Big Sister,' he said quietly. 'I don't think that he's simple. He may have been injured recently, though.'

He squatted down by the sitting Fred.

'Had a knock on the head lately, old fellow?'

Fred looked up. 'Think so. Not sure. Fred's had lots of knocks lately.' He was impatient to finish his chop.

'Mind if I take a look at your head? I promise not to hurt you.'

'Don't mind,' said Fred, still chewing busily. He smiled at Big Sister again. 'Nice, I like this.'

Geordie's long and skilful fingers explored Fred's skull gently. He soon found a tender spot. Fred winced and pulled away.

'You said that you wouldn't hurt Fred,' he mumbled reproachfully through his last mouthful of chop.

Geordie looked thoughtfully at him before breaking one of the diggings' major rules. 'Do you remember your home, Fred—where you come from? Did you live in Melbourne, or did you go there because of the gold rush?'

Fred pushed his empty plate away and hung his head, muttering, 'My head hurts when you ask me that, Geordie.'

His distress was so plain that even Kirstie began to feel sorry for him.

'Do you remember anything at all, Fred?'

'Yes.' Fred's voice was so low that they had to strain to hear him. 'But not much. It hurts when I try to remember.' He looked around him agitatedly. 'Where's my bottle? Who took my bottle away?'

Geordie stood up, shaking his head. 'It's all right, Fred, don't worry. You can tell me another time, perhaps.'

Fred shook his head agitatedly. 'No, no, nasty—Fred doesn't want to remember. No one was kind to him. They didn't give him chops—not like Big Sister.'

'What's wrong with him?' asked Sam. 'Is he ill? Or what?'

'Not exactly ill, no, but he needs looking after. He's lost his memory, you see. He might get over it, and then again he might not. It depends on whether he wants to.'

He looked sadly at Fred, who had cringed into himself,

his head on his chest and his knees drawn up to his chin. 'He's had a blow on his head, a severe one, and I think that that was what caused him to lose his memory. He's obviously forgotten who he is—or rather was.'

Big Sister was suddenly sorry for the unkind way in which she had spoken to Fred ever since they had freed him from the nick.

'He's not really ill, then, Geordie?'

'No, Big Sister,' said Geordie gently. 'He's not really ill, but he does need looking after.'

He looked sharply at her. 'I think that what he might need most of all is kindness.'

'Will he get his memory back?' asked Sam.

Geordie shrugged his shoulders. 'Who knows? He might, and he might not. Only time will tell.'

The gun went off when he finished speaking, so they couldn't put Fred to work that day, even if they had wanted to, or thought that he was fit to begin digging. When Fred uncoiled himself Bart took him on one side and explained to him that they had freed him from the nick, washed, clothed and fed him, and in return they expected him to work for their syndicate.

'We'll pay you a weekly wage, of course,' Sam added. 'We'll see you right.'

Fred nodded agreeably.

'I'll try to be good,' he said.

Geordie had hurt him a little, but these days his head had begun to pain him less and less. The vague feeling of unexplained misery, which had plagued him during his memory of his recent past and which had led to his drinking to forget it, was also beginning to disappear. Besides that, since the Moore party had washed him he had become aware of Ballarat for the first time, rather than seeing it as a blur of unmeaning noise and colour.

Kirstie watched him demolish another large plateful of

stodge with every appearance of pleasure, and his reputation as a man who loved his grub was already on the make.
He looked happily around while he ate and listened carefully to Bart, Sam, and Geordie when they told him what
they expected of him. None of them, even Geordie, had
any notion of how much of their instructions he understood.

In all directions lights had come on. There were small
fires everywhere. People sat in the open, eating, laughing
and talking. Music drifted from a big canvas tent nearby.
Ginger Tate, who worked the claim next to theirs, was playing a banjo; the hard drinking and high living which followed the day's work had already begun.

The lights pleased Fred. He stopped listening to the talk
around the fire and pointed his knife at near and distant
flames.

'Pretty,' he said to Big Sister who was gathering up the
dirty plates and cutlery.

'What is?' she asked him when he obediently handed her
his plate and tin cup.

'The lights.' He struggled a minute, attempting to find
words to express his pleasure. 'They're beautiful.' He
smiled at her so winningly that this time, despite herself,
she smiled back at him. She wondered what he would look
like if his long black hair and his straggling beard were
trimmed. He was certainly a fine figure of a man, justifying
Sam's belief that he would be an asset to the syndicate if
he were able to work properly.

'That's better,' he said encouragingly.

'What's better?'

'You. When you smile you look pretty. Do it more often—for Fred.' His artlessness robbed the words of any
ulterior meaning.

'I need something to smile at, Fred Waring,' she snapped
back at him, but it was only a little snap, nothing like those
with which she had treated him when they had fetched him

from the nick, before Sam and the others had cleaned him up and had discovered that he had lost his memory.

Allie helped her to collect the pots and carry them into the kitchen of the rude hut which the men had built for her. A large hand appeared in front of her when she bent over the washbowl. It was Fred's.

'Help?' he queried. 'You need help, Big Sister?'

Kirstie stared at him. Whatever their other virtues, the men took it for granted that all the chores around the camp—except for the digging—were done by her. None of them had ever offered a hand to help her during the long day which began at dawn and only ended when she was the last to retire, for now that Emmie's baby had been born, everything fell to Kirstie.

Here was Fred, though, saying uncertainly and looking anxious, 'Big Sister does a lot of work. Fred help?'

Sam appeared in the doorway, having followed Fred into the hut. 'Anything wrong, Fred?'

It was Kirstie who answered for him. 'No, nothing wrong, Pa. Fred came to help me.'

Sam began to laugh. He went outside to share the joke with the others, leaving Kirstie annoyed and Fred puzzled.

'Big Sister's got a kitchenmaid.' Sam smiled. 'Don't wear him out for tomorrow, mind.'

Kirstie bounced to the hut door. 'He's got more consideration for me than some I know, Sam Moore!' she shouted, bringing on another burst of laughter. Even Geordie Farquhar was looking amused.

She let Fred dry the pots, remembering what Geordie had said about kindness. When they had finished washing up Fred went back to the fire where Bart and Sam were passing a bottle back and forth. Geordie was repairing some tack.

'I need a drink,' Fred announced, and put out his hand for the bottle.

Geordie spoke before Sam or Bart could answer. 'No, Fred, you're not to drink.'

Fred's eyes filled with tears. So far Geordie had been kind to him: it was the other two who had been rough and thrown him into the water.

'Oh, I do so want a drink, Geordie. Please.'

Geordie walked over to sit by Fred. He took him by the right wrist, and looked hard at him, almost like the mesmerist in the little fair at the other end of the diggings.

'No, Fred. Drink isn't for you. You're poorly, Fred. Drink will make you worse, not better.'

'I feel better when I drink, Geordie,' said Fred, pleading with him.

'I know you do. But it's wrong, the wrong sort of better, Fred. Do you understand me?' He tightened his grip on Fred's wrist and looked even harder into his eyes.

'Bart and Sam are drinking,' said Fred in a sullen voice.

'It's not wrong for them. It's wrong for you. Look at me, Fred. Look into my eyes. Don't turn your head away.'

Geordie's stare grew even more piercing. Fred turned his head away to try to avoid it, but something drew him back again and, this time, when he looked into Geordie's eyes, he was lost. Kirstie, watching them, thought that the usually self-effacing Geordie had suddenly become hard and dominant: a man of authority. Sam and Bart were silent and fascinated spectators of his attempts to control Fred.

Fred dropped his head to break the spell which Geordie was beginning to weave around him. Geordie put a hand under his chin and raised it.

'Look at me, Fred, and repeat what I say. Geordie says that it's wrong for you to drink.'

Fred obediently began to do as he was bid—and then faltered. 'Geordie says it's wrong, but...'

'No buts, Fred. You understand me.' His grip on Fred's

wrist tightened, Geordie could feel Fred's hammering pulse. 'No buts, Fred, and no drinking.'

Fred looked sorrowful. 'No buts, Geordie, and no drinking.'

'Promise me, Fred.'

'I promise, Geordie. No buts and no drinking.'

They sat there for some moments, quite still, Fred drowning in Geordie's eyes until Geordie took his hand from Fred's wrist. He said, his voice low but firm, 'That's it, Fred. No more drinking for you in the future. You understand me? Say ''Yes, Geordie''.'

'Yes, Geordie,' Fred said, and then fell silent, inspecting his hands as though he were seeing them for the first time.

There was a moment of silence. Then Big Sister moved away and Bart and Sam started talking again, and although Fred watched the bottle sadly, he made no attempt to take it, or ask for it with Geordie glaring at him from across the fire.

Chapter Two

Whether it was the session with Geordie which disturbed Fred, or simply the consequence of his exciting day, he was too dazed to know. Only when he went to bed that night, lying wrapped in a blanket under the stars, he found himself trying to remember and recall who and what Fred Waring was, for all his memories were of the recent past. He was not even sure that Fred Waring was his name.

Geordie's voice echoed in his ears. Did you live in Melbourne, or did you go there because of the gold rush?

How to say that he had no notion of who he was or where he had come from when he found it difficult to say anything at all? What were his first memories? Try as he might he could remember nothing before…and he was back there again, where his memory began, standing in the dock of a courtroom in a place which he now realised must have been Melbourne.

He was feeling dreadfully ill, and was hardly able to stand upright. There was a horrible smell of drink. It took him some time to grasp that it was he who was the cause of the smell. His wrists and ankles hurt, too, which wasn't surprising since he was in chains.

Someone was asking him his name.

'My name?' he said. His voice sounded odd, and his mouth hurt. His lips and nose were so swollen that he could not breathe properly.

Someone said, 'He's been on a bender for four days. Constable Brown said that he came crawling out of an alley a week ago, too drunk and dazed to speak. He's been lying round the town ever since, begging. There's always some fool to throw him money. He promptly spends it all on drink.'

'He must know his name. Ask him again.'

Someone took him by the hair and thrust a grinning face into his, shouting, 'What's your name, cully?'

'My name?' He dredged a name from some pit whose bottom he had not yet reached. 'Fred!' That's it, he told himself. Fred.

'Louder, man,' said another voice.

'Fred, it's Fred.'

He looked around and the room came briefly into focus. A well-dressed man was sitting on a kind of dais: other men, some in uniform, were standing about. Where could he be? A courtroom? Yes, it was a courtroom. What was he doing in a courtroom?

'Fred what? You must have another name, man.'

'Not Fred what. Fred…Fred…Fred…Waring.'

He was not sure that was his name, but it was a name, someone's name, and since he remembered it, it might be his. It seemed to satisfy them, even if he didn't feel too happy with it himself.

If only his head didn't hurt so much he might be able to understand what was happening to him. The man on the dais began to drone at him. Then he stopped. The man on the right, who had seized him by the hair, now took him by the shoulders and began to push him out of the room.

'Where am I going?' he asked.

'You 'eard, chum. On the road.'

'On the road? What for?'

His articulation was so poor that, what with his head and his hangover, his guard could barely understand him.

'Don't worry. You'll find out soon enough.'

He was in a fog again. To some extent he began to grasp that something was very wrong. Trying to understand what the wrongness was, was beyond him.

'I need a drink,' he said pitifully.

Someone cuffed him. 'No, you don't. That's why you're here. You're a drunk.'

Yes, there was something wrong about everything because some remnant of his old self had him saying with great dignity, 'I don't drink.'

For some reason, when he came out with this the whole courtroom broke into laughter, and even the stern-faced man on the bench gave a great smirk. He began to protest— against what, he wasn't sure—and it took two men to haul the inebriated ruin he had become through the doorway and out of the courtroom.

He was suddenly in a yard in the open with no memory of how he had got there. He was chained to other men and standing in the cruel mid-day sun. It was so strong that it hurt him to endure it.

He started to fall but was hauled upright by an ungentle hand. He could hear people laughing. Even the other chained men were laughing at him. Out of some dim recess of himself that knew what was really wrong with him, he dredged up a coherent sentence that told the truth.

'I need a doctor,' he said, and then everything disappeared around him again.

His next memory was of being in a cart with other men. His neighbour kept complaining bitterly and tried to push him away when he fell, lax, against him, bawling, 'Sit up, can't you, mate. You weigh a ton.'

'Can't,' he said, and lost everything once more.

Then he heard someone calling out names. He was standing in a compound, surrounded by huts. He was still chained to other men. Guards stood about—somehow he knew that they were guards, though how he knew, he could not say. They were carrying muskets, old ones. How strange that he knew that they were old, since he knew so little of anything else!

Someone shouted 'Waring!'

The man next to him prodded him roughly and said, 'That's you, ain't it? For God's sake, answer him so that we can get this over.'

He said 'Yes?' but it was really a question, not an affirmation, and before he could register anything more the world went dark again, a nasty habit it had which frightened him.

He awoke to find that he was lying in the shade and someone was holding a tin cup of water to his lips. He drank it greedily. A voice said, 'This man's not fit for work today. He appears to be in a drunken coma.'

'No,' he said. It seemed important to say it again. 'I don't drink.' This time he was not greeted with laughter. Instead a hard face swam into view. 'You've drunk enough to kill a horse, man. You're sodden with liquor. Leave him to dry out. He should be fit tomorrow.'

After that he slept, or rather was unconscious, he was not sure which. Only that, in the morning when he awoke, for the first time since memory had begun in the courtroom he saw his surroundings quite plainly with an almost hurtful clarity, so that he wished that he were drunk again. Now this was an odd thought to have, and it disturbed him greatly, since he knew—how did he know?—that being drunk was something foreign to him.

The thought disappeared when the stomach cramps took him. After he had recovered and eaten a little, he was told to strip. He was given clean clothes—a coarse canvas shirt and trousers—and he put them on, shivering as he did so. He asked for shoes or boots—his had been removed, and the guards laughed at him.

'No need, chum, you're making roads, not walking on them.'

From some corner of his mind Fred grasped—if dimly— that he was part of a chain-gang building one of the new roads which was connecting Melbourne to the north. Not that he knew that he had been living in Melbourne when he had been sentenced to hard labour—he only found that out later.

He was clumsy and bewildered at first, because the whole world was strange, but one of his fellow prisoners was kind and helped him when they were fed at mid-day.

'Keep your head down, mate, and always eat your grub up. You'll not be able to work if you don't, and then they'll thrash you for being idle.'

His shrewd eyes saw more than the court officials or the chain-gang's guards and overseers. 'Ill, aren't you? It's not just the drink, is it?'

The man's voice was coarse but kind. Fred's short memory had no kindness in it, only curses, blows and kicks.

That night, for the first time, he dreamed of a tiger. It ran through his dreams, frightening him, while he looked for something which he had lost—and knew that he would never find again. This thought filled him with such desolation that it was almost worse than his fear of the tiger which nearly cornered him once.

In the morning the memory of the dreams stayed with him, and trying to remember what they reminded him of made his head hurt again—and the desire to drink almost destroyed him.

At this point in his effort to make sense of his brief past Fred opened his eyes and looked at the stars, bright above him in the clear night. He had seen them when he had been a prisoner in the chain-gang and in an odd way they comforted him. It puzzled him that he suddenly remembered some of their names quite clearly when he was not entirely sure of his own.

He had pointed the Southern Cross out to the man who had helped him, and who, when their time on the road gang was over, stayed with him when they were driven back to Melbourne and set free again. They were given a little money in return for their work, and Fred and Corny Van Damm, his new friend, turned into the first saloon they could find and within a few hours were lying dead drunk in the street again.

Corny looked after Fred, found him places to sleep where they wouldn't be disturbed and protected him from the roughs who tried to steal his pitiful store of money from him. It was Corny who arranged transport for them to Ballarat where he told Fred that there would be easier pickings than in Melbourne. Corny also comforted Fred when he became distressed, usually something which occurred whenever Fred seemed to be on the verge of remembering his lost past.

The trouble was that every time that this began to happen it was not only Fred's head which hurt him, but something else which seemed to be associated with his heart. This new pain was so strong that Fred found that the only way to overcome it was to drink himself into a stupor—whereupon it disappeared.

Corny also taught him to steal, beginning with fruit off stalls and barrows, but Fred wasn't as clever at this as Corny. He was clumsy and got caught and kicked for his pains, but Corny looked after him as much as he could. One day a very bad thing happened. Corny was helping a stupefied Fred to find a nice corner to lie down in, out of the sun, when a pair of policemen stopped them.

The bigger one took a good hard look at them. His eyes

widened when he saw Corny. 'I know you,' he said. 'You're Corny Van Damm. You went bushranging with Ryan's lot.'

Corny let out a shrill cry, dropped poor Fred and bolted. One policeman ran after him, and the other bent over Fred and hauled him to the nick. Neither Fred nor the police ever saw Corny again—self-preservation being the name of his game. Without Corny Fred was lost. People tripped over him, and he was dragged in and out of the nick until Sam and Kirstie had arrived to free him, feed him, and promise him something of a future.

Remembering all this not only made Fred's head hurt again, but disturbed him so much that when he finally slept not only did the tiger run through his dreams, trying to eat him, but somewhere in the background there was an old man who disapproved of him and frightened Fred even more than the tiger.

He shouted his distress and one of his new friends came to comfort him.

The odd thing was that when Fred woke up he remembered the tiger, but not the old man…

Sam decided that the new chum was to be put to work at once, and Fred, who had heard him tell Big Sister to feed him, was anxious to oblige him, never mind that Sam and Bart had thrown him into the water.

Fred had suffered from cramps in the night, and had begun to shout wildly in his sleep. Geordie, who shared a tent with Sam and Bart—Emmie and Kirstie slept in the hut for safety—heard him, and went outside to look after him.

He was thrashing blindly about. Geordie put a gentle hand on his shoulder and asked, 'What is it, Fred?'

Fred opened his eyes, clutched at Geordie's wrist and

gasped, 'It's the tiger, Geordie! The tiger's after Fred. Don't let it catch him.'

'Don't worry, Fred. Sam, Bart and I will keep the tiger away. I'll fetch you a drink of water and then you must try to sleep.'

'Thank you, Geordie. Don't let it catch *you*.'

'It won't, Fred.'

Fred drank the water down obediently and went back to sleep. The tiger was to run through his dreams for months but he never woke up shouting about it again, as though Geordie's reassurance had made it toothless.

He enjoyed his breakfast. His head had cleared even more, and while he sat eating and drinking he really saw them all for the first time.

Sam was fair, well built and powerful, both in mind and body, the true leader of the party. Bart was dark and ox-like. He depended on Sam and Geordie for leadership and advice, but he was a tireless worker—and reliable. He always did what he said he would. All three of them were dressed in guernseys and moleskins, and Sam and Bart were heavily whiskered.

Geordie was small and sallow and, Fred came to understand later, somewhat sardonic. He was one of the few men in the diggings who was clean-shaven. His eyes were watchful, occasionally moving over Fred, assessing him slightly. Fred didn't mind this. Geordie was his friend. He hadn't thrown Fred about as the other two had. Geordie had given him these nice warm clothes, and had been kind: the tiger had been chasing Fred in the night but Geordie had made it go away.

The diggings were alive with noise and movement while Big Sister and Emmie Jackson handed round the grub. Big Sister, Fred thought, was a puzzle. She was nasty-nice. True, she gave Fred his grub, but she wasn't pleased with him, Fred knew.

On the other hand, Fred could see how well she looked after everybody, even though she snapped at them, and cuffed large Pat and small Herbie when they were naughty. She had nice, fair hair even if it was screwed up. Her eyes were nice, too, bluey-green. They reminded Fred of someone, but every time he tried to remember who that someone was, he felt so sad and ill that he gave up trying to remember. He thought that he didn't really want to know if knowing made his head hurt.

Big Sister looked after baby Rod, giving him his food, tying him up to the kitchen-table leg with his reins so that he couldn't stray and get lost or hurt. In his new awareness he also saw that she looked after Emmie Jackson and her baby as well. It was a pity that Big Sister was so cross at times, particularly with Fred.

Still and all Fred helped her to clear away again, and would have done more except that Sam said, 'No, Fred. Leave that to Big Sister. It's time you started work. Pay for all the good grub you've eaten, eh?'

Geordie examined Fred's hands carefully before shrugging resignedly. It was apparent to him that, although Fred's nails were broken and his hands bore recent scars on the backs, palms and wrists, he had done very little manual work. His palms were soft and the calluses on them were new. His hands were beautiful and shapely, and Geordie thought that they had been cared for until not too long ago. All the marks of neglect on him were recent.

His body had been cared for, as well, and he had done very little physical labour. He was not unfit, but his muscles were not those of a man given to using them. For all his size—and his potential for strength—digging would, at first, be a hard task for him.

This soon proved to be true. Fred began enthusiastically enough in order to show his thanks to them, but he soon grew weary. His hands blistered and bled and he used his spade and swung his pick ever more slowly. He looked dismally at Sam, but Sam said, not unkindly, 'You've got to persevere, chum. We all went through this at the start, didn't we, Geordie?'

Geordie agreed, but he kept watch over Fred without saying anything or showing his concern overmuch. It was obvious that Fred was strong-willed behind all his artless charm—charm which even Big Sister grudgingly conceded he possessed. Once he grasped that they wanted him to go on, he bent to his task again, whispering to himself, 'This hurts,' but he still continued to dig, if slowly.

He had dug quite a hole when they stopped for a rest, a drink and more grub. Sam had hit a small pocket of gold-bearing quartz and Big Sister, Pat and Allie went down to the creek to wash it out. It wasn't a big strike, but with what they had already found between them it would make a fair profit on the week and would enable them to keep and pay Fred, and feed well themselves.

It was surprising how deft the women and children were at washing out and sorting the grains of gold. Sam showed it to Fred and told him that that was what they were looking for, and how he would know it when he struck it.

Geordie dressed Fred's hands and they started work again. The piles of muck around Fred's diggings grew, but he slowed down more and more when his aching shoulders and back began to add to the pain of his hands.

By the time the gun went off to signal the end of the day's work, Fred was so exhausted that he had to be lifted out of his hole by Sam and Bart. They laid him down on the ground and he only recovered a little when Big Sister brought him tea and grub, and said approvingly, 'Well done, Fred.'

Her voice was so kind that it nearly brought tears to poor Fred's eyes. So few people had been kind to him lately.

Sam agreed. 'Kept at it, Fred, didn't you? Many wouldn't.'

It was nice to hear them say it, but it didn't ease his bleeding and swollen hands much, nor his aching back and shoulders. Geordie dressed his hands again, and he too said, 'Well done, Fred,' and then, 'Are you all right, mate? Your head's not hurting you too much?'

'No,' said Fred. 'It's not my head today. It's my hands and my back,' and he made an almost comic face when he said it.

'You'll get used to it in time, and so will your hands.'

Fred was more than ready for his grub that evening and Big Sister was kind to him because he had worked so hard. Before supper Geordie treated his hands with spirits, which hurt, but Geordie said it would harden them sooner. He still wouldn't let Fred drink, which saddened Fred, but he tried not to mind too much.

Funnily enough, although Fred was so sad, he didn't feel able to disobey Geordie. Geordie told him that the more he worked the more he would be able to work, and the sooner his body would become work-hardened.

'Drinking won't help that,' Geordie told him. 'Quite the contrary.'

Although talk of the past was taboo round the diggings it was inevitable that a certain amount of harmless enquiry went on.

Bart said idly, 'How'd you get to Ballarat, Fred?'

Fred looked up from the damper he was eating with great enthusiasm. 'Don't know,' he said. 'Corny brought me.'

'Clerk, were you?' asked Sam, who, like Geordie, had noticed that Fred's hands were not those of a labourer.

Fred looked puzzled. 'Can't remember,' he said, after a minute's thought. 'Don't know.'

It became increasingly plain that Fred had, or claimed to have, little memory of a life before he had arrived in Ballarat. He had apparently worked on a road gang. He disliked the few police he saw, and was inclined to hide from them, crouching in his hole if they appeared when he was working.

Mac came along to watch him throwing muck about, and said, 'Congratulations, Geordie, think it'll last?'

Geordie shrugged his shoulders and said, 'Time will tell.'

Fred didn't object to Mac. He couldn't remember him as unkind, but the hard-faced man caused him obvious distress when he appeared one day.

Fred told Geordie that he thought that the police had been very unkind to him before he came to Ballarat, but careful and quiet questioning of him when the others were not about, continued to show that Fred's memories were all very recent.

Big Sister bawled at him once when he annoyed her by refusing to hand over a particularly dirty shirt to be washed. 'Brought up in a pigsty, were you?'

Great hilarity greeted his solemn answer, 'Don't know, Big Sister. Perhaps?'

'Can it be true?' Kirstie said to Geordie later, 'Can he really not remember anything? Or is it that, like some, he's quiet about the past because he's got a dreadful secret in it which he doesn't want to reveal to us?'

Like me, thought Geordie, but said aloud, 'I don't know why, Kirsteen. I thought that it was because he'd had a head injury that he couldn't remember anything, but I'm not sure that the injury was bad enough for that. I think that perhaps he doesn't want to remember. Don't question him. It makes him unhappy. Perhaps, one day…' and he shrugged. 'I think that he's already beginning to change a little, which is a good sign.'

Kirstie thought it all very odd. She continued to be kind to Fred that evening which made Fred very happy. Indeed, what surprised Kirstie the most was how contented Fred usually was—unless he was questioned about his past.

She remarked to Geordie that perhaps it was because Fred could remember so little that he was happy—which was not the first time that she surprised Geordie by her perception. She had already grasped that it was her memories which made her miserable, whether they were of the loss of her mother, or her dead older sister, Kathleen, or the farm, or her brother Jem, who had deserted them after his marriage to a wealthy farmer's daughter.

In the noisy press of their active life she and the others gradually forgot Fred's strange loss of his past, particularly since living with their little group began to educate him, to make him more responsible and a little less artless. It was not only Geordie who noticed that, when Fred stopped referring to himself as 'Fred' so often and began to use 'I' instead, much of his oddity disappeared.

He helped Kirstie in many little ways from that very first evening onwards. He also liked to tease her, as though she were his little sister, but he would always give over if he thought that it made her unhappy. As for his drinking, that had stopped altogether, and even though Geordie had hoped that his attempt to cure Fred might work, he was a little puzzled by how effective it had been. He had never seen a case like this since the days when…well, those days, anyway—he tried not to remember them.

What Fred did not tell Geordie, or anyone else, for they might think him mad, was that when he thought of having a drink a cold, hard voice in his head told him he was to do no such thing. 'You've had quite enough of that, Fred Waring,' it said. 'You don't need any more.'

Fred wondered who the voice belonged to. It wasn't Geordie's, that was for sure. Geordie's voice to Fred was always kind. This was a nasty voice. It belonged to a right nasty and arrogant bastard, the sort of person Fred disliked most. It reminded him of the magistrate in Melbourne, or the Commissioner and the police who rode about the diggings being unpleasant to people.

It was so harsh that Fred was frightened into obeying it. Who knew what might happen if he didn't do as he was told? Perhaps it was a pity that he didn't tell Geordie about the voice, for it would have confirmed Geordie's growing belief about what was really wrong with Fred.

Fred puzzled for a long time about who the voice might belong to, and then gave up the struggle. Life was too interesting, and there was so much fun to be had, that it would be a pity to waste it worrying about voices. After a time this one began to fade, but Fred was still careful never to take a drink—he didn't want it back again.

Fred discovered fun with women quite early on, and like everything to do with Fred, it came about in the oddest manner. Geordie Farquhar was one of the few clean-shaven men in the diggings; most could not be troubled to take the time, or make the effort, to shave off their beards and moustaches once they had reached Ballarat. Thus Big Sister's dismissal of men as large hairy monsters seemed particularly apt.

Geordie, however, always kept himself trim—he tried not to become too dirt-encrusted, even if, like everyone else, he fought a losing battle with mud and/or dust.

Fred, however, once he emerged from his liquor-induced semi-coma began to see the world—and himself—quite clearly. Consequently he started to chafe at his enforced dirtiness and to grieve over his damaged hands, but he had to accept that there was nothing he could do about them, committed to digging as he was. He also disliked intensely his unkempt and unruly black hair and beard. He was vaguely sure that there had been a time when he hadn't possessed them.

One day, watching Geordie shave, he came to the conclusion that he, too, would like to rid himself of his beard and shorten his long hair.

'Could you show me how to do that?' he asked Geordie plaintively.

'Surely,' said Geordie. 'Let me do it for you first, Fred, and then you'll know how to keep in trim yourself.'

It was a lengthy and painful business, Fred discovered, losing his whiskers, but Geordie's handiwork transformed him completely. Kirstie was not the only person to stare at the new handsome Fred it revealed to the world. That his teeth were good had always been plain, but that the rest of him was so personable was a surprise.

Beards could be grown to hide weak, lumpy, and ugly faces, and Big Sister often thought that some men were happy to grow them in order to disguise their facial shortcomings. Trimmed, Fred's hair fell into loose black curls, which added to the attractiveness of a strong and handsome face.

'Looks a different man, doesn't he?' said Sam to Bart. Both of them had 'run wild' as Kirstie disparagingly put it, and had luxuriant hairy growths.

'You could say so,' agreed Bart sadly.

It had been easy to patronise Fred when he was so vague and looked so wild, but the new man who had emerged from Geordie's ministrations—like a handsome butterfly breaking out of a cocoon—was not someone you could easily look down on.

Women turned to stare at Fred when he walked through the diggings, and Kirstie thought that this was what started Fred on his road to ruin with them. Not that Fred was vain. He seemed in some mysterious way innocent of most of the minor sins, vanity included. Perhaps what principally distinguished him was his happiness—it was difficult to upset him other than by being naughty with his food which

Kirstie sometimes was in order to punish him for anything
she thought was a misdemeanour. Kirstie considered all
those in her care, from Sam, Bart and Geordie downwards,
to be little more than her children to be kept in order for
their own good.

Fred liked to eat and, whilst not over-fastidious, he always looked glum if he was given the least attractive por-
tions or didn't get what he considered to be enough. He
was big, worked hard and loved his grub. He was always
ready for it, and was always the first to hold out his plate
for seconds.

'You're greedy, Fred Waring,' Kirstie snapped at him
once.

'Now, now, Big Sister,' said Sam mildly. 'Fred's a big
fellow. He needs his grub and he works hard. Don't grudge
it to him, girl.'

She half-flung more damper at Fred which he took thank-
fully. Damper wasn't exciting, but it was better than nothing. He decided that Big Sister for all her grudging manner
deserved a smile, so he gave her one. The effect was dazzling, but didn't mollify her.

'You needn't grin at me, Fred Waring! You'll get your
share, no more.'

'I don't want any more,' said Fred, who was feeling restless. He didn't know why, but somehow it was connected
with the sheep's eyes which several women had made at
him that day. He rose, and instead of helping Big Sister he
decided to take a stroll around the diggings and see life.
He might be able to walk the strange feeling off.

Geordie watched him go, and then joined Sam and Bart
in a card game around the fire. Big Sister finished the washing up, put the children to bed and began to mend shirts.
Emmie Jackson, more lethargic than ever, sat beside her,
making no effort to help.

Fred looked around him on his walk until he reached the

section where Hyde's saloon and gaming den was flanked by Fat Lil's Place. He had never visited either of them, although he had heard Sam and Bart chatting about them.

He stopped there—and caught the eye of Fat Lil herself.

It was the Yankees at the diggings who had christened the Madam at The Golden Horseshoe Fat Lil, and had changed its name to Fat Lil's Place. Not that Lil was really fat, just big all over. Junoesque, as Geordie had once described her to Bart.

'You know who?' Bart had said, puzzled. 'She's Fat Lil, isn't she?'

Fat Lil was very much the Madam. She kept the girls in order, and the place respectable, if a whorehouse could ever be called respectable. She often stood, or sat, outside, gathering custom, magnificent in her satins, with feathers in her hair, her face as highly painted as an Old Master, Geordie said, confusing Bart all over again.

Although Lil had once been on the game herself she rarely practised it now. Occasionally, if someone took her fancy when she sat outside, she invited him into her bed. 'Lucky for some,' laughed the diggers, since she never asked for payment—but this happened rarely.

Fred's restless mood had grown with every step he had taken. Lately he had found that looking at women, other than Big Sister, that was, made him feel—well—strange. He had a dim memory that doing something with women was very nice, but like many other aspects of Fred's life, his memory of exactly what that something was, was rather patchy.

Fat Lil watched him approaching. Everything about his handsome face and his beautiful body attracted her. When he drew level she returned his innocent stare with her knowing one.

'Hello! New chum, aren't you?' Then she realised that he was The Wreck, sobered off, and without all the hair.

A proper Apollo, as someone had once called a handsome man she had known, long ago when she had been Thinner Lil.

'Yes,' he said. 'Not all that new now, though.'

'No,' said Fat Lil, running her eyes up and down him. 'Like a bit of fun, would you? Free, too.'

Fred was immediately attracted by the prospect of a bit of fun.

'Yes,' he said, adding, 'my name's Fred.' He gave her his swooning smile, even more attractive now that he had lost his beard. 'A bit of fun sounds nice.'

'Right, then,' she said, taking him by the hand, for he seemed a little unsure of what to do next. She led him to her own quarters which were unexpectedly comfortable and pleasant, in contrast to the stark appointments of the girls' rooms.

Fred thoroughly enjoyed having fun with Fat Lil. Once in her bed he found, much to his surprise, that he knew exactly what to do, and that he was rather skilful at it, judging by Fat Lil's pleased reactions.

Fat Lil was surprised as well as pleased. She thought that although it was some time since Fred had enjoyed a bit of fun—and she was right about that—he was still very considerate of his partner, both before and after the fun. She thought this was a little surprising, too. Great hulking diggers were not usually so thoughtful in her experience.

'Nice, wasn't it?' said Fred dreamily, afterwards, thinking that he had been missing a lot in life by not remembering what fun was before. He sometimes wondered why he had such difficulty in recalling things. Whenever Geordie asked him questions about the past to test whether his memory was returning, his usual reply was, 'I can't remember, Geordie.'

Geordie, indeed, was curious to know why it was that Fred had lost some things completely, and yet remembered others quite well. It had been obvious to him for some time that sex had flown out of Fred's universe, and he had sometimes wondered what would happen when—and if—it flew back, and why it had disappeared at all.

That first night Fat Lil was so pleased with Fred that she allowed him, nay, encouraged him, to pleasure her for longer than usual, so it was quite late when he finally trotted off to the only home he could remember. Not that Fred had much idea of time and its importance—that was something else which he had mislaid.

Big Sister was still up when Fred rolled home, a look of stunned happiness on his face. Sam and Bart had abandoned the card game and had gone to Hyde's for a quick drink—which always seemed to turn into a slow one, Kirstie noticed sardonically.

Geordie was teaching her to play chess. He had tried to interest Fred, but Fred had said distressfully, 'It makes my head hurt,' when Geordie had begun to explain some of its basics to him. The chessboard lay on a mat between them, and Fred's arrival came at a crucial point in the game.

'Remembered you had a home to come back to, did you, Fred?' Kirstie said sharply to him. The sharpness was partly because Geordie had her Queen pinned down again.

Her sarcasm flew over Fred's head. He was still in such a state of delight that nothing could disturb him.

'Oh, yes,' he said simply. 'I don't forget that.'

'As a matter of interest,' Kirstie asked, more to delay the fatal moment when her next move—whatever it was— would result in her losing the game than real curiosity about Fred's doings, 'where have you been and what have you been doing?'

Fred, who had sat down in front of the chessboard, opened his mouth to tell her about his adventure with Fat Lil—and then closed it again. He was not so far gone that he did not remember that fun with women like Fat Lil was not something which you talked about to a pure and innocent young girl like Big Sister.

Not that she didn't know about them—you couldn't live in the diggings and be unaware of their presence, but there was a pretence that somehow young virgins never saw them and knew nothing about them and their activities.

He desperately tried to invent some explanation of where he had spent the last three hours, and began to sweat with worry that he might come out with something wrong.

'I...' he began, and then, water running down his face, he pulled his handkerchief out of his pocket and tried to mop it up. He looked at the chessboard as though it might give him inspiration. Not that it did, but what it did do was drag a memory from the distant recesses of his mind.

'If you're playing with white, Big Sister,' he said judiciously, 'you could mate Geordie instead of him mating you, if you let him have your Queen, and then you moved your rook to the square opposite his King—seeing that his taking your Queen leaves your Bishop covering his King as well, and so his King has nowhere to go and you've won the game.'

There was an intense and stunned silence. Both players stared at the board. Geordie, an old chess hand who was certain that he had won the game, saw immediately that Fred had spotted a major weakness in his attack—probably because he had not been concentrating very hard against a novice.

He looked across at Fred. 'Now, how the devil did you know that, Fred?'

Fred had spoken without thinking. He looked at the board and tried to think but nothing happened. The game of chess was once more as mysterious to him as it had been when Geordie had tried to teach him.

'I don't know,' he said, mopping his sweating forehead

with his handkerchief again. 'Why did I say that, Geordie? Does it mean anything?'

'Yes,' said Geordie, 'It means that you were once a better player than I am, and I'm a good one. Are you sure that you can't remember anything more?''

Kirstie, who had been watching Fred and his handkerchief closely, gave a short scornful laugh. 'I think that Fred has remembered another game,' she said. 'Lend me your handkerchief, Fred, I'm hot, too.'

Fred obediently handed it over to Big Sister. He invariably tried to oblige her. Too late, he remembered that Fat Lil had given it to him as a memento of their highly successful encounter, and that Lil was embroidered in one corner. It reeked of powerful perfume, too.

Kirstie saw the name and smelled the perfume.

'Well, well, Fred Waring,' she said softly. 'So you ended up at Fat Lil's Place, did you? Were you there all the time you were gone?'

Fred sighed and said stiffly, 'A gentleman never talks of such things, Big Sister. Particularly to a good woman.'

I wonder where he dredged that piece of etiquette from, thought Geordie who was watching Big Sister's stricken face.

'If it is Fat Lil's I certainly don't want it, Fred Waring, and you can have it back,' and she tossed it into his lap.

Fred said anxiously, 'If you want a nice clean one which isn't Fat Lil's, Big Sister, I have one in my other pocket.'

Geordie didn't know whether to laugh or to cry at this artless answer. Big Sister's response was to snap, 'No, thank you, Fred. I'll take your advice about the chess game, and then leave you to talk to Geordie about those things which a gentleman never talks about to good women but can, apparently, discuss with good men.'

She rose agilely to her feet and stalked to the door of

her hut where she turned to bid them both a haughty good-night.

Fred said anxiously to Geordie, 'Why is Big Sister so cross with me? I tried not to tell her about Fat Lil, but she insisted.'

Geordie hesitated a moment before saying, 'I can't explain to you now why she's so cross with you, Fred. I don't think that you would understand. But I'm sure that one day, perhaps soon, you might be able to work it out for yourself.'

Fred nodded. He wasn't sure that he understood what Geordie was telling him, but said in an earnest voice, 'I do try to be good, you know, Geordie.'

'Yes, I do know, Fred. Don't worry about it. Go to bed yourself. Tomorrow is another day.'

Fred nodded his head and did as he was bid, leaving Geordie to wonder what the future held for Fred and the Moore party now that Fred had remembered one of the reasons why women had been put on earth.

Chapter Three

The immediate future for Fred was a happy one. Women were attracted to him, as Fat Lil had been, and Fred Waring soon gained a name for himself as a man for the ladies, particularly since he was always gentle and courteous when with them. He never pestered them if they weren't interested in him, but when they were, proved to be a joyful and happy lover.

In short, he took to women as he had taken to the bottle—'As though,' Geordie said once to Sam, 'he's making up for lost time.'

He also thought that, one day, Fred's desire for women might go the same way as his desire for drink and disappear. He was still not sure how much his treatment of Fred had stopped him from drinking and how much it was due to Fred himself. Could it be that the man he had once been before he had lost his memory occasionally took him over—which he had done on the night of the chess game?

Big Sister was in despair. 'Who would have thought it?' she wailed. 'All those weeks—and nothing. Now this! You ought to try to stop him, Pa. It's not right.'

Her father looked kindly at her. 'He's a man, Kirstie,'

he said. 'Fred needs his fun. It was right odd that he never seemed to need it before.'

'Oh, you're all the same,' she raged. 'All that you can think of is drink and women.'

'And gambling and smoking and horseplay,' said Geordie, laughing gently at her.

Big Sister rounded on him, too. 'Oh, you're as bad as the rest, Geordie Farquhar, for all your education! You should be helping Fred, not encouraging him to go round lifting women's skirts.'

She realised that her anger with Fred was making her indelicate, and she began to wonder why she was so cross with him since, after all, he was only doing what the rest of the hairy monsters did.

She was prevented from answering this question by Allie running in and announcing that Fred had made a strike, and they were all needed to wash the gold out. Organising this, and standing in the creek, overseeing the little ones, collecting the fine grains, and sharing in Fred's pleasure at his first substantial strike, drove her annoyance at his womanising temporarily out of her head.

Instead, Fred ended up that night with the choicest chops and Johnny cakes as a reward for being a good hardworking mate. Later, Pa gave him a share of the gold on top of his pay and Fred bought himself a new straw hat and Big Sister a ribbon for her hair.

'A bluey-green one to match your eyes,' he told her.

She could scarcely be cross with him after that, particularly as he never said a wrong word to her, or tried to take advantage of her in any way. He was still his usual kind and gentle self, trying to help her a little, so that the entire care of their small party did not fall on her shoulders.

She was cross later, though, when she found that he had gone to Fat Lil's Place wearing his new hat, and Lil had seen him in it, and Fred had had a great deal of fun with Lil celebrating his strike.

Fred's going out on his own to Fat Lil's had another consequence since Sam, Geordie and Bart began to include him in their forays into the night life of Ballarat. But he was not only beginning to alter mentally: the physical changes in him were even more striking. After a few weeks of hard labour his body and hands had both hardened: he was all muscle and had become a powerful man, larger and stronger than the majority of those in the diggings.

Will Fentiman, who ran the boxing booth next to Hyde's Place, walked round to the Moores' claim one afternoon to watch them at work. He was particularly interested in Fred.

Fred had been driving himself hard that day. It was hot and he had stripped off his shirt to reveal his powerful torso. He was about three feet down and, later that day, he was to strike a thin vein of gold which would help them to make a profit that week.

After watching him swinging his pick for a little, Fentiman said, 'You're a big fellow, Fred, and powerful, too. You've got a good body there and you use it well. Have you ever thought of taking up the Fancy?'

'Bit old for boxing, isn't he?' commented Geordie, who didn't want Fred's head hurt again before he was fully recovered.

'Depends,' said Fentiman. 'There aren't many his size. I'd like to see him spar. Can you spar, Fred?'

Fred stopped and looked puzzled before he found some memory from somewhere. It was odd what he could sometimes dredge up.

'Think so. A bit.'

'Come round this evening,' offered Fentiman. 'I'd like to see you in action.'

* * *

'No,' said Big Sister sharply to Fred when he proudly told her of Fentiman's invitation during their evening meal. 'You'll get hurt again.'

This saddened Fred who liked to please Big Sister, but also liked to please himself. He was proud of his new-found powers and strength and wanted to try them out.

'I would like to go, Big Sister.'

'Oh, let him spar a bit,' said Sam. 'He's worked hard, let him have a bit of enjoyment.'

Even Big Sister's flouncing couldn't change the men's minds so they all went round to Fentiman's with him, even Geordie, who privately agreed with Big Sister, but after all Fred was a grown man, even if a slightly strange one.

There was quite a crowd there watching Fentiman's stable work out. Later he would ask members of it to try their luck against his men. There was always some fool, Geordie said, who was willing to risk getting his stupid head knocked off in an attempt to gain a few pence.

Fentiman saw Fred and called him over. 'Have a go with Dan'l here—he'll be careful with you until he's seen what you're worth.'

Dan'l was known as Young Mendoza after some famous fighter of the past, Geordie explained later. He was smaller than Fred, but much more skilful. He danced around Fred saying, 'Loosen up, loosen up.'

This had an odd effect on Fred—Mendoza was kind and didn't really hit him hard, but after they had shuffled about a bit and Mendoza shouted, 'Loosen up,' again, it was as though a kaleidoscope shifted and the scene before him changed.

It wasn't dark Mendoza opposite to him at all, but a laughing sandy-haired giant, blue-eyed and confident, bigger even than Fred, who was saying, 'Come on, come on, loosen up, you're tight.'

And then, suddenly, Mendoza was back again and Fred

really had a go at him, remembering what the giant had said. After a few moments of this Fentiman said, 'That'll do. Well done, Fred.'

Fred walked over to the others, puffing and blowing a bit, and laughing at them. 'Wasn't too bad, was I, once I loosened up? I enjoyed that.'

Fentiman said. 'You were right, Fred. You have sparred a bit. It's a pity you aren't younger I could have made something of you. Not a champion, but something.'

'He doesn't want his brains addled,' muttered Geordie to Bart.

'Thought they was addled already,' grunted Bart.

'No,' said Geordie, half to himself. He asked Fred a quick question, to try to catch him off guard when he often had insights into his forgotten past. 'Do you remember when you last sparred, Fred?'

Fred looked at him, surprised. 'No,' he said, 'but I know that I was once in the ring with a right big 'un. A fair giant he was with a grin all over his face. He was a real hard one, though. Kept shouting orders at me.'

It didn't do to push him too much. Geordie thought that when Fred wanted to remember he would, and Geordie wanted to be around on that day and find out what the true man was really like.

After that Fred often worked out in Fentiman's gym, not enough to damage his hands or head, but enough to keep himself in trim. With each new skill that he recovered he grew and changed a little.

Big Sister fussed over him, and scolded him severely once when he got a black eye through failing to dodge a blow.

'She doesn't want him to spoil his pretty face, does she,' grinned Bart who wasn't always blind to what was going on and, not being so near to Big Sister as Sam was, realised what lay behind Big Sister's half-scolding, half-affectionate manner to Fred—something which Big Sister had not yet grasped herself.

As a result of going to Fentiman's Fred made new friends, principal among them being Young Dan'l Mendoza. Mendoza wasn't so young, being in his mid to late thirties like Fred: he was a man who had almost made it to the very top in England, but not quite. He had joined Fentiman's after he had come to the diggings because he found it easier to earn a living in the boxing booth than breaking his back down a hole.

Sparring with Fred late one afternoon, he towelled off with him afterwards. He knew of Fred's inability to remember his past, but asked him idly, 'Can you remember who taught you to spar, Fred? It was someone who knew his trade, I can tell you that. I'd not say that you were a natural fighter, mind, but you've got brains as well as skill and courage.'

'Oh, I wasn't like my brother. He was really good. He could have been a champion,' said Fred unthinkingly, pulling on his red flannel shirt. He was momentarily in the dark where, oddly enough, the kaleidoscope occasionally shifted and a brief enlightenment often followed.

'Your brother?' queried Dan'l. 'You had a brother who fought?'

Fred's head emerged from his shirt and he blinked at Dan'l, the brief memory already gone. For a moment he had recalled that he had a brother who was a real fighter...but... 'Did I say brother, Dan'l? I can't remember.'

He puzzled a little and tried to bring the memory back, but like the tiger in the night—it hadn't run so often lately—he could not catch it, although one day, like the tiger, it might catch him. He surprised himself by having such complicated unFredlike thoughts these days.

Once he was dressed again—he was slower than Dan'l who had had more practice at taking his clothes on and off—he suddenly stretched and yawned. Dan'l laughed at him and said, 'How about going to Jameson's for a drink, Fred, make a night of it?'

Fred said, 'You're on, Dan'l,' even though he knew that his drink would be a soft one, and they joined the watching trio—Geordie always accompanied Sam and Bart in order to keep an eye on Fred in case he was hurt. Dan'l was kind, though, and tailored his skills to test Fred rather than to knock him about for the fun of it.

Jameson's was in full swing when they arrived there. At one end of the big tent was a small improvised stage on which some minimal entertainment was provided. Jameson claimed that this meant that he was running a music hall. His customers usually ignored the entertainers but that night for some reason each third-rate act was being greeted with rousing cheers.

Fred drank his lemonade—it was pitiful stuff—and didn't join in the ironic cheering. He rather felt for the poor creatures struggling through their acts. They were giving of their best, even if it was inadequate.

Dan'l said quietly to Geordie, 'Fred spoke of a brother today.'

Geordie looked sharply at him. 'Did he say anything useful?'

'Only that he was a really good fighter. He couldn't remember any more and I didn't push him.'

'Best not,' agreed Geordie. 'Fred doesn't strike me as having a member of the Fancy as a brother, though.'

'No,' said Dan'l. 'But at some time someone who really knew the game taught him, I'll say that. Fred can box, but he's no fighter. He has no instinct to kill. The brother had, apparently.'

One more piece of the puzzle that was Fred. Geordie and

Dan'l abandoned discussion of him when a juggler ran on stage. He was so unskilful that he was unintentionally funny and they joined in with the sardonic applause which greeted each failed trick.

Fred said mildly, 'The poor chap's only doing his best.' His kindness seemed to embrace everything and bore out Mendoza's judgement of his lack of a killer instinct.

'His best isn't good enough,' said Sam, laughing. The rowdy mood of the crowd grew and the juggler began to curse them when he lost his clubs in mid-flight again. One hit his foot so that his pained hops accompanied his oaths.

'Damn you all,' he roared.

'And damn you, too, chum,' roared back a sturdy digger at the front, 'if that's the best you can do.'

A man sitting near to him took exception to this. Like Fred, he was sorry for the inept juggler, and said so, drunkenly and loudly, until the big digger aimed a blow at him.

In a flash the stage was forgotten when the fight this started spread happily to other tables, and before long swept down the room. Work-toughened, hard-drinking men struck anyone who was near to them with no idea of why they were doing so—except that it seemed a good idea at the time.

The swirling brawl overturned tables and drink, and at last reached the Moore party. Their table flew sideways when yet another burly digger, set on by two others, crashed into it.

Angered, Dan'l, now half-cut, roared, 'Watch that!' and he struck the larger of the two men who were responsible for his drink disappearing. In a trice the whole Moore party became engulfed in the mass of struggling, fighting, laughing and cursing diggers, striking out in their turn at they knew not who, or what, and being struck at in reply.

At first Fred was bewildered. He was somehow aware that this was a totally new experience for him. He took no part in the brawl to begin with until a mild-looking little man sprang at him from nowhere and struck him, quite without reason.

This was too much, even for equable Fred. Letting out a roar he struck back, and suddenly found himself in the midst of the mêlée, taking part in it with the same unthinking joy as the rest.

Jameson and his bruisers were powerless to quell the riot, which was rapidly wrecking the tent. The fight streamed through the doorway and ended up in the alley outside. Fred threw a last punch at a one-eyed man which was hardly fair of him, he thought later, but he enjoyed doing it at the time. He subsided, laughing and breathless, on to the ground where Geordie found him a little later.

'You all right, Fred?' he enquired, putting out a hand to haul him up.

Fred came upright, laughing helplessly. 'Never had so much fun in my life,' he gasped. 'I could never understand Alan when he said how much he enjoyed the Macao run, all that fighting and wenching!' He shook his head. 'But now…' and he laughed heartily again.

'Alan?' asked Geordie, his eyes watchful.

Fred's laughter ran down. 'Alan?' he repeated, a question in his voice, too. 'Who's Alan? I don't know an Alan.'

It was interesting, thought Geordie clinically, how often Fred spoke of his lost past when he wasn't attending to what he was saying. It was almost as though he blocked it off when he was fully conscious and awake. An odd thought that.

So the brother who could fight had been a sailor, had he? On the Macao run? Geordie found this as difficult to believe as that he had been a boxer. He had his own ideas of what Fred might have been in his lost life, but it might be some time, if ever, if he discovered whether they were right or wrong. In the meantime, they had to get home before the police arrived.

Fred had enjoyed the horseplay, even if he'd lost his new hat in it. He'd been lucky, too, in surviving relatively unmarked. Sam had acquired a black eye, and Bart, beer-covered, torn clothing. Only Mendoza looked as though he had not taken part in the scrimmage. After his first few blows, he had quickly crawled out under the canvas side of the tent, not wanting to damage his hands and body which he needed to keep professionally whole.

Big Sister reprimanded them all when they finally reached home again.

'It's the wages of sin,' explained Geordie. 'Men love horseplay, but they have to pay for it afterwards.'

'They don't pay enough,' she said nastily. 'The grub's cold, and you'll have to eat it cold. It was ready for you at the right time.'

'Cold or not,' said Fred, 'it's welcome.' He sat cross-legged on the ground, grinning happily while he demolished cold stodge and looked at the friendly stars.

Oh, this was the life, and it was good indeed!

After that night, Fred's enjoyment of fun of all kinds grew with each passing week. The harder he worked the more fun he wanted. Kirstie grew used to other women teasing her about Fred or arriving at the claim trying to get a glimpse of him. It was difficult for her not to know what was going on, even if he did exercise a fair amount of discretion.

Some of the women threw themselves at him, which was not always wise. He would turn away from them, and it became clear that he liked to be the one who was the initiator. He did not like bold women.

One of their neighbours, Lew Robinson, had a wife named Annie who made eyes at him, but always from a distance. Fred ignored her at first because Lew was a chum whom he liked. Then he learned that Lew was given to beating her if she as much as looked at anyone else, whilst running after other women himself.

After Fred found out that Lew was cheating Annie with one of Fat Lil's girls he felt differently about her. 'Fair's fair' was his motto, and Lew wasn't being fair to Annie. If he, Fred, made Annie feel happy again, then that would be a good deed as far as he was concerned.

He kept quiet about this, though, for he knew that Big Sister disapproved of his goings-on, which made him feel very unhappy, but not unhappy enough to change his ways—except that after the first few delirious weeks he steadied down and began to pick and choose a little.

'Why did I forget about fun with women, Geordie?' he said one day. They were sitting together before the fire amid the evening hum of activity going on all around them.

'That I can't tell you, Fred. What made you remember, do you think?'

'Oh, that's easy,' returned Fred confidently. 'That was Fat Lil. She liked me, didn't she—and then I remembered. What else have I forgotten, d'you think?'

Geordie could not tell him. Only that he might yet recover skills and knowledge which he did not know he possessed, and would not until they flew back—as having fun had done. Until then, Fred enjoyed himself hugely.

One afternoon he finished work early and went for a walk. He was feeling restless again and a bit of fun seemed called for. He thought that he knew where he might find some and who would happily oblige him.

He stopped at a stall and bought a fairing, a cluster of ribbons made up around a paper flower. Annie would like that, he knew, and he thought that it would be a good idea to visit her armed with a present.

The hut Annie shared with Lew—who might, or might not, be her husband—was a little way away from the Moores and this was convenient, too. He didn't want Big Sister to know about Annie.

There were times when Big Sister's patent disapproval made Fred think that what he was doing was wrong, no matter how much he and his partners enjoyed themselves. But he had seen that Lew was busily engaged elsewhere on a task which would take some time and he congratulated himself on his cleverness in noticing this.

He looked through the improvised window of their hut into the kitchen, but Annie wasn't in. This was disappointing, so he walked round to the back, and there she was, feeding the chickens inside the picket fence which Lew had built for her.

'Hello, Annie,' he said, the fairing hidden behind his back.

'Hello, Fred. Why aren't you working?'

'Finished early, didn't I? Sam said that I'd been good and had done enough for today.' His smile was engaging. 'Guess what I've got, Annie? Make me a cup of tea and I'll show you.'

She looked at his smiling face, and knew at once that it wasn't a cup of tea he wanted. She also knew that whatever he wanted, she wanted, too.

'You're on, Fred. Come in.'

Her kitchen was small, but neat and clean. There was even a little iron stove on which she boiled a kettle. Fred sat down and Annie brewed the tea. After that Fred produced the fairing.

'That's for you, Annie. You can have that for the tea.'

She took it and pinned it to her dress. Fred smiled his dazzling smile which had all the women in the diggings swooning at his feet—everyone but Big Sister, that is.

He picked up the teacup and drank it appreciatively. He

put it down, took her hand and said gently, 'Have fun with Fred, Annie?'

'I thought that the fairing was for the tea, Fred.'

'Oh, it was, it was. But we can have fun as well.'

Annie debated for a minute while she went to a small mesh cage, fetched out of it a cake—a rarity in the diggings—and cut him a large piece which Fred ate with relish, his eyes still on her.

Oh, yes, she wanted fun with Fred, but there was Lew to consider. He might return and she did not want another beating. She had always been faithful to him up to now, but she knew that he had been having fun with the girl from Fat Lil's, so why should she not enjoy herself?

Fred leaned persuasively across the little table. 'Kiss me, Annie, please.'

The kiss was long and satisfactory. It was soon evident that Fred wanted much more than a kiss—and so did Annie. She pushed him off regretfully.

'No, Fred, not now. Lew will be back soon.'

'No, Annie. He and his crew went off to do a job, Sam said. They'll be late home. Be kind to Fred, Annie, and Fred will be kind to you.'

He did not push or force her but simply put on a comically sad face. They were standing close together now.

She put her arms around his neck. 'In the bedroom, then.'

His smile was impudent. 'I can't wait, Annie. Nor can you, either. What's wrong with the wall?'

'Oh, Fred, you're wicked!'

But she didn't argue with him further. He began to kiss her more urgently. His hands were all over her, undoing her in more ways than one.

'Oh, Fred, please. Oh, Fred, no, Oh, Fred, yes, please, yes. Oh, please…' and on that last word her voice rose an octave as Fred Waring had his wicked way with yet another woman.

* * *

'Who have you been misbehaving yourself with today, Fred Waring?' Big Sister asked him acidly when he arrived home late that afternoon.

'I don't know what you mean, Big Sister.'

'Oh, yes, you do, Fred Waring. I know your face when you've been enjoying yourself. Cock of the walk, you don't hide it,' exclaimed Big Sister coarsely, wondering at her own anger.

'Now, now, Big Sister. Little girls shouldn't know about such things.'

'Little girls, my foot,' said Kirstie inelegantly. 'I haven't lived among men all my life without knowing about their many nasty tricks. And you're the trickiest of the lot, and no mistake. Is any woman safe with you, I ask you?'

'Well, you're safe with me, Big Sister,' said Fred, laughing, being naughty with Big Sister for once, but she obviously needed reassuring that he had no designs on her virtue.

Big Sister, however, felt a terrible desire to weep on hearing that she was safe with Fred.

'I wouldn't have you, Fred Waring, however hard you begged me.'

'Shan't ask, then,' said Fred obligingly, grinning at her over his warmed-up stew.

If only he weren't so handsome. And good at *it*, too. All the women in the diggings said so, and were mad for him. Damn him, she thought suddenly. If he made half a move I'd be all over him. No, I wouldn't. I've more sense. Oh, damn him again!

'Feeling better now, Big Sister?'

'What?'

'Now that you've sent me to hell in your thoughts.'

'And damn you for being a mind reader, too,' she said

aloud. 'You're a right bastard, you are, Fred Waring, for all your pretty ways.'

His eyes were teasing her, but not unkindly. She was his little sister, after all, not his big one.

'Temper, temper,' he said.

Kirstie began to laugh despite herself. 'Oh, damn you again, Fred.'

'Such language, Big Sister. What would the parson say?'

'Parsons, Fred Waring? What do you care about parsons? It's all without benefit of clergy with you.'

'Parsons are for you, Big Sister, not for me.'

At this she threw her wooden spoon at him. He caught it and threw it back at her. She caught it again and with a swear word of complete reproachability she threw it clear across the little kitchen.

Herbie, the next to youngest, sitting in the corner, thought that this was a new game. He caught it deftly and threw it back to her. She caught it for the last time, sat down, flung her apron over her head and began to cry. For what, she had no idea.

A large hand lifted the apron from her face.

'Kiss it better, then,' said Fred helpfully as though she were no older than the baby.

She slapped his face. He had no right, no right at all, to see her as a child. He caught her hand and kissed it, quite impersonally—I might as well be little Rod for all he knows—and as she thought this he said, his voice quite different, 'When did you do that, Kirsteen?'

'That? Oh, the burn—yesterday.'

'It should be dressed. You don't want a permanent scar there.'

His voice was quite changed, something which had happened once or twice before. It was not amused, or joking, but quiet and serious. He sounded like quite a different man.

He let her hand go. 'I'm sorry, Kirsteen, I shouldn't have teased you so.'

'So you should be, Fred Waring, so you should be.'

'You should be kind to Fred, Big Sister.' His eyes were teasing her: he was careless Fred again.

Kirstie rose and cleared the table with such exasperation that the noise made Fred's head hurt.

She began to wash the pots with unnecessary vigour. Rod, sitting by Herbie, in the corner, sensed Big Sister's anger—why was she so cross with Fred?—and began to cry loudly.

It was too much. Kirstie bent her head, tears coming into her eyes. She took her hands out of the water and prepared to comfort Rod. The crying stopped suddenly.

She found that Fred had picked Rod up, was bouncing him on his knee and making faces at him to amuse him. He was being so kind and Fred-like that all Kirstie's anger drained out of her at the sight. Oh, let him have as many women as he wanted, if *that* was what he needed, she thought sorrowfully.

Fred bent his head and whispered to Rod, 'Mustn't bother Big Sister, chum. She has too much to do as it is, looking after us all,' and he gave her his most charming smile.

'He's so good, Fred is,' said Kirstie sadly to Geordie Farquhar later when Fred had taken the little ones down to the creek so that Big Sister could have some time to herself. 'Oh, I know that sounds strange and silly when he used to drink heavily, and now he chases after women. But he means no harm by it. When I reproached him the other day he looked at me and said, "But they enjoy it so much, Big Sister, how can it be wrong?"'

Geordie's respect for Kirstie's perception grew. 'I know what you mean,' he said. 'And you're right. There's an innocence about him—as though he were new-born. And, Kirstie, if it comforts you, I think that there's a good chance that the chasing after women may go the way of the drink.'

He thought that he knew what was wrong with Kirstie. For Fred, Kirstie was Big Sister, nothing more.

Small Rod was fretful in the night and the water jug in the hut was empty. Kirstie tried to comfort him, but he lay restless in her arms, until finally she put him down, picked up the jug and the ladle and went outside to the water butt, dodging the sleeping Fred.

Fred was making strange noises—half-sobs and muttered words which made no sense at all. Pa had once said that Fred was a noisy sleeper and he had put it down to the drink at first—but it couldn't be that now. When she passed him he tossed and turned, flinging out a questing hand.

Suddenly Kirstie felt sorry for him. So long as it had been the drink which caused the trouble she had felt little sympathy for him, but now, when he sighed and groaned, moved by pity she bent down, took him by the shoulder and whispered, 'Be quiet, Fred, there's a good boy. There's nothing wrong.'

Fred sat up abruptly and looked at her with blank eyes, so she knew that sleep still claimed him, and that he did not recognise her. Before she could stop him he put his arms around her and drew her down to him. His actions, his voice when he spoke to her, were so unlike Fred that she hardly knew him.

He held her to him so gently and lovingly, and kissed her cheek with such care that the wild, rowdy Fred of the daytime seemed a different man.

'Oh, my love, my love,' he whispered in her ear. 'I thought that I'd lost you. There was a tiger running through my dreams. Let me hold you, my darling heart.'

Kirstie was so surprised that it was a moment before she

pushed him away from her. She saw his face change when she disengaged herself: more than that she understood that he had recognised her and was the daytime Fred again.

His face puzzled, he said, 'It's Big Sister, isn't it? For a moment I thought…'

The puzzled look grew stronger before it cleared and he said in his usual frank, almost childish way, 'I had a bad dream. About a tiger—and I thought that I had lost something precious. I can't think what it might have been. Was I noisy?'

'Yes,' she whispered. 'But only a little. Go to sleep, Fred. Try to forget the tiger—it was only a dream and it can't hurt you.'

'Oh, I will, I will,' and he lay down again. He looked up at her and said simply, 'You're kind really, aren't you? I like it when you're kind to poor Fred.' He put his head on his arm and fell asleep immediately.

Poor Fred, indeed, thought Kirstie, ladling water into the jug for Rod. Poor Fred—making half the women in the diggings happy. A tiger, of all things—and something he's lost. I wonder who he thought I was? Geordie had said that Fred was an enigma and he had explained the word to her. But it was hard to think of Fred as someone complicated, particularly after he had spent the afternoon with Annie.

The thought pained her so greatly that for the first time she asked herself why she found Fred's wenching so distressing. The answer came immediately and it explained so much that she knew that it was true.

She was in love with Fred and had been for some time without knowing it—or rather she had refused to know it for she had determined that she would pin her affections on no man, and least of all on anyone as unlikely as poor, lost Fred.

But there was no controlling the body's call, she knew desolately. In some way which she did not understand and could not explain he had become the centre of her world, and his arms about her, unknowing of her, had told her plainly that she wanted from him that which he gave to other women so carelessly.

She loved him for his looks, his beautiful voice, his kindness and consideration for others, his hard work, but most of all because he was just Fred. Fred, who only saw Big Sister, never Kirsteen Moore. Big Sister, who was sometimes cruel, sometimes kind, but never someone to love.

She also knew why Geordie occasionally looked at her with such pity, and why she hated it so when he did.

Chapter Four

Sydney, Villa Dilhorne

Lachlan was too young to miss his father, and even had he been older, Hester thought, Thomas's involvement with him had been so minimal that Lachlan would hardly have noticed his disappearance from his life.

Only Hester's resolute will kept her tears from falling when she watched her grandson at play. Neither she nor Tom had expected Thomas to return happily from Melbourne: what they had not expected was that he would not return at all—something which was beginning to seem extremely likely.

The documents relating to the railway agreements, signed and sealed by Thomas, had arrived, but no Thomas came with, or after them—nor did he send them a personal letter. The only one which they had received related strictly to business.

Even then Tom did not worry overmuch. He was hopeful that his son had taken his advice, after all, and had decided to enjoy himself a little before he came home. It was only when a letter arrived from Roger Herbert, one of his new partners in the railway venture, plainly assuming that

Thomas had left Melbourne for home some time ago, that Tom began to worry.

It was impossible for him to keep much from Hester, nor did he wish to. After he had given her Herbert's letter to read she had said bluntly to him, 'What, then, *has* happened to Thomas? He should have returned home long ago. There has been no word from him, or of him. Even allowing that he departed in such anger it is not like him to leave us in ignorance as to his whereabouts.'

Tom looked steadily at her. 'I propose to write today to Melbourne, asking for enquiries to be made about him. It seems that both Herbert and his partner, Redmayne, believe that he has returned home. It is plain that he is no longer in Melbourne.'

Hester had closed her eyes. 'If he is not there, then where is he? Oh, Tom, I am afraid for him.'

Tom was afraid, too, but he did not say so. His son had become almost reckless in his pride and his arrogance, that he did know. He was fearful of what danger he might have put himself in. Hester knew it also and, watching Lachlan, her fears had grown greater with each day that had followed the arrival of Herbert's letter.

The door opened to admit her husband. His face was grey, almost defeated. He looked his years.

'You are back early from the counting house?' Her voice rose a little. 'Is something wrong?'

'Yes.' He would not temporise with her. He respected her too much for that. 'You must be brave, Hester, my dear.'

'It's Thomas, isn't it?'

'Yes.' He closed his eyes in pain. 'I told you that I had written to Melbourne for enquiries to be made. I have heard from both Redmayne and Herbert and the police. It seems that Thomas was last seen at a dinner at Herbert's, given to celebrate the agreement over the railway. They did not expect to meet him again, nor did they. Their assumption was that he was to return home on the following morning—he had already made all his arrangements to do so. But…'

He paused. He did not want to say the unacceptable.

'Go on,' she said. 'It may be hard for us both, but you must tell me the truth. Everything.'

'So far as the police can discover he disappeared after the dinner. He went home with a Mrs Theresa Spurling. He stayed there for a short time before leaving her to walk back to his hotel, which was only a short distance away. But he never reached it. His luggage is still in the hotel, unclaimed. They are in such disarray because of the gold fever that they did nothing about it—other than put it into store.

'They probably thought that he'd gone home without it for some reason—if they thought at all, who knows? Things are chaotic there, I understand. There's worse, though, I fear. I sent a list of his personal valuables to Melbourne. The police searched the pawnshops and found these.'

He opened the parcel he had been carrying and showed Thomas's mother what it contained.

Hester stared at Thomas's seal ring, at his ruby stick-pin and, worst of all, the gold half-hunter given to him by Tom and herself when he had reached twenty-one. She picked it up and gazed blindly at the inscription on the back of its case.

'No,' she said with difficulty. 'I don't believe it. He cannot be dead, I would have known.'

Tom took the watch from her and placed it on the table beside him. 'My love, I can offer you no false hopes. The most likely explanation is that he was attacked and killed, either deliberately, or accidentally, for his valuables. The pawnshop owner remembered that the watch and the other things were brought in by a big digger, that's all. He says that there are thousands like him in Melbourne and Ballarat.

The name left was Smith—and plainly by the description of him he was not Thomas.'

'But they haven't found his body, have they? You are not keeping that from me, are you?'

'I have never kept anything from you since I deceived you over Jack Cameron. I said then that I would never do so again, and I have kept my word. But it is now over six months since he disappeared. We have to face that fact and what it implies—in the light of the discovery of these,' and he placed his hand gently on Thomas's mute possessions.

Hester was shaking but tearless. 'I still do not believe that he is dead. But you must write again.'

'I wrote to Melbourne today, before I left for home, saying that I intend to pay a visit there. We have already lost so much time. I can offer you little hope, for if he is alive, where is he? Furthermore, I can imagine no circumstances in which he would willingly part with his treasured possessions.'

'But his ring. The ring Bethia gave to him—that is missing.'

'The robber probably kept it, my dear.'

'Of course, I am being foolish. Oh, poor Lachlan, his father and mother both gone.'

Tom pressed her hand lovingly. 'I am so sorry that I had to bring you this news—but I could not lie to you.'

'No, you must never deceive me, however worthy the motive.' She paused and looked at him, her eyes glistening with tears. 'I still do not believe that he is dead. I would have known if he were,' she repeated.

Tom looked at her sadly. He had heard this said before, by others, and it had meant nothing more than a refusal to accept the inevitable.

'My dear, when I reach Melbourne I shall do my best to clear this mystery up—unless we hear any news of him before I am due to leave.'

'If they do not find his body, you mean? Or if he does not come home.'

It was not like Hester to be unable to face reality. It was hard for her to accept this loss, coming as it did after Bethia's untimely and tragic death.

'My dear, so much time has passed that I fear my journey will be a fruitless one, but until we know the worst we can always hope.'

Hester rose and picked up Lachlan.

'I cannot accept that he has gone forever, particularly when we should not have let him leave us in the state he was in.'

Tom picked up his son's watch. He saw again Thomas's angry face on that last morning.

'You cannot reproach yourself more than I reproach myself, for it was I, not you, who sent him to Melbourne. I thought that it was for the best, but now…'

'I do not reproach you, Tom. You were doing what you saw as your duty.' She hugged Lachlan to her. 'I shall try to be patient.'

Tom rose in his turn and took the child from her. 'He has left us Lachlan, and we must care for him.'

Fred sat watching Geordie, Sam, Bart and Ginger Tate play poker one evening after supper. None of the four cared to risk much by playing at Hyde's. Instead, they indulged themselves by wagering beans instead of money. Very small quantities of money were paid out at the end of the game according to the number of beans won or lost, and a player could retire at any time if he began to lose consistently.

Fred was bored: a new condition. When he had first been rescued by the Moores, simply living had been enough to keep him happy. He had greeted each day with zest and an artless wonder. A game of snap with the kids had been enough to please him and help him to pass the time. Lately, though, he had begun to change.

That night Big Sister sat by him repairing shirts—her hands were always busy with some much-needed task—while Emmie rested idly, dreaming of the past and leaving Big Sister to care for the children who were enjoying a last play before retiring for the night.

Geordie looked up from his hand to find Fred's eyes on him. Something there, something not seen before, alerted him. When the round ended Geordie scooped up the beans he had won from the others before saying, 'Would you like to take a hand, Fred?'

Sam said with a laugh, 'Knows how to play poker, does he?'

Sam had only learned to play the game on coming to the diggings where the Yankee miners had brought it with them. Bart was a poor player, Sam was much better, Ginger was your stolid average man, and Geordie was skilful enough to win at Hyde's when he cared to play there—which wasn't often. He was careful with his money, particularly now that they were beginning to make a little, although they were still waiting—and hoping—for a really big strike.

Fred nodded eagerly at them. 'Yes, I've just remembered that I've played poker before.'

Geordie remarked, apparently idly, 'When, Fred?'

'I can't remember, Geordie. But I do know that I've played the game and what the rules are.' He paused and then said dreamily, 'The Patriarch taught me, I think.'

'The Patriarch, Fred? Who was that?'

'I don't know.'

As usual when challenged directly, Fred looked unhappy. 'Somebody, I suppose. May I have some beans, please, Geordie?'

Fred rarely forgot his manners. Geordie pondered the

many paradoxes of Fred's condition—knowing and not knowing. Forgetting the important things of his life, but remembering the inconsequential.

What was becoming plain, however, was that Fred was slowly beginning to recover more and more of his lost past. One day he might even remember who he was—or rather, who he had been.

Fred played uncertainly at first. Losing did not please him. He knew—how?—that he was not used to losing. He began to concentrate on what he was doing. The hard determination which had recently begun to surface above his artless charm was suddenly in evidence.

Slowly, Fred began to win. Geordie—from playing in a way which allowed the others a share in the game—suddenly discovered that such tactics were useless against Fred. He was having to try to stay with him, and gradually the beans began to accumulate before him.

Kirstie put down her sewing to watch them. Fred's joy in his success was manifest. He scooped up his beans with a smile on his face. His pleasure in recapturing a skill which he had not known he possessed was so artless that the others could not feel offended.

The game ran out with Fred the winner. He sank back, refusing the others' money at the end. 'No, I don't want it. Oh, I'm so tired. That was hard work.' But there was no doubt that he was happy. 'You see, I was right. I had played before.'

'Yes,' agreed Geordie drily. 'You've certainly played before. Do you remember any other games?'

'Yes,' smiled Fred, 'other games, too. The Patriarch said that I was a natural with cards—not like boxing.'

He lay back on the ground, his hands behind his head, admiring the stars. Night had fallen while they played and Kirstie had lit the lanterns for them after putting the kids to bed.

Dreamily Fred let his mind run loose: the concentration of the last few hours had made him feel as though he had run a marathon. Geordie, recalling the game, thought that Fred's recollection of cards played and odds for and against was remarkable.

Fred fell asleep while they watched him. Sam picked up the cards and wondered, 'Now who would have thought that? I never would have believed that he'd sit so still or play for so long, or, for that matter, would play so well. He knew every card that fell and when to call—and not to call.'

Kirstie had resumed her sewing in the light of a nearby lantern, but she looked up several times in order to watch Fred sleeping so quietly. Sam had told her that recently Fred wasn't suffering so many disturbed nights, and now the effort of the game, and the satisfaction he had achieved, had quietened him ever further.

'Queer customer, Fred,' said Ginger Tate. 'He's like a child sometimes. But I've never known a child who could play poker like a card sharp. Not that he was cheating, mind,' he added hastily. The Moore lot didn't like Fred to be criticised: he was one of theirs.

Geordie yawned and rose. He walked across to Fred and threw a blanket over him. 'A pity to wake him when he's so sound off and quiet. Let him sleep.'

Which they did and Fred had a night without alarms and excursions and tigers: it was to be the first of many.

After that he was included in the poker school, and he agreed to start with less beans to make it more interesting for the rest of them. Even so his skills visibly improved with time until Geordie said to him one evening, 'How about going round to Hyde's, Fred? Try your luck there, why not? We could all pitch in and give you a stake to start with.'

Fred's face shone. He looked at Geordie who had always been kind to him when he was poor Fred at the beginning of time, and he was still kind now that Fred was no longer poor, but was becoming more and more a partner in their enterprise—although still somewhat irresponsible and happy with it.

'I'd like that,' he replied. His face was alight with joy when he set off for Hyde's with the rest of the Moore party escorting him. He was well turned out: Big Sister had given him a clean white silk scarf to wear, even though she privately deplored the whole risky enterprise.

However, she saw that she had no way of stopping it, so she gave them all her blessing and watched them go. Fred was on equal terms with the others for the first time, and was off to try out his newly remembered skills, learned, God knew when or where, for Fred certainly didn't!

Edward Hyde watched the Moore party walk into his place. He knew Geordie Farquhar and that he was a skilful, if careful, player. He was not a true gambler for he would never risk all. Hyde thought that Geordie had probably risked a lot once in the game of life and had lost all. Being a loser in life's lottery, Hyde knew another when he met him. He knew Fred by sight and was surprised to see him with the others. He was even more surprised when he joined Geordie at the tables.

Hyde was a heavy, dark man, clean shaven with a hard, clever face. He ran an honest gaming house: Hyde thought that you made a greater profit that way. Several games were on offer, including a wheel of fortune as well as the poker tables where men won, but mostly lost, their hard-earned gains from the earth. Well, if the Moores wanted their big dummy to lose his small poke, it was their worry, not his.

He smoothed his broadcloth sleeve with his hand and watched Fred buy counters from the bank. Playing, Fred changed. His artless look of happiness remained—it was almost better than the conventionally expressionless poker face, more than one rueful punter was to think. His concentration was absolute. Geordie's luck ran out early that night, but Fred's held good and Hyde, coldly studying the game and the players, soon grasped that the Moores' dummy was a natural.

'Play poker like a damned accountant, don't you,' said one disappointed player who left the game when all his counters had disappeared, 'for all your silly grin?'

The words awoke an unpleasant memory in Fred. His face clouded over. 'I'm not an accountant,' he said with dignity. 'I'm a member of Sam Moore's syndicate.' He gathered his winnings together. 'I've had enough,' he announced. 'Father always told us, leave off before you lose. Winning streaks don't last.'

'Your father taught you, Fred?' asked Hyde, who knew nothing of Fred's strange lack of memory. It was a conversation he was conducting, not an inquisition. 'He must have been a good player.'

'Yes,' agreed Fred, 'he was. The Patriarch taught my brother and me to play cards.' The frail memory vanished—who, he thought, was the brother? And the Patriarch, whose name he kept remembering, who was he?

'I like winning,' he offered happily. Hyde looked at him sharply. He was not used to innocence, and this was Fred's distinguishing feature, which was odd in a man who showed such guile in playing cards, but so little in life.

'Do you play piquet, too, Fred?' he asked and when Fred nodded an eager 'Yes', Hyde said, 'I'll give you a game next time you come here.' Now this was an accolade, for Hyde rarely played cards with anyone but he was curious to test Fred's skills.

'Father taught us to cheat,' Fred said suddenly to Geordie

on their walk home. 'But he ordered us never to do it—
only to watch for it and allow for it.'

He fell silent again and none of them questioned him
further, for he was so tired that they had to help him to
bed.

If Kirstie had any misgivings about this latest addition
to Fred's repertoire of fun she kept them to herself. One of
the unintended consequences of her discovery of her feelings for Fred was that she suddenly became attractive to
other men.

It was as though they glimpsed through the sharp face
which she showed to the world her true beauty and the
kindness of heart which she resolutely withheld from public
view. Pa's prediction that she would not lack for suitors
began to come true.

The first to arrive was Young Dan'l Mendoza, who often
visited their claim and had joined the poker and beans
school through his friendship with Fred. Until then she had
been merely part of Dan'l's background—someone who
flitted in and out of view, scolding the children and keeping
the men in order. Spending more time at the Moores' claim
gave him a different picture of her. He watched her caring
for poor, overwhelmed Emmie and all the others in the
party. He saw her working in the creek, sewing, knitting,
cleaning, cooking, making and repairing shirts, trousers,
vests and socks, and ensuring that everything was correct.

Oh, yes, he saw a woman whose whole face softened
when she looked at the men laughing and talking, who
came alive in their presence, and he knew what she might
look like if she were cared for, instead of caring, if she
loosened her pretty blonde hair and wore the attractive
clothing of the more fortunate.

Dan'l did not realise at first that the soft looks at the
men, unknowingly given by Kirstie, were meant for Fred

alone. He only knew that he hoped that they might be for him. Kirstie liked Dan'l despite his profession. She thought that most men, whatever their age, were like great puppies. They never really grew up.

Sam and Bart were not young but they loved horseplay and joking. They cheered Fred and Dan'l on when they wrestled and fought in mock play after the poker game was over, and Dan'l had lost to Fred and demanded his revenge.

If Dan'l fell out of the game early he invariably went over and talked to Kirstie. He never called her Big Sister— that was for the Moores only. She asked him about London and his life there for she had a sharp curiosity to learn as much as she could and, like Geordie, Dan'l tried to satisfy her.

She listened and worked as he told her of the gas-lit city and of its roaring life, of the gymnasia, and of the men and women he had met during his brief career as a coming fighter. Some of them were famous—even Kirstie had heard of them. He had no woman of his own now, and Kirstie took note of his ripped and damaged clothing and offered to repair it for him.

'Only if you let me pay you,' he said.

She shook her head, but the next time he came around carrying a shirt which had nearly lost its collar, and a scarf for her if she mended it—which she did.

Fred was not sure how he felt when he saw Dan'l with Kirstie, especially when he grasped that Sam quite approved of their growing friendship. Sam wasn't sure whether he wanted Kirstie to marry Dan'l, but at least it was better for her to have a suitor and a personable one— for Dan'l was the first to show an interest in her. It might make her look at men in a different light.

Fred, now, he definitely thought that Dan'l was not good enough for her. Big Sister deserved—well, what did she deserve? Someone who would care for her as well as she cared for others, and Dan'l was hardly likely to be able to do that from a boxing booth at Fentiman's.

Dickie Vallance, the storekeeper, was different, but he was not good enough for Kirstie, either, Fred rapidly decided. He was too old, for one thing. There was no doubt that he had an eye on her despite being in his early fifties. He was looking for a useful second wife and Kirstie's hardworking care for everyone attracted him.

He saved the best of the food for her, occasionally dropped the price, and the Moores' grub was the better for it. Kirstie, however, was short with Dickie, which, far from discouraging him, had the opposite effect.

One evening he turned up at her hut and asked to take her to The Palace Theatre which, for all its grand name, was really only an extra-large tent. Kirstie wasn't sure that she wanted to go with him, but she could tell that it would please Pa if she did, so she said, 'Yes', even if a little unwillingly.

Dickie waited while she changed into her best print dress, the one with the blue and white stripes, put on her new bonnet which had a silk rose on its brim, and the pretty scarf which Dan'l had given her. Thus splendidly outfitted she went off with him, Fred looking glumly after them.

'What does she want to go out with that old man for?' he asked Geordie.

'Kirsteen needs a bit of fun, too, Fred,' said Geordie, watching him.

'Surely not with Dickie,' said Fred anxiously, taking the phrase 'a bit of fun' literally. Kirstie was not one who would have that sort of fun lightly, he thought.

'Dickie will behave himself,' said Geordie, 'and Kirsteen will enjoy herself, I'm sure.'

Geordie was right again. Dickie did behave himself. Kirsteen Moore was a good girl, he knew, and he brought her home untouched. Even though she had enjoyed herself at the theatre, laughing at and applauding the clowns and jugglers, and crying at the sentimental ballad-singer, it was not Dickie she wanted to be with, and the next time that he asked her out, she told him that she was tired.

Dan'l and Dickie were not the only men who began to hover about her, but they were the most persistent and it was soon evident that she wanted none of them. The only man she did want glowered at all those who danced around her, but made no move himself and continued to see her as only Big Sister, even if he were a little puzzled as to why he resented her would-be suitors so bitterly.

These days, though, he didn't seem to have time to do a great deal of thinking and puzzling, for his life had become extremely busy. He had begun to supplement his earnings at the diggings by going round to Hyde's Place and playing for money. He never staked a great deal, but played cautiously enough to ensure himself a small, if steady, income.

From being someone who found it difficult to concentrate at all he was now capable of sitting for hours, contemplating the game, studying the cards, coldly aware of what had been played, of the nature of the men against whom he was playing, and calculating the odds 'like a damned money-lender' as more than one defeated man said, echoing the loser on his first night at Hyde's Place.

He soon acquired quite a reputation. The Yankees came to Hyde's to play against him. Geordie Farquhar and Edward Hyde agreed that they had never seen such a remarkable transformation.

'A few months ago he could barely play snap with the Moore kids and Big Sister,' said Geordie, 'and look at him now!' Changing all the time, he added to himself.

He was, in many ways, still artless Fred for all that, unless he was roused or angered, which was rarely.

* * *

The night that Geordie Farquhar particularly remembered afterwards started innocently enough. Fred sat in his usual place, the only man without a bottle beside him. There were a large number of strangers, newcomers to the diggings, there. Regulars were beginning to avoid playing against Fred. His childish delight at winning was particularly galling when he had been so disgustingly cunning in order to win.

He was seated opposite to a large heavily-built digger who kept looking at him with an odd, slightly puzzled expression on his face.

'Anything wrong, then?' asked Fred in his frank way. 'There's not something strange about me, is there? Everyone here knows Fred Waring—ask Ned Hyde.'

The man shrugged and decided that he must be mistaken. It was an odd likeness, surely, nothing more, but the likeness was so strong it troubled him—for a number of reasons. He began to lose heavily and grew more and more angry. He put his cards down at the end of one losing game, grumbling and muttering while he did so. His big left hand was splayed, firm against the table.

Fred stared at the hand and, moving with surprising speed, pinned it down with his own right hand. He spoke, his voice high and angry. 'Why are you wearing Fred's ring? That's my ring you're wearing.'

'Oh, come now,' said the ring's wearer uneasily. 'I've had this for years.'

'No, you haven't. It's mine. I wondered where it had gone to. How did you steal it from me?'

His behaviour was typical of Fred: it was innocently straightforward and to the point.

The big digger appealed to Hyde. 'You're in charge here. Do something about this blasted lunatic.'

'I'm not a lunatic! And that's my ring.'

'Hang on, mate,' said Hyde to the digger. 'Fred doesn't

usually lie. He's a straightforward chap, is Fred. Let me have a look at the ring.'

'Be damned to that,' said the digger angrily, his hand still pinned to the table. Fred's strength after months working with pickaxe and spade was formidable. For the first time since Geordie had known him he looked dangerous.

'It's soon checked,' said Geordie, interested by what he suspected was something out of Fred's lost past. 'Is there anything distinctive about the ring, Fred?'

Fred screwed up his face. 'Words inside,' he said excitedly. 'Yes, I remember now, words inside—and on the front.'

'Anyone can see that,' said the digger, sneering.

'But it says that it's mine inside.'

'We can soon check that,' repeated Geordie. 'Let's see. Take it off, if you would. You can't object to that. If Fred's wrong, he'll apologise.'

Hyde leaned forward, interested, staring at the pinned hand, and at Fred, silent, but still visibly seething. He said, 'We all know Fred, but who are you? New chum, aren't you?'

'The name's Walker, damn you,' snarled the digger. 'What's with the lunatic that you all support him?'

'You can end it,' said Geordie. 'All you have to do is give Hyde the ring, ask Fred to tell him what's inside, and let Hyde check whether or not he's right.'

Walker looked round at all the inimical faces. At Hyde and his bouncers watching him, their faces impassive. He knew a losing situation when he was in one.

He shrugged in his turn. 'First make him let me loose,' he ground out.

'You heard, Fred,' said Hyde.

Reluctantly Fred let the hand go. Equally reluctantly Walker pulled off the ring and handed it to Geordie Farquhar. 'You look at it,' he snarled. 'Not him,' pointing at Hyde.

Geordie held the ring to the light from the oil lamp hanging above the table. He looked from Fred to Walker. 'Yes, there's lettering inside. Can either of you tell me what it says?'

'Bought it off a chum recently,' grated Walker. 'I've never looked inside.'

'You said that you'd had it for years.' Geordie's voice was dry.

'Oh, but is it the lunatic's?' demanded Walker savagely. 'Go on, Fred, if that's what you're calling yourself now. You tell us what it says. If you can.'

Fred's face clouded. 'I'm sure it's mine, Geordie,' he muttered slowly. 'But you know that I'm not good at remembering. I'll try.'

He dropped his head and dredged his memory. Nothing. He looked at the ring in Geordie's palm, closed his eyes this time—and suddenly the kaleidoscope shifted.

He was in a big room, full of light. The tiger was there—but how could a tiger be there? Opposite to him was the prettiest girl Fred had ever seen. She had red hair, a delicate white skin, bluey-green eyes, and a loving expression. The ring was on her palm, and she was handing it to him.

'See what it says inside, my darling.'

'B.K. to her loving T.D.,' he read aloud, and then felt himself drowning in her beautiful eyes.

'What did you say, Fred?'

The voice was hard. It destroyed the vision of loveliness before him. He looked around to find himself in a strange room, surrounded by people whom he had never seen before. He thought that he was going to faint—and then the kaleidoscope shifted again and he was staring at the ring in Geordie's hand.

A feeling of the utmost desolation and loss swept over

him. He spoke. His voice was strange to himself and to the watchers.

'It says "B.K. to her loving T.D."'

Geordie looked keenly at the ring and then at him. 'So it does, Fred. It's your ring,' and he held it out to him.

Walker had begun to shout that the initials had nothing to do with Fred Waring, either, when Fred, with an expression of the most bitter rage and hate on his face, sprang on him, battering him with his fists, and would have killed Walker if the bouncers had not pulled him away.

The bouncers ran the protesting Walker to the door. Once there, Walker turned and shouted desperately, 'You should have been dead by now, damn you, Fred Waring, or whatever you're calling yourself these days.' He was still shouting when the bouncers threw him into the alley.

Hyde turned to Fred, who had sunk back into his chair, the ring in his hand. 'If you have any further trouble from him, Fred, let me know. I'll see to him for you.'

But Fred was listening to no one. He slipped the ring on to the third finger of his left hand.

'She gave it to me,' he murmured slowing, stroking the ring.

'Who was she, Fred?' asked Geordie quietly.

'The girl with the bluey-green eyes. Not Big Sister—another girl. I told you that it was mine.'

He looked up at Geordie, his eyes full of tears. 'I do remember that I told her that I would always wear it. That's all.'

He looked across at Hyde. 'I've played enough tonight,' he said. 'I want to go home.'

Chapter Five

Ned Hyde had not been aware of Fred's loss of his past and the episode of the ring intrigued him. Some nights later he sat in his comfortable back room, talking to Geordie Farquhar, two lost souls together.

'Now, Geordie,' he said abruptly, 'explain to me how Fred Waring came to own a ring with someone else's initials in it, has trouble remembering them, but did recognise the ring the moment he saw it.'

'The answer is, I can't,' said Geordie. 'All I know is that Fred remembers virtually nothing before he arrived in Ballarat and that the Moores try to protect him as much as they can. They're very decent people. As to why and how he lost his memory, that I can't tell you. He had been struck a bad blow on the head, but I can't be sure that's the sole reason for his trouble.'

He hesitated before going on. 'I used to try to treat similar victims, Ned, and it was difficult because we know so little about the brain and how it works. It often seemed to me that some sufferers from loss of memory *wanted* to forget their past for some reason or other. I used to be laughed at for saying that, but I'm sure that I am right. Fred, or whatever his name is—T.D., I suspect—may be one of them, since trying to remember distresses him so. I also think that he's slowly recovering himself.'

Hyde stared at him. 'That seems very odd to me, Geordie.'

'It is odd, Ned. What may be even more strange is that the man Fred was may not be at all like Fred as he is now. More than that, when, or rather, if, his memory returns he may change yet again into quite another man. I saw that happen once or twice.'

'Can no one say why?'

'No one. We might know one day, Ned, but that doesn't help Fred Waring now. ''There are more things in heaven and earth...'' you know, Ned, ''Than are dreamed of in your philosophy.'''

Hyde nodded. He was an educated man and knew his Shakespeare. 'There's no use in questioning him, I suppose?'

'None. It might even damage him. It's interesting, you see, that he hates questions: they upset him. You saw that over the ring.'

'But why did he remember the ring? Why that?'

'I suspect that it meant a lot to him, and he wasn't thinking when he recognised it. He just saw it and knew that it was his without even trying to remember. That's all.'

Hyde shrugged. 'Well, you've explained what's been puzzling me. Poor devil is all I can say. Well, someone taught him to box, Dan'l says, and he plays cards like a master.'

'He remembers that his father taught him how to play,' Geordie said. 'He recovered that but nothing else, no memory of the man himself, or when or where he learned. Time, Ned, that's what he needs.'

'Time,' said Hyde shortly. 'I doubt that. Time does for us all in the end.'

'Maybe, but in the short term Fred may find himself and I want to be there when he does. I think that Fred was someone out of the common run. Don't ask me why I think that. Just his hands, his speech—when he talks without thinking and is no longer careless Fred—and his looks. He was someone who cared for himself, whatever he had turned into when the Moores sprang him from the nick. I'm sure that he hadn't been a drunkard long.'

'Well, you're the expert,' said Hyde, fetching out a clean pack of cards after drinking the tea which he had been sharing with Geordie. 'Time for a friendly game of piquet.'

'Only if you give me a start,' said Geordie. 'I'm not Fred's equal at the game.'

'Come to that—' Hyde smiled '—neither am I now that he's fully remembered how to play. And if that isn't odd, what is? To forget who you are, but to remember how to play cards!'

'He forgot more than that,' said Geordie, laughing, but he did not amplify further. He did not care to tell anyone that Fred had forgotten what men did with women—and what did that tell you, if anything, about why Fred had thrown his past away?

Something, he was sure—but what?

It was ridiculous to be in love with Fred, thought Kirstie despairingly. But there was no doubt about it, she was. She was quite certain now of what was wrong with her—if being in love with Fred was wrong.

She had lived among men all her life and they had never troubled her before. Men were great, hairy, smelly creatures who scratched themselves, made vulgar noises, laughed and sang and swore. Creatures who would never have washed themselves, or worn clean clothing, fed themselves properly, or been respectable at all, if it weren't for the ministrations of women.

They were exasperating, too, finding things funny which any sane woman could see weren't funny at all. Even Geordie Farquhar joined in helpless laughter with Sam and Bart at jokes—jokes?—which left her staring.

Take horseplay, for example. Men loved it, engaged in it, and then what happened? Women had to clear up the mess which they had made, just as they had to clean up the mess after everything men did. And then men thought that it made everything right again if they handed you some ribbons or gave you a quick kiss.

Kirstie had been very sure that she would never fall in love. All that that got you was marriage, and soon after, babies, and what did that mean except more mess—and more cleaning up!

Once Fred came along, though, it was as though Kirstie's kaleidoscope was shaken, too. There she was, content and reasonably happy, and the next thing she knew was that she was getting these extraordinary feelings. First of all she felt extremely cross all the time. She had always been fiery, but jolly with it.

With Fred, however, it turned into a choking black anger so that when she saw him enjoying himself by having fun with women she began to feel almost sick with rage.

One afternoon recently Fred had found her cleaning the hut. He had been his usual kind self, and said, 'Let me help you, Big Sister.' She had answered 'Yes,' because to say 'No' would have made him unhappy. He had given her his slow sweet smile and her heart had turned over.

She had thought that she was going to explode. It was as though all the breath had been knocked out of her. For a moment she thought that she was sickening for something, and then she had known that it was simply Fred's smile. What was worse was that she had understood immediately that the dreadful rage which she had been experiencing lately was black jealousy. She had come near to knowing this on the afternoon on which he had been out with Annie, and now she had no doubt at all.

It was quite dreadful. For what she wanted most in the world was for Fred to come over and put his arms around her and kiss her and... Her senses almost reeled. She pushed away the thoughts of what Fred might do next after the respectable part of love-making was over.

It was not a particularly hot day but Kirstie was overwhelmed by one vast blush. She felt that she was wearing too many clothes, and every time that Fred came anywhere near her she thought that she was going to faint.

'Are you all right, Big Sister?' he asked her anxiously when he carried back inside the boxes which served as stools, and handed her the blankets which she had earlier washed and which had dried in the sun.

'Have you been overdoing things? Why don't you sit down and have a bit of a rest.' He put out his hand and touched her gently on the wrist.

Oh, dear! Kirstie nearly fainted on the spot, the effect it had on her was so powerful. There had been nothing wrong with Fred's attempt to touch her: it was just a Fred-like act of comfort. It was not his fault that she was reacting so strongly to it.

'No,' and her voice sounded odd to her, but not apparently to him. 'It's just the heat.'

'Heat?' said Fred, staring at her. 'It's not very hot today, Big Sister.'

Then there were the other, gentler, feelings. She wanted to look after him, fuss over him, make sure that he didn't overdo things, wanted to wash his clothes for him, feed him—anything which would make him feel happy.

She worried about him all the time. If he were late back at night she found herself lying awake, fearing that he might have fallen into one of the holes which made the diggings look like a battlefield, Geordie said.

She hated it when he occasionally sparred at Fentiman's. Most of all she wished that these feelings would go away, but they didn't, they got worse.

Why did she love him? Why did anyone ever love anyone? She hadn't loved him at first when they had fetched him from the nick—or had she? Could she really have loved The Wreck, loved him that first day? Had it begun then, when they had washed him and given him clean clothes, and she had half-thrown the chops and damper at him, and he had given her his first slow smile? Was it his smile which had touched her heart so?

Kirstie knew now that she had begun to love him even before he had shaved off his whiskers and she and the other women had seen how handsome he was, like a gentleman in one of Ma's old novels. Was it because he was so kind and mannerly and would never let the kids tease and annoy Big Sister?

For all that, he never looked at her as he had looked at the other women. Did she tell him to settle down, not because she wanted him to, but in the hope that he might then look at Big Sister in love, and not in kindness and friendship? Why was it that she loved him so when loving him was so hopeless?

Perhaps it was because of his voice that she loved him. She'd know it anywhere. No, no, it wasn't that at all. She must be honest. When he was working in the diggings, stripped to the waist, his body as well as his face beautiful, she knew why women married men and had their babies. It wasn't fair. She yearned to touch him, to stroke him, and yes, she might as well admit it, to kiss him and...

No, it wasn't fair! She didn't want these powerful feelings. They made her cross with him because if she were kind there was the danger that she might throw herself at him. Why in the world did all the songs and poems go on as though love were a sweet and gentle thing? It certainly didn't make her gentle. It made her wild, and it wasn't sweet, it was fierce and powerful.

Kirstie knew that little of this showed. Only Geordie knew something of what she was feeling.

'Don't look at me like that, Geordie Farquhar,' she had shouted at him once when she had been yearning after Fred just before he had trotted off to one of his women. It was the worst thing of all that she was giving herself away to Geordie.

She had burst into tears, sat down, and thrown her apron over her head. It was always her refuge. Geordie had been kind. 'Never mind,' he had said comfortingly, 'one day things might change, Kirstie.'

Kirstie had pulled her apron down and showed him her tear-streaked face. 'It's only that I'm tired, Geordie. Sometimes this place is too much for me. Oh, I don't want to live in the diggings forever.'

That was true—but it wasn't why she had cried and Geordie knew it.

So when Young Dan'l, Dickie Vallance, and Jack Tate, Ginger's brother, who had joined Ginger and his wife on their claim, throwing up his clerk's job in Melbourne, hovered around her, and asked her out, she sometimes said yes.

Jack took her one evening to the Dance Hall, another of the big tents set up for pleasure. She had often passed it and had never thought that she would enter it. Nellie Tate lent her a pair of light shoes and she wore her new pale blue poplin dress, with frills around the hem—she had never worn frills before. The dress was the result of Sam's having some money to spare for the first time, and spending a little of it on Kirstie.

She loosened her abundant fair hair and bound it with the blue ribbons which Fred had given her when he made his first strike. Jack brought her a flower to put in her hair when he called for her. Altogether she looked like Kirsteen Moore, not like Big Sister at all.

Jack was quite a good-looking boy with brown curly hair, not fiery red like Ginger's. He was only a year older than Kirstie and he seemed young and callow to her after the men she was used to, but he gazed admiringly at her and gave her his arm as Dickie Vallance had done. Fred had already left, so he had not seen the new Kirstie in her finery, which disappointed her a little, but, never mind, there would be other times.

She and Jack walked side by side to the dance. Jack told her about his life in Melbourne and how dull it was compared to the bustle of the diggings. He had already made a small strike and, unlike Ginger and Nellie, he seemed steady enough to keep what he had gained and would not throw it all away on drink and gambling. He took care to tell her that he didn't care much for drink.

The Dance Hall surprised Kirstie a little. From reading her mother's novels she had expected it to be decorous, not something uproarious and rowdy. She found herself in a huge room. A small band made up of a harpist and fiddlers sat at one end, and down its sides there were trestle tables, covered with grubby white cloths where you could buy food and all kinds of drink.

The band was playing a jig, and a group of Irishmen were dancing in the middle of the floor. Some of them were already half-cut, or worse, and the crowd was cheering them on, clapping and whooping in time with the music. It was noticeable that the few women present were smartly turned out, but that most of the men still wore the clothes in which they worked when digging.

The jig ended amid uproar, and there was an interval during which the dancers rushed to the improvised bar and the band were treated to drinks by the Irish party. Even some of the fiddlers seemed to be none too sure of what they were doing, they had been treated so often.

Jack took Kirstie on to the floor when the band began to play again—they called it a country dance, although she knew that it was really The Lancers. She knew that was its true name because she, Nellie Tate, Emmie and the children had learned it together at the diggings one day.

Kirstie had just joined hands with Jack and was waiting for her turn to pass under the dancers' raised arms when she saw Fred enter with Fat Lil beside him. Lil was wearing a low-cut gown in cream and gold with great, spreading skirts over several petticoats. Her hair had a white feather in it held in place by a jewelled pin and she carried a large cream and gold fan secured to her wrist by a light gilt chain.

Fred was his usual handsome self—much cleaner than most of the men there. Kirstie had washed his deep blue shirt and his white silk scarf herself, all so that he might take Fat Lil to the dance, she thought bitterly. Jack was quite diminished by him.

It was no consolation to see that Fat Lil, although not really fat, was old. It simply showed Fred's bad taste, as did his immediately buying her a drink at the bar, even if he only drank lemonade himself. They stood together laughing and talking, Lil's hand possessively on Fred's arm while they watched the dance. Neither of them recognised Kirstie, capering with Jack in her new finery.

Jack bought lemonade for himself and Kirstie when Kirstie told him that she did not like liquor. He thought how pretty she was, looking up at him, drinking her lemonade, her face pink with exertion and pleasure. Despite Fred and Lil she was enjoying herself, happy to be away from the cares and tasks of her everyday life.

The band began to play a waltz. They put down their empty glasses and Jack swept her on to the floor, whispering into her ear, 'You're as light as a feather, Kirstie. Who taught you to dance?'

'Ma,' she told him. He whirled her around the tent, demonstrating his agility by narrowly missing Fred and Fat Lil and a score of others by inches. The music played faster and faster, so that Kirstie began to feel exhilarated, particularly when the music stopped and they ended up near Fred and Fat Lil. Fred was also laughing and panting after the excesses of the dance.

He suddenly recognised her.

'Big Sister! What are you doing here?'

He stared at her, sounding almost displeased at the sight of her in her pretty blue dress, her hair loosely escaping from its confining ribbons, her face soft and her blueygreen eyes blazing at him.

'Jack brought me,' she announced defiantly, taking Jack's hand in hers again since Lil had seized hold of Fred's. Lil gave Kirstie a hard professional glare, assessing her as a woman, not as a little girl.

Big Sister, indeed! thought Fat Lil. What next? She's a pretty young woman, not a child for all her name. She suddenly felt desperately old before such shining innocence. She was instantly aware of what Kirstie felt for Fred and was amused by it. Like most men, though, Fred was blind to something which any woman could see immediately.

Kirstie knew at once that Fat Lil had divined her secret.

Oh, please God, she thought, let her not say anything to Fred. I couldn't bear that.

She need not have worried. Fat Lil was not going to tell Fred of what another woman felt for him. Particularly when she was such a young and pretty one, who was so often with him.

'Well, be careful then, Big Sister,' said Fred, suddenly losing his carefree expression.

'You're not my keeper, Fred Waring,' she snapped back at him. 'Jack will look after me, won't you, Jack?'

Jack put a proprietorial arm around her shoulders and said cheerfully, 'Don't worry, Fred. I'll take good care of her.'

Fred wasn't sure that he wanted Jack Tate to take care of Big Sister. He didn't know why the sight of the two young people together disturbed him so—even if Fat Lil did.

She took him by the arm, 'Oh, come on, Fred. I could do with another drink.'

Kirstie watched them walk away. She didn't see Fred and Fat Lil again and concentrated on enjoying herself feverishly until Jack walked her home and tried to kiss her in the moonlight.

At first, because of her sore heart at the sight of Fred with Fat Lil, she let him. Also she wanted to find out what kissing a man would be like. Ralph, a previous suitor of hers back at the farm, had never got that far. She soon found that, although she liked being with Jack, she didn't like kissing him very much.

The fire that shot through her when Fred touched her ever so lightly was missing when Jack ground his lips against hers and put a hand to her head to stroke her silky ash-blonde hair. She twisted away from him in order to end the kiss as soon as she could.

'Oh, come on, Kirstie,' Jack said, disappointed. 'Don't stop now. Let's enjoy ourselves for once.'

'No,' she told him fiercely. 'That's enough, Jack. I enjoyed our evening, don't spoil it for me.'

He was a decent young man and let her go. Ginger had warned him that she would not be easy and he had been proved right.

The sight of Kirsteen Moore had cast a slight damper over Fred and Fat Lil's evening for quite different reasons. Fat Lil felt old and soiled in front of Kirstie and Fred worried about Big Sister being out with a possible tearaway like Jack Tate. They danced for a little until Fat Lil said that she was tired.

'Come home with me,' she said. 'I'll make you a cup of coffee. Dickie Vallance had a little in this week and he let me have some as a favour—at a price, of course.'

She thought that Fred might stay the night if she were kind to him. The idea appealed to her. It conferred a kind of respectability on an affair when one of the lovers did not rush home immediately after the fun was over, but put an arm around his partner and they fell asleep together like a true married couple.

That, she thought, or rather hoped, was what they looked like after she had made coffee for them on her little stove and Fred sat in the big armchair, half-asleep in the warmth of her comfortable room, a candle throwing its kind light on her face and on Fred's. He often looked serious when his face was in repose, although it lit up again when she handed him his coffee and they sat drinking together.

She was well aware that their affair had not much longer to run. She had been the first woman in the diggings he had taken up with and a queer business that had been. At first she had thought that he didn't know what to do when she had taken him to her room, and then he most definitely did. Better still, he had been the most kind and considerate lover she had ever entertained and she would be sad when, inevitably, she lost him.

She had watched him run through the women in the diggings, amused but pleased when that palled and he had come back to her.

'You're worried about Kirsteen Moore,' she said, why, she didn't know. 'You shouldn't be, she's no child. I thought that she was when you called her Big Sister.'

'She's a child in experience,' he said gravely, sounding quite unlike any Fred Waring she had ever known.

Fat Lil gave a grating laugh. 'A child! I'd been on the game for years, God knows, when I was her age.'

'And would you wish that on her?' he asked, still strangely sober.

Fat Lil didn't feel like Fat Lil at all. She felt like crying. He must have sensed this, for he put down his empty coffee cup, opened his arms, and she went over to him and sat on his knee.

He gently took the jewel and the feather from her hair and loosened it until it fell about her shoulders.

'That's better,' he said. 'Fred likes that.' He drew her to him, making no attempt to begin to have fun, merely holding her as though she were precious to him until they were both nearly asleep.

'Stay, won't you?' she murmured into his neck. So he carried her to bed and it was exactly as though they were an old married couple, and Fat Lil wondered what would have happened to her if things had been a little different all those years ago.

I'd probably be dead of babies and overwork by now, and then, just before drifting into sleep, I'll enjoy this while I've got it—even if it doesn't last.

* * *

In the morning he was carefree Fred again, nothing like the man he had been the night before, or in the night itself. For the first time when he was with Fat Lil the tiger had run through his dreams again, and he had woken up sobbing and holding her. He had lost something he said, and could not find it—but he could not tell her what it was that he had lost, and he fell asleep again without remembering.

This made the carefree Fred of the morning all the more difficult to understand—and when she questioned him about the tiger he had forgotten that, too.

After the night he took Kirstie to the dance Jack Tate's interest in her grew, rather than lessened. By rejecting his advances she had attracted, not repelled him, much to Ginger's amusement. He guessed that Kirstie had been, as he had warned Jack, not easy.

To Ginger's slight mockery Jack's answer was that a really good girl would make a hardworking and faithful wife—a belief shared by her other admirers. They were well aware that many of the women in the diggings took advantage of the freedom it offered them to engage in personal licence. There were many Annies using their new-found liberty to behave like their husbands. Pretty and hard-working girls, who were virtuous as well, were a rarity.

After a time, though, they all became convinced that she was basically cold and incapable of love because she always rejected immediately any attempt to go beyond the most innocent kiss. Dan'l in particular had come to this conclusion, but he was to discover, quite by accident, that there was nothing wrong with Kirstie when it came to loving. It was simply them that she did not love.

Revelation came because Walker, the big digger who had been compelled to give Fred his ring back, burned for revenge. He waited until the rest of his chums followed him to Ballarat before planning any move against Fred. He was well aware that Hyde was a powerful figure in the diggings, and that most of the other important people in Ballarat were protective of Fred. Why, he could not understand. Well, he would deal with Fred when they were not around to help him.

Hyde had warned Fred that Walker might want to take his revenge, but Fred was as happy-go-lucky as he always was, and soon forgot the incident even if he did continue to treasure his ring now that he had found it again. Sometimes it gave him a good feeling when he looked at it, at other times it made him feel sad. Perhaps everyone had these contrary emotions but said nothing of them, he concluded. He still did not understand how much he was marked off from his fellows.

One night he gambled at Hyde's against a crowd of Yankees. They had brought a big red-headed fellow with them who had been a noted poker player out West at the time of the strike there, and they claimed that he had the beating of anyone—including Fred, whose fame had spread throughout the camp.

Big Red's game with Fred was fast and furious. It attracted a large crowd who sat, fascinated, while Fred, his confident grin pasted on to his face, played the Yankee card for card, pot for pot, neither of them winning or losing, neither of them giving way to the other.

Their styles were completely different. Big Red was as wild and reckless as his appearance. He sported a great red-gold beard down to his waist and looked like someone left over from the Viking invasion, as Geordie said afterwards, and then had to explain who the Vikings were.

Fred was his usual cautious self, playing the percentages, a game completely at odds with his own carefree appearance. Like others before him Big Red found that a man who seemed to be so artless had an advantage when playing a game as guileful as Fred's.

The evening passed like a dream and at the end they agreed a draw. They drank together after it was over, Fred indulging himself for the first time since Geordie had sobered him. He liked Big Red and Big Red liked him, so a drink, for once, seemed to be in order

'Come back to the States with me,' bellowed Big Red cheerfully, 'and we'll set up together and take on the world. We could make a fortune.'

The rest of Fred's party had long gone by the time the pair of them left Hyde's, Big Red barely able to walk and Fred, tired by the long night and the effort of concentration in little better case, even though he had limited himself to one drink.

Arm in arm and singing happily—Big Red was teaching Fred 'Dixie'—they walked down Regent Street, for so the diggers had named the alley containing Fentiman's, Hyde's, Fat Lil's and the Palace Theatre. At the end of it Big Red bade Fred a fond and loving farewell, promising him another bout in the near future. 'Although I usually hate a game where no one wins or loses,' he declared, 'so I'll have your scalp next time, Fred Waring, just you see. I can't be held by a cheapskate who plays like an accountant.'

But his roaring was friendly and Fred did not take offence at it. He waved Big Red a cheerful goodbye and set off on the last lap of his journey towards the Moores' claim which had now been christened 'The More the Merrier' by irreverent neighbours who had noted the Moore party's extreme good humour.

His attackers were waiting for him just at the point where the main set of tents ended and a clear space of open ground stood between them and The More, as it was usually now called.

Fred saw them coming and by some instinct knew that they were not friendly. He began to run back towards Regent Street, shouting for help. Walker, who was ahead of the rest, caught up with him and struck him, and the others, arriving in his rear, were ready to finish Fred off.

By great good fortune he was saved by a group of men who had just left Fat Lil's and were making for home. Young Dan'l was in the party, and, led by him, they made short work of Walker and his henchmen, who ran off as soon as they grasped that they were taking on half of Fentiman's stable.

It was only when Young Dan'l picked Fred up from the ground that he realised who it was that they had saved.

'Fred!' he exclaimed. Fred stared at him groggily. He had been hurt enough to be dazed, and had an eye that was rapidly swelling and would turn black. He was so confused that he had no notion of where he was. He did not recognise Dan'l, nor any of the others with whom he had sparred at Fentiman's. He was too shocked to thank them.

'Best get him back to The More,' said Dan'l practically. They walked him home to find that Geordie, who had missed Fred's return to the tent which they now shared— Sam having moved into one of his own—was out looking for him. He was a little worried, for Fred, not knowing of Big Red's arrival, had earlier told him that he would not stay long at Hyde's.

The noise Dan'l's party made returning him, combined with Geordie's worry over Fred's dazed state, not only roused the Moores, but also brought out Jack and Ginger Tate, who came to find out what was wrong.

'Let's get him into bed,' urged Geordie, a little frightened because Fred did not recognise him and kept asking him who he was. At this point Kirstie, who was always a light sleeper, came out to see what all the commotion was about.

Her first sight of Fred was of him hanging between Geordie and Young Dan'l. Before she could stop herself she cried out, her voice shrill with anxiety, 'Oh, God, Fred, what has happened to you?'

Her face was ashen and her distress was patent when Fred peered at her and, whispering something incomprehensible, called her by a strange name, obviously mistaking her for someone else.

'What have you been doing to him?' she demanded of Dan'l, assuming that for some reason Fred had been boxing at Fentiman's and had been badly hurt.

Both Dan'l and Jack stared at her. It was immediately apparent to both of them why Kirstie had not welcomed their advances. The secret which she had kept with such care had been revealed. It was Fred whose advances Kirstie wanted, and now not only Geordie, but her pa and all her suitors knew what she had not wished them to know.

At the time she was aware of none of this. Her tears, her agitation at the sight of the injured Fred, were so great that Geordie asked Sam to help Dan'l get Fred into his bed on the floor of their tent while he attended to the distracted Kirstie.

'Don't worry,' he told her gently. 'He's not badly hurt. Walker's lot attacked him, but fortunately Dan'l and his friends happened to be about and saved him. He's dazed and doesn't quite know where he is or who we are. He'll be better by morning.'

'He doesn't know me,' sobbed Kirstie. 'He called me by a strange name.'

'You probably reminded him of someone he once knew,' said Geordie, wondering whether Fred *would* recover in the morning—although he hardly knew what he meant by recover. Would Kirstie be pleased if Fred was physically better, but had found his original self, and lost all knowledge of the diggings and his friends there at the same time?

He made Kirstie drink a glass of spirits to calm her and to help her to sleep. He saw her back into her hut and emerged to discover that Fred had been put to bed and had fallen asleep at once. He didn't know whether that was a bad, or a good, thing. Only time would tell.

So that's it, thought Young Dan'l glumly. She's not cold at all. She just wants a man who has never seen her except as a child. Jack Tate was thinking the same thing. Each of them was wondering whether it was worth persevering with their suit. Both of them, seeing the agony on Kirstie's face at the sight of the injured Fred, were inclined to think that she was a prize worth winning.

Chapter Six

Fred woke the next morning still groggy, but his knowledge of the diggings was back with him. He recognised Geordie immediately when Geordie woke him up, and he remembered the beginning of the attack on him. He had a beautiful black eye and a swollen face, but fortunately he had suffered no permanent damage.

He remembered nothing after the first blow Walker had given him. He was quite unaware that Dan'l and the others had rescued him, and was also unaware of how he had returned to The More. He certainly had no memory of seeing Kirstie and had no knowledge of her acute distress

'You really ought to take more care of yourself, Fred Waring,' she stormed at him when she handed him his breakfast. 'I expect that you had been misbehaving yourself with that Yankee Jack told me of, and weren't thinking about what you were doing. A right clown you looked last night when Dan'l brought you home.'

She had to be cross with him because she was in danger of crying all over him if she were kind.

'I'm really sorry, Big Sister,' said Fred humbly. 'Ned Hyde told me to be careful because of Walker and his mates, but so much time had passed that I thought that I was safe.'

'Safe, Fred Waring! You'll never be safe. You only live for the moment, that's your trouble. You need a nurse-maid—and even then you'd be sure to make a fool of your-self somehow.'

Big Sister's anger with him always bewildered Fred. He tried so hard to please her, but he had to admit that he managed to land himself in some trouble or other however hard he tried. She never seemed to be so cross with Geordie and the others, though, when they did wrong things. For instance, Bart came home one night in the small hours, blind drunk, and woke the whole diggings when he tried to get into old Mrs Horsforth's tent, mistaking it for his own. Kirstie's only comment the next morning had been a kind, 'Well, boys will be boys, I suppose.'

'I'm a bit big for a nursemaid, Big Sister,' he assured her. 'But I promise you that I'll be good in future.'

'Easily said,' she retorted, filling his tin cup with tea. 'The only thing that you're good at, Fred Waring, is eating.'

'And playing cards,' he told her proudly. 'Even Big Red said that we could make a fortune together. It would be easier than digging, too.'

'That's it, then,' she said, flouncing by him. 'Be off with you. The Yankees can have you, for all I care.'

Which wasn't true at all. It would break her heart to lose him. For all that, nothing he could say would mollify her. She had had too big a fright for that, and she was uneasily aware that she had betrayed her feelings for Fred, not only to the Moores, but to Jack and Dan'l as well. Perhaps they hadn't noticed how extreme her distress had been, she thought hopefully. Fortunately Fred had not remembered how stupidly she had behaved over him, which was just as well. Goodness knows what he would have made of it.

She didn't think for a moment that he would go off with Big Red, for he was still aware that he needed looking after, however much he claimed that he didn't. Not that he needed as much looking after as he had done when he had first been rescued from the nick. His progress to normality might be slow, but it was still progress.

Fred's affair with Fat Lil, for instance, ran its course exactly as Lil had foreseen. They became friends rather than lovers. Much of Fred's interest these days was centred around the card-table. Hyde twitted Lil about this, but she simply shook her head at him, unwilling to admit that she had lost Fred. No, she thought, I haven't lost him, I never really had him. In some way he needed me and when that need was fulfilled, it was over.

She was a shrewd woman and, like Geordie, she had noticed that Fred's passionate involvement, first with drinking, and then with women, had followed a similar pattern. Once the compulsion had gone, it was as though he could take it or leave it—with leaving it being his usual habit. She could not help wondering how long his gambling fit would last. It was difficult to know for while it was true that men's behaviour was predictable—and women's too, for that matter—that of any particular man or woman was not. Fred was either purging himself, or looking for something, and it was hard to tell which it was.

Kirstie was delighted to learn that Fred and Fat Lil were no longer lovers—even though Geordie let slip that they were still friends, because Fred is kind, he had added. Perhaps it meant that he would settle down to a more sober way of life, and, indeed, for a time, work and playing cards seemed to be all that he was interested in.

But just as Kirstie, in consequence, began to feel happier about him, posters went up all over the diggings advertising Rosina Campbell's coming visit. 'An Evening with Rosina' they boldly announced in black and red type, and Kirstie had no idea what a threat to her happiness Rosina was going to be.

Like everyone else she was intrigued by the news that this world-famous beauty was actually coming to Ballarat and to The Palace Theatre. It was bound to add a certain cachet to the place to have someone like Rosina appear there.

Before her arrival, the acts and turns who had appeared were poor, to say the least, but if she were successful other great performers would be eager to visit Ballarat.

Rosina and her supporting troupe arrived in town in great style. She had hired a special pair of coaches. One was for Rosina and the leading players, another carried minor characters and the special props they needed. Bullocks hauled two drays containing the scenery and Rosina's personal possessions.

She behaved exactly like visiting royalty when her party drove up Regent Street, waving and smiling through the open window at the welcoming crowd. She jumped nimbly out of the coach when it stopped outside The Palace Theatre to reveal herself in all her glory. She was dressed in a silvery blue and grey ensemble, with a bell-shaped skirt, matching hat, parasol, and a tiny muff with a spray of artificial forget-me-nots pinned to it.

Her manoeuvring of the muff and the parasol was a turn in itself, thought Kirstie acidly. She had not been able to resist leaving the claim in the day for once, in order to say that she had seen the great Rosina. She was wryly amused when Rosina stood on the makeshift steps of The Palace Theatre which, despite its grand name, was only a canvas structure like all the buildings in Ballarat, including the Commissioners' quarters, and blew kisses at the crowd, before going in on the manager's arm.

From where she stood Kirstie thought that Rosina looked very pretty, although it was difficult to tell how old she really was. Geordie had told her the night before that she was not very young, but he had no idea of exactly what her age might be.

Well, that was that! Kirstie went back to the claim to help to wash out the gold. She had become very dextrous at panning and wielded the big tin plate with panache, Geordie had once said, explaining to her later what the word meant. He was as good as a book, was Geordie, and was one of the few men who actually did any reading in the diggings.

Rosina and her show caused a great deal of excitement—in more ways than one. Every man in Ballarat fancied his chances with her.

'The trouble is,' drawled Ned Hyde, who was seated in his main room, watching the action, 'is that it's not an evening with Rosina Campbell at all, ever. She saves herself for the nobs in Melbourne, I'm told. I got nowhere with her last night. I had supper with her and then—nothing.'

He looked across at Fred who was fiercely concentrating on his hand, but was otherwise in a characteristic Fred pose. He was lying back in his chair, slightly sideways, quite relaxed, his grey felt hat on the back of his curly black head.

'I'm willing to bet that even our Fred couldn't have his way with her—any wager you like, Fred,' he added, raising his voice since Fred appeared not to have heard him.

Fred looked up on hearing his name and shook his head.

'Fun's fun,' he said briefly. 'I never bet on fun with women, it spoils it.'

'Come on, Fred,' prodded Hyde, 'don't be a spoilsport. Bet you anything you like she won't let you into her bed.'

Fred put his cards down. His expression changed completely. One might almost have said that cheerful, carefree Fred Waring looked dangerous.

'You heard me, Hyde. I don't want to say it again. Pleasing women is one thing, betting on 'em's another. Don't push me.' The last sentence came out as a growling threat.

Hyde shrugged. He needed to please his customers and Fred was a good customer who brought the crowds in whenever he played.

'Have it your own way, then.'

'I like having my own way,' said Fred simply, his old charming self again. 'I haven't seen her yet, anyway. Worth it, is she?'

'She's pretty, can sing a bit, and dance a bit,' said Hyde, and laughed to himself. He'd like to bet that he'd intrigued Fred enough to make him try to win the woman, even if he wasn't prepared to bet on her.

He was not far wrong. On the following evening, telling Kirstie that he was off to Hyde's Place, Fred went to The Palace Theatre instead.

The theatre was packed. The whole diggings had buzzed with the news of Rosina's arrival. Her fame as a beauty, and, as the diggers put it, as a high-class tart, was guaranteed to give her a full house every night. Even the tiny local newspaper carried a piece about her, unkindly suggesting that her notoriety was greater than her dramatic talent.

Rosina, never one for missing an opportunity for self-publicity, had turned up at the editor's office armed with a pistol, and had frightened the life out of him by carelessly waving it about while she demanded a full apology in the next edition.

Satisfied that she had got her way she left the office to find herself faced by a crowd of cheering diggers, and shouts of 'Go get 'im, gal,' which all resulted in even bigger audiences all eager to admire the lovely termagant.

Fred found that the entertainment her company offered was varied in nature. Apart from her solo singing and dancing Rosina also took part in a one-act play, a farce designed to please the diggers. There were other good-quality acts there to ensure that she did not have to spend the whole evening on stage.

Fred enthusiastically joined the audience in having innocent fun. Men called to her when she first appeared and she was not slow to answer them. On her first night the painted flats behind her had collapsed, missing her by inches. She had never flinched, nor fluttered, had merely flirted the great fan which she was carrying and informed the diggers that the strength of their welcome was too much for the scenery.

'Show us yer legs, dearie,' a drunken digger bellowed at her. He was sitting near to Fred, who had to restrain himself from immediately punishing such an insolent swine who was insulting the delicate creature on stage.

Rosina needed no assistance from her audience. She was well able to defend herself. Her riposte had the crowd cheering with her and not at her, when she snapped her fan to, pointed it in the drunk's direction and sweetly informed him that, 'You'd need to pay more than the admission fee for that!'

Oh, she was a right pretty lady, thought Fred who was cheering with the rest. Her eyes were fine, and her ankles were well turned—hinting at even lovelier legs. It was reasonable to suppose that the rest of her, which her sumptuous gown hid, was as beautiful as the parts of her which you could see.

You could also see why she had charmed kings and princes, even though the status of her audiences had shrunk down to hairy, unwashed diggers. But the diggers loved her. They threw coins and flowers on to the stage when she performed her wild Spanish dance, flirting and waving her fan at them. Their appreciative roars drowned the music of her small orchestra.

Oh, yes, here was a classy piece and no mistake, thought Fred. Fun with her would definitely be worth having if she would consent to favour a poor digger like himself—which Ned Hyde obviously thought doubtful.

He felt a little guilty when he bribed a backstage hand, with whom he occasionally sparred at Fentiman's, to let him into her dressing room. Like Hyde, the hand was curious to see whether Fred Waring would manage to have it off with Rosina.

Fred had recently promised Big Sister that he would be a good boy and not run after women any more, but he felt sure that she'd forgive him once she saw how beautiful Rosina was.

Her dressing room turned out to be small: it contained only a curtained alcove for her costumes, a dressing-table, a chair before it, and a couch. He hid behind the curtains among the scents of Rosina's dresses and waited patiently for her. He guessed that she would be tired after her long evening, and was not surprised when the first thing she did was collapse wearily on to the chair to examine her face in the dressing-table's mirror.

Fred let her relax for a moment before he put his head through the curtains, saying, 'Peek a boo,' in his most engaging manner before emerging into the room.

On hearing his voice Rosina jumped, let out a little

scream and then stared at him, surprised beyond belief. Her first instinct had been to call for help and have him thrown out, but on suddenly seeing his face quite plainly, her expression changed to one of acute distaste. Her memory took her back several months to an unpleasant encounter at the Criterion Hotel in Melbourne…

She had just arrived there, causing as great a stir in the town as she had done in the diggings—with the difference that most of the wealthy entrepreneurs in Melbourne were well aware of her history, which was romantic in the extreme. Although no longer young, she still retained much of the beauty and grace which had enabled her to have such a remarkable career.

The daughter of a Scots adventurer of good family, she had married an Army officer when she was only seventeen. She had then run away from him with an even more handsome friend but had subsequently been abandoned by him in Paris where she had set herself up as a top-rank courtesan.

In her early twenties she had become the mistress of a king and the power behind his throne in one of the tiny German states. In 1848, revolution had overwhelmed most of Europe and it swept away both the king and herself. Her twenty years of glory ended in a few moments and she had been lucky to escape with her life.

She could sing and dance and, using her romantic story as an entrée, she toured the world, earning some kind of living. From the gold field of California she had come to Australia with a rich Yankee digger who, tiring of her, had left her in Melbourne.

Now she was seeking another wealthy protector and Thomas Dilhorne had been pointed out to her. He was not only rich, it appeared, but extremely handsome. Fortunately he was staying at The Criterion and Rosina decided that he was to be her next target. She took every opportunity that came along to try to intrigue him, but he seemed to be the only man in the hotel—or in Melbourne—who was immune to her charms.

One morning when she was leaving The Criterion she dropped her handkerchief before him in the lobby. It was one of the oldest tricks in the book of seduction and it had no effect on him at all.

He had picked it up and handed it to her. 'Yours, I believe, madam.' His manner could hardly have been more brutally perfunctory.

'My thanks, sir. It would have been most provoking to lose it. A fine day, is it not?'

His stare had been glacial and his manner equally so when he said shortly. 'It usually is, madam, at this time of year, being summer.'

It was obviously an answer designed to kill the conversation stone-dead on the spot.

Rosina was not accustomed to having her manifest charms ignored, particularly by enormously rich and handsome gentlemen, so she had persevered all the more in her attempts to snare him.

'How droll you are, Mr Dilhorne!'

'Droll, madam?' he asked in a voice which demanded of her how she had known his name.

'Indeed,' she fluted at him. 'It suits you. Most men are too smooth, too flattering.'

'I agree. No one would accuse me of either fault.' His voice and his expression were ice, his answer evidently designed to end the conversation once and for all.

'Flattery is alien to me, madam, so pray do not trouble me with it,' he added and, giving her a half-hearted bow to show that their conversation was at an end, he made to move away.

Annoyance at this, and his whole contemptuous tone, made Rosina persist—most unwisely—in her attempt to win him over.

'To me also, sir, I assure you.'

His impatience to be off made her adversary churlish. His fine black brows rose haughtily. 'You surprise me, madam. I would have supposed that it was meat and drink to you.'

His whole manner was now so killingly bored that for a moment Rosina scarcely registered the insult. When she did her face flamed scarlet.

'Allow me to inform you, sir, that you are no gentleman.'

His answer when it came was brutally savage. He uttered the unspeakable. 'Then we are well matched, are we not? For you are certainly no lady.'

She was not to know that he regretted the words the moment that he had uttered them, but the dreadful mood which had held Thomas Dilhorne in thrall ever since the scene with his father had deepened rather than lifted.

The scarlet had drained from Rosina's face, but the dignity which she had never lost was still with her. She knew what she had been, and she knew what she had now become, but she had always been discreet. Off the stage she had never flaunted herself and, if her pursuit of one of the Dilhorne heirs had been a trifle open, she was now the one who regretted it the most.

Her head lifted proudly. 'You shame yourself, sir, not me. I wish that you may not live to regret what you have so rudely said to me. You, too, have passions and desires— like all humanity—and may one day need a little forgiveness yourself.'

The only effect that this had was for him to bow to her

and say before he turned on his heel and left her, 'I doubt that very much, madam. It is not my intention to engage in unseemly romping.'

...And now, months later, here he was, in her room, smiling at her, and behaving as though he had never met her before.

'You!' she exclaimed. 'I never thought to find you here—and dressed like that.'

She had, she was compelled to admit, been impressed by both Thomas Dilhorne's looks, his splendid turn-out, and the manner in which he had walked through The Criterion as though he owned the hotel and all Melbourne.

A bewildered Fred felt injured by this remarkable response to his kindly meant offer of fun. He looked down at his best corduroys and his newly cleaned boots. Big Sister had washed his shirt and his best blue guernsey for him and his white silk scarf was spotless. He had seldom been so well turned out.

'There's nothing wrong with poor Fred's clothes, is there?' he said with great dignity. 'I only came here because I thought that you might appreciate a little fun.'

'Fun!' Her gaze was scathing. 'I thought that you never engaged in unseemly romping.'

Fred's surprise shone out of him. 'Unseemly romping? What the devil's that? No, I thought that you might like cheering up after all that hard work. I'm rather good at cheering up pretty ladies.'

Rosina looked carefully at him. She was almost sure that he was the man who had been so savagely rude to her in Melbourne. But the coldly handsome face was now so innocently happy, and the superb body which she had appreciated back in Melbourne—if he were Thomas Dilhorne, that was—was now so evident through his grotesque clothes, and his desire to please her was so plain, that she was half-lost.

Fred, he had called himself. She must be wrong, although twenty-odd years of knowing and pleasing men of all degrees told her that she was not. What silly masquerade was he engaging in? Was this how he enjoyed himself when he was being a stiff prig, insulting women in hotels?

'What are you doing here?' she said shortly, remembering the wealth and consequence which had surrounded Thomas Dilhorne.

'Well, I came to see *you*. Geordie said that you were worth seeing, and he was right.'

Rosina closed her eyes, before opening them again to find that his striking blue eyes were approving her warmly.

'I meant what are you doing here, in the diggings? Why are you in Ballarat of all places?'

'Oh, that. I'm Sam Moore's top mate. I work for him and Big Sister. I make a bit of pocket money gambling. I'm rather good at that, too. Why are we wasting time when we could be having fun?'

'If you want to keep up this masquerade—' she began.

'Masquerade?' Fred was injured again. 'These are my best clothes, I'll have you know. I put them on especially for you.'

It was useless. Rosina looked at him. He was remarkably desirable, something that had scarcely registered at the hotel where she had come to see him as unattractive because of his coldly imperious manner. This face, unlike Thomas Dilhorne's, was eager and alive, amusement playing round the eyes and mouth.

She was also tired and bored. An unseemly romp with this splendid animal might be, as he had said, fun. She had not had any real fun for a long time. She really deserved something after the hard and tedious grind of her stage life. There was a knock at the door.

'I'm resting,' she called. 'Go away. I'll ring for you when I want you.' She turned to Fred. 'Seeing that you've changed your mind as well as your clothes, why not?'

'Changed my mind?' Fred was puzzled, but not indignant, as they sank on to the couch together. 'I've not changed my mind. I knew what I wanted the moment I first saw you.'

A statement which was perfectly true—and even truer than Fred Waring could have consciously known.

Chapter Seven

Of course, the lad at The Palace Theatre talked—it was too good a tit-bit to keep to himself. Before long everyone on the diggings knew that the apparently untouchable Rosina was the latest woman to fall to Fred Waring.

Neither of them made any secret of it after the first night. Rosina was happy to show her audience that she was as pleased to have a poor digger for a lover as a prince—it brought in the crowds. Fred did not flaunt his conquest but he was round at the theatre every night to meet her after the show was over. He was so pleased with himself that even Big Sister could not distress him.

'You said that you'd reformed, Fred Waring. You said that you had settled down.'

He was all dignity. 'That was before I met Rosie.' He refused to call her Rosina. She was his girl Rosie, his sheila, not the international courtesan.

Ned Hyde tried to twit him when next he played at his Place. Fred stared at him and said, 'Leave off,…Ned, or I'll play elsewhere. What Rosie and I do is our affair.'

Hyde had laughed at that and said later to Geordie, 'There are times when Fred comes on so strong you'd think that he was used to giving orders.'

Geordie had looked at him queerly. 'Have you ever noticed that Fred's habits don't last? First he gave up drinking, and now, he's almost over wenching. If I'm not mistaken, he'll soon stop altogether.'

Hyde said derisively, 'You're joking, Geordie. For God's sake, he and Rosina Campbell have been hard at it ever since I told him about her. It's a good thing that he didn't take on my bet.'

'I know,' said Geordie, and refused to say any more.

Rosina soon gave up worrying about Fred and his extraordinary likeness to Thomas Dilhorne. Fred said to her on their second night together, 'I don't know why you keep calling me Tom when we're having fun together. It's not very flattering. The name's Fred, and don't you forget it, Rosie.'

That had amused her. Apparently Thomas Dilhorne had attracted her more than she had thought, and his cutting refusal had rankled more than she had known. It was a form of revenge on him to enjoy herself so thoroughly with Fred, as well as a pleasure in itself. Curious about him, and the life which he said he was living, Rosina put on her finery and took her splendid person along to the Moores' claim.

It was a sunny day and, parasol up, she paraded along, flattered and amused by the admiring stares which she gathered. She ignored the occasional coarse comment which floated into her ears. Nothing ever disturbed her lovely calm: she had learned to contain herself in a hard school, to present a beautiful picture to the world—and when it was necessary to give as much as she got.

Ballarat pleased her, the show was successful, and life for the moment was good. Fred was kind and loving and possessed a delicacy which sat at odds with his claim to be a lowly digger—hence the visit.

The Moore party was hard at work when she arrived. Only Geordie Farquhar, suddenly tired, was reclining and resting. The iron butterfly, for so he had privately named her, had come to see Fred working, and he wondered why.

'Mrs Campbell!' He sprang gallantly to his feet when it was plain that their claim was indeed her destination.

Rosina turned her fine eyes on him. She saw immediately that his appearance was unlike that of most of the diggers and that his voice, with its upper-class drawl and vowels, was also different. As with Fred, she had the impression that she had met him before. It was not such a strong impression, but it was still there.

Geordie dragged up a box for her to sit on. She accepted it graciously.

'Improvised, but better than nothing,' he said.

'We have met before, I think, Mr—'

'Many years ago,' he told her ruefully, which was hardly gallant but the truth. 'In a London drawing room. We were both very young.' There, that piece of untruthful tact should help matters. 'You were with your husband. Geordie Farquhar at your service, Mrs Campbell.'

The name meant nothing to her. It was faces which she remembered. They were her trade.

Rosina looked about her at the labouring men. Fred had not seen her. He was standing in one of the holes, and had stripped off his shirt for the day was hot. There was no doubt that he had been telling her the truth. He was certainly a digger, and by the state of his splendidly muscular torso had been one for some time.

She watched him and the others who were all so engrossed in their work that they had not seen her arrive. Sam was busily engaged in examining lumps of quartz and clay, and his abrupt bellow of 'Big Sister!' brought Kirstie from the hut where she had been baking bread.

Advancing on Pa, Kirstie suddenly saw Rosina, sitting in the sun, her eyes wary and calculating, watching and assessing her from under the shade of her parasol.

Kirstie recognised her immediately as the beauty she had seen on Rosina's first day in Ballarat. She was even more elegant than she had been then. She was wearing an expensive silk dress and a tiny bonnet with lilac ribbons whose trimming of a bunch of violets echoed the colour of her whole ensemble. Her delicate parasol possessed an ivory and silver handle and her expensive leather shoes were also violet in colour. Seen near to, however, her face, although imperious in its beauty, bore the unmistakable marks of age.

Why, she's old, thought Kirstie, no one told me that. One thing's for sure, she'll never see forty again.

She was aware that she was staring, and that her stare was inimical. How can Fred trouble with her? The thought of him having fun with Rosina was agonising, and showed on her face.

Rosina stared back at Kirstie. She knew jealousy when she saw it and was amused, but she was also pained. Through the unflattering clothes, the clumsy shoes, the scraped-back ash-blonde hair and the pretty mouth set hard against the world, Rosina saw something which she had lost and could never regain.

This chit was a delicate beauty and, properly dressed, she would be outstanding. She was also young and fresh, and, without a doubt, untouched.

On the other hand, she possessed something which the chit did not, and that was Fred. Fred who had just seen her, Fred whom the chit, by her agonised expression, fancied, even if he didn't fancy her—and she was obviously painfully aware of that. Fred, whose face was one smile, and who was hauling himself up out of the hole, was picking up his discarded shirt, and pulling it on, denying her the sight of the powerful body which had pleasured her so often.

'Rosie!' he exclaimed, ignoring the stares of the others

who turned to look at him and her together. He bowed over her hand, remembering some etiquette once practised, and kissed it tenderly. Kirstie's agonised stare seared his unheeding back.

'Rosie, what are you doing here?'

She let down her parasol. 'I came to see you working, Fred. I couldn't quite believe you when you told me that you laboured here, but now I have seen for myself that you do.'

She put out a hand to touch his bare arm. 'You are so strong, Fred,' she sighed at him.

Oh, yes, let the chit see that she possessed him: to demonstrate her power over men was a pleasure which she had always enjoyed, and it was an even greater pleasure to discover that she could still exercise it in the face of this rustic beauty. She had not missed Kirstie's visible distress when Fred had kissed her hand.

She might only be sitting on a box but Rosina behaved as though she were back in her royal audience chamber. Her subjects were brought to her, one by one, to be introduced. By now Jack and Ginger Tate had joined the Moores, determined to join in the fun. Geordie, sardonic, watched them and thought that it was as good as a play.

Only Kirstie hung back, finally turning to enter the hut again. She had barely reached the door when Geordie said to her, his eyes watchful, for although he was usually kind to her, he could not resist teasing her a little, 'Don't you want to meet her, Kirstie?'

'What? Meet that old woman! Whatever for, Geordie Farquhar? I'm no man to make a fool of myself over her. She's nothing but a flytrap.'

'She's a legend, Kirstie. A king's mistress. You can tell your grandchildren that you met her.'

'My grandchildren, Geordie Farquhar? I shan't have any to tell. I don't want to know her, she's not nice.'

'I grant you that, Kirstie, but that's not the point.'

But Kirstie was not to escape meeting Rosina; watching them, and guessing the subject of their conversation, Rosina walked over to where Kirstie stood, and detained her.

'Now, Mr Farquhar, pray do me the honour of presenting this young woman to me. Mr Sam Moore's daughter, I presume?'

'I'm Kirsteen Moore, who looks after this lot and sees them fed and cared for,' said Kirstie belligerently before Geordie could answer. She would have liked to have added, 'And you're Fred's whore,' but seen close to there was something so sad in Rosina's face that the sight of it shocked and silenced her.

'Indeed, and you do it well, I am sure.'

Rosina's answer to Kirstie's was one of such queenly patronage that Kirstie stiffened and might have said something unforgivable after all, had not the pressure of Geordie's hand on hers restrained her.

He said gently, 'Big Sister is our mainstay, Mrs Campbell,' and his eyes on Kirstie implored her to be good because Fred was approaching them in order to take Rosina's arm and offer to show her the creek.

'It's where the women and children work,' Fred told her, not even noticing poor Kirstie before he walked Rosina towards the water. 'They pan the gold and clean the muck away from it.'

Kirstie was left looking forlornly after them. Fred was all that was gallant and Rosina a model of charming animation.

'Oh, the fool,' she said desolately to Geordie. 'Can't he see what she is?'

'Yes, but he also sees what she was. And, for the moment, that's what he wants.'

'But she's so old,' wailed Kirstie despairingly.

'That, too,' said Geordie, 'and you must know that that doesn't matter, either.'

'Oh, but she wears him like a trophy.'

'And she's his,' said Geordie acutely.

He was not being unkind, but it was as well that Kirstie knew the way of the world. It was as though she read his mind, for she flung at him, 'Oh, you're an old devil, Geordie Farquhar, and no mistake. You're educating me again, aren't you? I'm to let Fred have his fun, is that it?'

'Something like that. You can't stop it, so why not accept it? Suffering is a part of living, Kirstie. No one can escape it and the other part is all the better for having known this.'

'So you say, Geordie Farquhar, so you say. Big Sister goes to prepare the dinner while the men play with the pretty women who have nothing to do but please. Yes, I can see that's the way of the world.'

To prevent herself from crying she went into the hut and cooked the dinner with vigour. She saw Fred kiss Rosina's hand again just before she left, so she made sure that he got the burned chops.

That would teach him that he couldn't have everything!

Geordie took Kirstie to see Rosina's show at The Palace Theatre after she had visited The More. There was no doubt that she was more distressed by Fred's affair with Rosina than by his light-hearted involvement with the women of the diggings, or even his association with Fat Lil—who was as amused as anyone that Fred had made off with Rosina.

'Clever devil with all his pretty ways, isn't he?' said Lil. 'He never has to pay for his fun, either.'

Fred could not have afforded Rosina in the normal way of business, and one had to assume that she regarded him as her personal cavalier while she played at The Palace.

The trouble was, that Fred, in his own way, was quite serious in his affair with Rosina. He never looked at anyone else, refused to talk about her, stayed with her overnight, and treated her almost reverently.

What can he see in her? thought Kirstie despairingly. That old woman—which was an exaggeration, she knew, but Rosina was certainly older than Fred. When she saw her on the stage, however, the mystery of her attraction for him, and for men generally, was solved.

For a fleeting moment the unparalleled beauty of the young Rosina was revived before the improvised footlights of The Palace Theatre. It was easy to see why kings and princes had fought for her favours. No little girl from the diggings could hope to compete with such a nonpareil. Rosina's singing voice was good, her dancing less so, but neither mattered. Her attraction, as Kirstie could plainly see, was the woman herself: and for the moment that woman was Fred's.

Suppose she remained Fred's? Would he leave the diggings with her? For Rosina was certainly not going to stay.

Kirstie said nothing of this to Geordie, who himself felt the pull of Rosina's attraction when she dominated the stage and the tent. The diggers rose and roared at the end of her show as they had done in California. Mirthful before the crudely painted back-cloth, Rosina blew kisses at them, pirouetting before she finally sank to the ground in a great curtsy, exactly as she had sunk before her king.

Never mind that the time left for her to exercise her charm was short, that there would be few more Freds, and certainly no more princes, she accepted their applause graciously and was happy with it. She knew that Fred waited for her in her dressing-room to confirm that she could still attract and that she could still take a lover for joy and not for profit. What she was earning at The Palace would keep her for a time, and then she would move on, as her whole life had been moving on, but she had always tried never to think of the future.

'So that's what she was like,' said Kirstie when Geordie walked her home. She was moved to be honest as she always was with Geordie. 'I can see the reason for all the fuss about her.'

'Yes,' he said. 'I met her when she was about your age. She was the most beautiful creature I have ever seen, or shall see. But unhappy, Kirstie, never forget that.'

'Unhappy!' She was suddenly scornful Kirstie again. 'Unhappy! But think what she was.'

'What was that, Kirstie? She has no home, no husband, no chick nor child—only the cheers of the diggers left and memories like mine. Is that happiness?' Geordie knew that he was speaking of himself as well as Rosina.

Kirstie was silent. Geordie could always make her think, and persuade her not to be over-hasty in her judgements. It was plain that he pitied Rosina. She said thoughtfully, 'Is that what Fred is, Geordie? Sorry for her, as well as having fun with her, I mean.'

'I'm not sure, Kirstie. I have the feeling that Fred's involvement with Rosina has some deeper significance—but what, I can't imagine. I only know that you should not envy or be jealous of her—whether Fred cares for her or not. Would you change your life for hers? Hard though yours is, hers is harder, and will become more so.'

Kirstie had not thought of that. Geordie was right. She is old and men will soon see that she is, and what will she do then? She did not say this to Geordie, she did not need to.

'Why are you here, Geordie?' she asked him. 'This is no place for you. You were not meant to live a dog's life in a colonial mining town.'

He stopped and turned to look at her.

'I am like Rosina. There is nothing left for me but this. I made a wrong choice once and I must pay for it. Never forget that, Kirstie. Nothing is free. We pay for everything, and for some the payment is hard. We are wrong to think that we can take what we wish and forget the morrow.'

She was not sure what he was trying to tell her. 'Fred must choose, then. And I, must I choose, Geordie? But I have no choices.'

'Oh, we all have choices, Kirstie, but sometimes we do not recognise them. I think that you will know yours when they arrive, and you will not choose lightly. You chose to come here did you not? Sam said that you could have married the neighbouring farmer who offered for you.'

Kirstie had never thought of her rejection of Ralph as a choice, but, of course, Geordie was right. 'I did not know then that it meant that I would end up in the diggings. I thought that I was choosing to stay at our farm.'

'Yes, that is another problem for us, Kirstie. We do not know where our choices will take us. Remember that.'

Later, much later, Kirstie was to remember what Geordie had told her, and to think that he had spoken more truly than even he could have known. At the time she simply nodded her head because they had reached the Moores' claim and it was plain to her that, yet again, Fred had chosen to stay the night with Rosina, and for the first time she accepted this without resentment, even if the knowledge made her unhappy.

Jack Tate watched Fred squire Rosina, happiness in his heart since it gave him the opportunity to press his suit with Kirstie who must surely now give up her hopes of winning Fred. He thought that Fred must be mad to run after such an overblown creature as Rosina when pretty, hard-working Kirstie was there for his asking—if only he had the wit to see it!

For there was no doubt about Kirstie's prettiness now. Whether it was living in the diggings, or falling in love with Fred, or the attentions of her many suitors, she had suddenly blossomed.

The slightly pinched look had gone and, almost unconsciously, she had begun to make the most of herself, to loosen her hair, to put a flower in it, to make and wear more feminine dresses, using the money which Sam gave her from one of his richer strikes, all of which served to show the world what a pretty woman she had become.

Jack turned up at The More to ask Kirstie to go dancing with him. For a moment she almost said yes, but then she knew that if she did it would only encourage him in his hopeless attempt to court her, and so she said regretfully, 'Oh, Jack, I'm so tired I couldn't do a dance justice.'

She didn't look tired, and it was so plainly an excuse that Jack said reproachfully, 'Oh, come on, Kirstie, enjoy yourself. You'll only be young once. You can't spend all your life looking after folks.'

He put a would-be loving hand on her arm. 'It's such a waste, Kirstie, particularly when you're so pretty.'

It was typical of her that she didn't simper at him when he told her this, but just looked gravely back. 'It wouldn't be fair to you,' Jack,' she told him at last. 'You're serious about me, but I'm not serious about you.'

'I'll take my chance on that. You might change your mind.'

She shook her head, her bluey-green eyes large and solemn, 'I don't think so, Jack.'

Jack took a deep breath. He could not stop himself from saying savagely, 'There's someone else, isn't there? That's why you won't walk out with me. It's Fred, isn't it? It's true, I'm sure I'm right. It's Fred you fancy.'

'No,' said Kirstie, her face ashen, 'No, you're wrong—and it's no concern of yours who I fancy.'

Far from silencing him, this simply served to urge him unwisely on. 'Oh, I saw your face, Kirstie, the night he was attacked. You couldn't hide it then. How can you fancy *him*? He's too old for you, and he's not steady like me. I've got plans, Kirstie, great plans. I don't intend to be someone else's man all my life. When I make my strike I shall use it to advance in the world…'

She turned away from him, because of what he had said about Fred, but he took her by the arm to prevent her from leaving him.

'No, listen to me. I do love you, and you'd make me the sort of wife I've always wanted. Someone serious and hard-working, a proper partner, not a drag like Ginger and Bart's wives. Marry me, Kirstie, and make us both happy.'

The tears Kirstie was holding back began to fall in earnest.

'I'm so sorry, Jack. I wish that I could say yes. I like you, but it wouldn't be fair to marry you. I've seen too many marriages made because girls were desperate and thought that liking was enough—but it wasn't.'

'I'm ready to take that chance, Kirstie. You're good. You'd come to love me, I'm sure. Don't throw everything away because you fancy a man who used to be a drunkard, who spends his spare time gambling and who can't let women alone.'

This last sentence was too much. It echoed so strongly what she was always telling herself about her passion for Fred: and it was useless. Reason had nothing to do with being in love: nothing. She could not marry Jack for safety, for friendship, when she had to force herself to kiss him and when she did, could only think what it might be like with another man.

That way unhappiness lay because she could not imagine herself loving Jack more when they married, only less, because if she had to force herself to kiss him now, then what would more serious love-making do to her—and to him—when he discovered her revulsion.

'No, Jack, I won't go out with you, and I won't marry you. It's no business of yours how I might feel about Fred—or anyone else for that matter.'

He shook his head. 'I shan't take that as your final answer, Kirstie. I won't torment you, I like you as well as love you. I shan't talk to you about Fred again, even if I think that I am right about him.'

There was a quiet dignity about him. He had dropped his hand from her arm some time ago. Now, remembering how Fred had treated Rosina, he picked up her work-scarred hand and kissed it.

Kirstie didn't wrench it away as she might once have done. After all, he felt for her what she felt for Fred, and just as hopelessly. They were partners in the miserable, not the triumphant, side of love. She wished that his kiss on her hand had excited her, but nothing happened. It had had no more effect on her than the embrace of one of the kids would have done.

She was right to refuse him, but the refusal gave her no pleasure, it merely increased her own sense of desolation. Big Sister was growing up at last. Increasingly she was Kirsteen Moore to herself, not the mere servant of her family and friends. Had I not been Big Sister from the beginning, she thought, would Fred have looked at me then?

Fred and Rosina were lying in bed together at the hotel where she lived. They had even made a little suite for her, away from the common rooms and the dormitory where the rough beds were set out in rows, and the long table where everyone, rich and poor alike, sat together to eat.

But for Rosina nothing was too good. Her rooms were full of her own possessions, brought in by bullock dray from Melbourne, giving her the illusion of privacy. She had brought silk sheets to put on the bed, china and silver, and from somewhere someone had produced flowers as well as vases to put them in.

Her nightgown was as pretty as a ball-dress, and was trimmed with lace so fine it was like a whisper. At the moment it lay abandoned on the floor where she had thrown it. Her lustrous black hair was down and clothed her to the waist. She lay languorously back on the pillows, temporarily satisfied.

Fred was propped up on one arm. He had just finished plaiting a long strand of her hair and she was idly undoing it again.

He spoke equally as idly to her. 'Big Sister doesn't approve of our goings-on, but I told her that she can't expect to tell me what to do about everything now that I can look after myself properly. I do intend to reform one day, but I'm enjoying myself with you too much to start now.'

This artless confidence started Rosina laughing wildly. How could she ever have thought that he might be staid, articulate and self-controlled Thomas Dilhorne? She had earlier poured out two glasses of lemonade, but matters had become so urgent after his arrival that they stood neglected on her bedside table.

She handed him one, and drank from the other, saying afterwards, 'Big Sister—I suppose you mean Kirsteen Moore?'

'That's right, Big Sister.'

'But why that name?'

'Because that's what she is. She looks after Sam and the little ones, Bart and Emmie and their little ones, and Geordie and me. Fits her, doesn't it?'

Rosina looked at him, contentedly drinking his lemonade. She was again overwhelmed by his whole remarkable presence and by his easy, innocent and child-like charm.

'They say that you used to drink a lot, Fred.'

He squinted at her over the top of his glass. 'Yes, odd

that. I can't bear spirits now, though they do say that one glass of wine should be enough for a gentleman, preferably at dinner.'

She felt like laughing at the magisterial way in which he came out with the last sentence. There was an echo of Thomas Dilhorne in it, something which intrigued her.

'We'll have champagne on our last night together, Fred, and find out whether you like that. Did you drink much before you came to the diggings?'

As usual, such a direct question about his past troubled him. 'I can't remember anything before the diggings, Rosie.' He looked at her severely. 'Stop talking, Rosie. Let's enjoy ourselves again.

Later she was to remember his answer and wondered what he meant about his lack of memory, for no one had told her of it. At the time her question went unanswered because he gathered her to him so tenderly, and began to make gentle love to her—quite different from their earlier passionate frenzy.

Afterwards, looking down at her lying in the crook of his strong arm, he asked her, 'Enjoyed yourself, did you?'

'Yes,' she said truthfully, 'always with you.'

'I thought you did. Me too.' He lay down beside her, saying indignantly, 'Unseemly romps, indeed, what a way to describe having fun.'

'Unseemly romps?' repeated Rosina hazily. She had barely got her breath back after their last session and for the moment Thomas Dilhorne and his peculiar attitude towards her and life had flown out of her head.

'Well, you said it,' replied Fred reasonably while he stroked her gently in gratitude for her being such a good chum. 'Not at all like you to say such a thing about having fun. Where in the world did you get it from?'

A curious smile passed across Rosina Campbell's face.

Thomas Dilhorne's double was tickling her lovingly under her chin.

'A man I once met,' she said looking him in the eye. 'A most unpleasant man. He didn't like the idea of unseemly romps at all—or perhaps he liked them too much and didn't want to admit it.'

'Must have been a damned stupid ass to call having fun unseemly romps,' said Fred derisively. 'Come closer, Rosie, I want to go to sleep now, and it's better when we're spoons.'

'Spoons?'

Rosina felt that as was usual with Fred she either spent her time being thoroughly pleasured, or laughing with him, and at him, or being amused by his artlessness. Not that there was anything artless about his love-making.

'Yes, that's what we called it when we went to sleep around one another. Spoons together in a box,' he murmured dreamily, his eyes closed.

He sat up abruptly, his eyes wide open, and asked her in an agitated voice, quite unlike his normal one, 'We, Rosie! What do you think I meant by that? I don't remember a we at all.'

He looked so distressed that it was her turn to soothe him, who had so frequently soothed her in the feverish aftermath of performing. 'I don't know, Fred. Lie down, there's a good fellow. I want to sleep, too. You and I are "we" at the moment, aren't we? Let that be enough.'

Chapter Eight

Kirstie was at a loose end. The evening meal was over and the men had all gone off to have their respective versions of fun, leaving her alone with her sewing. Fred had been the last to go and she knew that his destination was Rosina and The Palace Theatre. He always thanked her for his dinner before he left, even when she gave him the burned food—someone had once taught him good manners of a kind which few in the diggings possessed.

She had watched him stroll away, determined not to mind too much—after all, Rosina's engagement in the diggings was nearly over. He had barely turned the corner in Regent Street before Dan'l Mendoza appeared, smartly dressed and obviously making for the Moores' claim.

'You're too late,' she told him, looking up from one of Fred's socks which she was busy darning. 'They've all gone.'

'Oh, I didn't come for them,' he said. 'I came for you.'

He didn't add, Particularly now that Fred's gone off with Rosina again, but he thought it.

Earlier that day he had gone into Dickie Vallance's store and chaffed him about his glum face, and Dickie told him that Kirstie had again refused him the night before, despite Sam's approval of his suit.

'Acourse,' said Dickie, 'Sam's particularly eager to see her married, now.'

Dan'l was immediately interested, 'Why's that, then? I thought that she was too useful to the Moores for them to want to lose her—seeing how much she does.'

Dickie gave Dan'l an exaggerated wink. 'Ah, well, you see, Dan'l, it's on account of the Widow Clancy, isn't it? Sam's been hanging round her for some time and she seems to have taken a fancy to him. Not surprising since he's a steady and well-set up man. You can see the problem, though.'

Dan'l, who had never married, couldn't.

'He can't have two women running his household, can he? Kirstie's been doing it so long that Sam's hard put to bring in Kate Clancy and put Kirstie down. Even if it did mean that she'd have less to do, she'd be bound to feel it. Can't have two women in one kitchen, can you?'

Dan'l saw at once why Sam had changed his mind about Kirstie acquiring suitors. Well, where Dickie had failed, he might succeed.

'Does Kirstie know? About Kate, I mean.'

'Not she,' grinned Dickie. 'Probably thinks that Sam's past it. Now Kirstie, she's hankering after that big brute, Fred Waring, God knows why. What does he have to offer her? She could have had a silk dress if she'd married me. She'd have to do her share, mind, but nothing like what she's doing now. She'll be old before her time if she's not careful. Besides, Fred Waring's only got eyes for madam at The Palace Theatre. Lucky for some, eh?' and he gave Young Dan'l yet another conspiratorial wink before he served the next customer.

Dan'l walked thoughtfully away from Dickie's, determined to set his cap at Kirsteen, who was a real prize

whichever way you looked at it. Like Dickie Vallance and
Jack Tate, he wondered at Fred for passing Kirstie over.
No time like the present then, while Fred was fooling with
Rosina, he might as well take the opportunity to secure
Kirstie for himself. Perhaps it was because Fred only saw
Kirstie as his Big Sister who had alternately scolded and
looked after him ever since the Moores had rescued him
from the nick that he didn't recognise her true worth.

He put on his best suit, and a clean shirt, combed his
hair down and set off to woo Sam Moore's pretty daughter
by asking her to go dancing with him. It was his good luck
that he found her alone.

Kirstie put down her sewing. 'You came for me?'

'Yes, I thought that you might like to go to the dance
hall with me tonight. You deserve a little pleasure after
your hard day's work.'

For a moment she hesitated, and then almost defiantly—
although who she thought that she was defying, goodness
knows, Fred and Rosina, perhaps—she said, 'Yes, I'll go
with you, Dan'l, but you'll have to wait while I change.'

'Be a pleasure, my dear.'

So she was his dear now, was she! Feverishly, Kirstie
dressed herself in her best blue dress. At least, this time,
she wouldn't see Fred, since he had gone off to spend the
night in bed with his fancy piece, his ageing flytrap.

Alas, she was wrong. For once The Palace Theatre had
an evening without a performance and Fred and Rosina had
decided to have a night on the town—if Ballarat could yet
be described as a town! So it was that Kirstie found herself
fated to go to the Dance Hall on yet another night when
Fred was entertaining his current bit of fun.

Rosina had thought it a splendid wheeze to go slumming
there with Fred, as though she were truly only a digger's
fancy piece. She had not dressed up much, more likely

dressed down, as Kirstie rudely said later when describing the evening to Emmie and Mrs Tate.

'Thought she was giving us all a rare treat by being there at all,' she said savagely, remembering with dreadful clarity what had happened after she had seen Fred cavorting on the floor with the flytrap.

Dan'l had gone to the bar to buy himself a light ale—he rarely drank too much because he needed to keep in condition—leaving Kirstie at the soft drinks table with a glass of lemonade in her hand when Fred and Rosina walked to it, arm in arm.

Rosina waited until Fred went to the other end of the counter in order to find something genteel for her to drink—as Kirstie put it later when telling the tale.

'Ah, Miss Moore, is it?' she breathed prettily with an air of the most determined patronage.

'Yes,' countered Kirstie grimly. 'And who are you?' smiling defiantly at Rosina as though she had never seen her before. She looked at her rival who was decked out like a pig's head on a plate, decorated with parsley—her later inelegant description of Rosina to her entranced hearers. She was actually wearing a tartan dress trimmed with white, and heather made of silk was fastened in her hair and to her waist, and her elegant black shoes were adorned with silver buckles.

Kirstie paused for a moment before coming out with her most killing insult, 'Have a job at the theatre, do you?'

This piece of insolence nearly did for Rosina, who had been known to horsewhip rivals for less. Before she could answer Fred returned with two full glasses.

'Fred brought you, did he?' demanded Kirstie nastily. 'You'd better make sure that he's got enough money on him to pay for all you might want to drink, dearie. It wouldn't do for you to be left paying his bills, would it? Or perhaps you're used to that.'

For one glorious moment the watching crowd around them thought that the two women were on the verge of scratching one another's eyes out: the light in Rosina's was nearly as dangerous as that in Kirstie's.

Fred handed Rosina her drink, saw Kirstie, and said in surprise, 'What are you doing here, Kirstie?'

Consumed with black rage Kirstie thought, Does he always think that I have no right to go dancing? and her answer flew out of her mouth before she could stop it.

'I'm playing leapfrog, of course, Fred Waring,' she snapped back at him. 'What does one usually do in a dance hall?'

'Lose one's manners apparently,' said Rosina, thin-lipped. Fortunately at that moment Young Dan'l returned and read the situation at a glance. Before she could object he took Kirstie by the waist and swung her into the waltz.

'And what do you think that you're doing, Daniel?' hissed Kirstie, deprived of her prey.

'More like I should ask you that,' returned Dan'l, amused but determined. 'I shouldn't cross swords with Rosina, if I were you. She has a habit of winning such bouts.'

'Oh, has she? Well, she wasn't winning that one—I would have won it if you hadn't interfered.'

Dan'l stopped dancing. 'And what good would it have done if you had?'

'I should have felt better than I do now, Daniel Mendoza.'

'No, you wouldn't,' retorted Dan'l, swinging her into the dance again. 'You would have felt worse, much worse. How do I know?' he added, sensing that Kirstie was preparing to attack him verbally again. 'Because I'm older than you are, Miss Moore, and I like you. I don't want to see you make a cake of yourself over Rosina, who is here today and gone tomorrow. Do you want to make a fool of yourself for the whole camp to laugh at? Remember, you will have to live here when she's gone.'

Kirstie's good sense returned with a bang after she had heard this reasoned answer. 'I suppose that you're right,' she conceded grudgingly. 'But she's such a…flytrap.'

'And you're twenty-one years old and the prettiest girl in the room,' said Dan'l. 'That must break an old tart's heart, you know, whoever she's got in tow.'

It was as near as Dan'l dare go in hinting at Kirstie's interest in Fred. He was older and wiser than Jack Tate, even if he were never going to end up with the fortune which Jack was determined on.

Kirstie danced on in silence for a little. Then she gave Dan'l her heartstopping smile. 'You're right. She's not worth it.'

The music stopped. A drum rolled and the MC made an announcement, lost in the cheering before the band played a Scottish tune and Rosina favoured the audience with a solo turn: the Highland Fling, for free.

The cheering grew even more tumultuous: the diggers rushed at her and chaired her round the room, before handing her back to the amused Fred who took her on to the floor when the band segued into yet another waltz.

'You see, Kirstie,' said Dan'l, who had been cheering and clapping with the rest, while even Kirstie felt constrained to acknowledge the woman's power to please. 'That's what you're up against. She's a professional charmer. It's her line of business. Just like the poor boys, twice as strong as I am, who come up against me, and only last a few minutes in the ring: it's no contest. Besides, she's nothing to lose, you have.'

Kirstie did not tell Emmie and Mrs Tate that just after Rosina had danced the Highland Fling, she and Fred had been cheered while they whirled around the room and a big digger had shouted, 'Rosina forever,' and she had at last seen the folly of crossing swords with her rival.

This was particularly so when Fred came up to her when she had stood at the drinks table with Dan'l and had said quietly, 'You weren't very kind to Rosie, Big Sister. She doesn't mean you any harm.'

He then echoed what Geordie had told her, although Kirstie was sure that he had not talked to Geordie about her, 'She's got no chick nor child to love her, or for her to care for.'

It was all Kirstie could do not to say acidly, 'No, but she's got a tent full of cheering diggers instead,' but Fred looked so sorrowful when he spoke that she resisted the temptation to spark at him.

'Oh, go and have fun with her, Fred,' she said wearily, 'and I'll enjoy myself with Dan'l.'

This had an even bigger effect on Fred than she had intended, as the idea of Big Sister having real fun with any man was abhorrent to him. She was like the girl with the bluey-green eyes whom Fred had seen on the night when he had recovered his ring. She was definitely not someone with whom you had idle fun. He felt quite agitated at the mere idea.

Then, when he had looked across the room at Rosina who was dancing with a burly digger who was already half-cut, a beatific smile on his face, he knew that he had no right to tell Big Sister what to do while he was squiring Rosie. All the same, watching her defiantly enjoying herself with Young Dan'l gave him a queer feeling.

He told neither Rosina nor Big Sister about this, nor did he ask himself what it meant. His slow recovery of the man he had once been had not yet reached that point.

Fred's affair with Rosina Campbell lasted as long as she stayed in Ballarat. Big Sister continued to flounce about giving him the burned chops and the stale dampers, and handing out the johnny cakes to anyone but him.

It was typical of the way in which Fred was changing that he accepted this treatment from her without complaint: an earlier Fred would have objected artlessly. The new Fred was resigned—and a little amused.

He knew that he had very little time left with Rosie and this made him sad. In the same way that, during his last days with Fat Lil, he had lost a lot of his cheerful thoughtfulness, his mood with Rosina in the week before she left was one which could only be described as elegiac. Long after she had left Ballarat, Rosina thought that it only served to increase the mystery which was Fred.

She had already noticed that Fred was a different man when he relaxed in the evening. He became serious and thoughtful. On her last night at The Palace Theatre this was particularly true.

He was lying on the couch in her dressing room, watching her put on her theatrical make-up.

'I don't like you smearing that stuff on your face, Rosie,' he said quietly.

'I don't like it myself, Fred, but the footlights would kill me without it—and I'm getting old, too.'

Fred sat up. 'No, Rosie!' he protested.

'Yes, Fred.' Rosina shivered. She had been a king's mistress, and had come down to singing and dancing in the gold fields of the USA and Australia for uncouth miners, and her latest lover was one of them. But, echoing Fat Lil again, she had never known a kinder or more considerate partner.

'Come with me, Fred,' she said on impulse.

He thought for a moment before saying, still sober, 'It wouldn't do, Rosie.'

She looked at him again. He was sitting there quiet and still and serious, with little of rowdy Fred Waring about him. His likeness to Thomas Dilhorne was stronger than ever. He looked older, too.

'You're sure that we've never met before, Fred?'

'Yes, Rosie. I wouldn't have forgotten you.'

'You're right not to come with me,' she conceded. Rosina knew that she had nowhere to go but down.

'I'd like to come with you, Rosie, but there's Sam to consider.'

'And Big Sister?' queried Rosina derisively, thinking of the beautiful termagant who had baited her at the Dance Hall.

'Yes,' he said gravely. 'Her, too. They looked after me, you know, when I needed it. Now I ought to look after them—and Geordie Farquhar.'

Earlier in their affair she would have laughed at such an odd statement, but now, looking at him, she saw that he was quite serious.

'We should have met long ago, Fred.' But that would not have answered, either. She was nearly ten years older than Fred, and there was no way in which they could have been lovers on equal terms.

Fred did not answer her. He walked over to where she was sitting and held her to him. 'Let's not spoil our last night together, Rosie. We've had fun, haven't we?'

Rosina's departure should have left Fred at a loose end but, oddly enough, didn't. No one was more surprised by this than Fred. Without his even thinking about it he suddenly gave up wenching. It wasn't a conscious decision, it was more as though he became aware that, pleasant though it had been, it was not something which he wished to remain a major part of his life.

The main thing which puzzled him was how many things he suddenly wanted to do which he had never wanted to do before, responsible things, things which had seemed impossibly grown-up to the old Fred, like saving his money—previously he had always spent his wages from Sam as soon as he received them.

He spoke about this to Geordie, who told him gravely, 'I think that it's because you're slowly getting your memory back, Fred.'

'You mean that I wasn't always like I am now—or how I was when I first came here?'

'Perhaps,' said Geordie. 'Who knows? Don't let it trouble you, Fred—but there may be more changes ahead.'

'What if I don't want to change? I like being who I am now.' He said this with some of his old artlessness—the artlessness which he was rapidly losing.

Whether or not Geordie's answer satisfied him, he stopped pursuing women. He was still jolly with the girls, teased them and was kind, but he never went beyond that. The day after Rosina left he bought Big Sister a new bonnet with his winnings at Hyde's.

Kirstie took it from him, admiring the pink roses pinned to the broad white ribbon round its straw crown. She looked at him with a strange expression on her face and leaned forward to kiss him on the cheek.

'Oh, thank you, Fred, it's beautiful.'

His answer surprised her.

'I've reformed, Big Sister. I told you that I would.'

She would once have replied tartly, 'Early days, Fred Waring, early days. We'll see,' but that day she said nothing, merely watched him when he took his place in the circle round the fire. It was a balmy summer evening and, like many others, they were going to eat their early evening meal in the open.

For once she gave Fred the choicest victuals, wondering while she did so what had prompted his gift of the bonnet.

Fred could not have told her. He was already feeling the loss of Rosie—she had formed such a large part of his life over the six weeks of her visit—and, passing the little dress and bonnet shop recently set up in the alley which the diggers had christened Bond Street, he had seen the pretty straw hat—and had immediately thought of Kirstie.

Oddly enough, it was her blazing, bluey-green eyes when she had taunted Rosie that he remembered, and he had laughed to himself at the defiance which she had spat at the world on the night of the dance.

Leapfrog, indeed, he thought, she deserves a present for that alone, although it had grieved him at the time. It pleased him mightily that before she had served them their food she had run into the hut to try the bonnet on, and had admired herself in the small glass hung in the corner of the room before she had bounded out to show them all how much it suited her.

After his good meal, sitting there comfortable and re- plete, he said to Sam, 'I want to buy into the syndicate, Sam.'

'What with?' Sam asked with a laugh.

'Well,' Fred said in a measured voice, 'what with my winnings at cards and the money I'm being paid to look after Hyde's books and Dickie Vallance's at the store, I have more than enough.'

They all stared at him in wonder, even Geordie Farquhar.

'Yes,' he said, surprised at their surprise. 'Didn't I tell you? I haven't been spending all my time with Rosie.'

If they had not known artless Fred for so long, they might have thought that he was being devious.

It had happened nearly a fortnight ago, just as the real- isation that he was soon to lose Rosie had come hard upon him. She was being entertained by the Commissioner that night, and there was no room at the table for the poor digger who was her fancy man. He had gone to Hyde's Place to his corner table, and had taken up his usual lazy position stretched between two chairs.

Ned Hyde was seated in his corner, his face *distrait*, his ledgers open before him.

'What's up, Hyde?' asked Fred cheerfully when Hyde groaned for the third time.

'Damned book,' grumbled Hyde. 'I can calculate any odds you like, but book-keeping…' and he shrugged his shoulders impressively.

Fred had just finished playing a hand. He rose, ambled over to Hyde and stared at his books. Memories which he did not know that he possessed revived themselves within him.

'Let me,' he asked, and put out a large hand to turn the ledger which Hyde was studying towards him.

Hyde stared at him. Well, he thought, let Fred look. Little he'd learn. Hyde didn't like strangers looking at his books—but Fred! He pushed the ledger at him. Fred gave him his slow smile and looked down.

'Want them added up, do you?'

'It's usual,' returned Hyde, winking at the amused company.

Fred read rapidly down the columns. He picked up Hyde's quill pen and began to enter figures equally rapidly.

'Here,' exclaimed Hyde, 'leave that, Fred. What the devil do you think that you're doing?'

'You said that you wanted 'em added up, so I've done it for you,' replied Fred, his voice injured. 'Changed your mind, have you?'

Hyde stared at him. He swung the book round, slowly began to add up the column himself before staring at Fred's accurate, beautiful figures at the bottom of the page, figures which he had written with surprising speed.

'Can you do that again, Fred?' he asked, his voice disbelieving.

'Easy,' said Fred, so Hyde turned the page and pushed the ledger towards him again.

Fred repeated his trick.

'Now where the devil did you learn to do that?' Hyde demanded. The crowd around them had fallen silent.

'Don't know. Can't everybody do it? It's easy.'

There were several present who had witnessed Fred's surprising skill and wondered whether it might be of use to them. One of them was Dickie Vallance, who ran a money-lending business out of his store as well as selling dry goods, provisions, and buying gold on the side.

He stopped Fred in the long lane between the canvas flats of the saloons and the gaming dens on the next afternoon. Fred had finished his day's work and was off to do Hyde's ledgers for him.

'Fred, come here, Fred.'

Fred walked over and smiled at Dickie. He liked him. Long ago, at the beginning of time, Dickie had been kind to Corny and Fred, giving them some damaged provisions to eat, and once or twice he had thrown coins at them for drink.

'What is it, Dickie?'

'Could you do that trick with my books, Fred? They'll be more difficult than Hyde's—at least the ones to do with the money-lending business. Can you keep quiet about them, about what you see?'

He looked doubtfully at open, cheerful Fred, who always said exactly what arrived at the end of his tongue.

Fred considered. 'Yes, I'll try, and yes, I'll not talk, Dickie. Fred knows what's what.'

'Then, when you've finished with Hyde's, come and have a look at mine. I'll pay you good money.'

Fred spent that evening tidying up Dickie's books. His speed and precision were such that Hyde and Dickie agreed later that he ought to do it as an act in a fair.

'Where'd you learn to do this, Fred?' asked Dickie, while

Fred calculated percentages and added up columns of figures as fast as he could read them.

'Can't remember,' said Fred. 'It's not difficult, though. By the by,' he added, frowning at Dickie, 'you aren't charging enough in the store, you know. You could get nearly twice as much with food as scarce as it is here. Bad business, that.'

His voice was so hard and short and his stare so penetrating when he came out with this that Dickie hardly recognised him. The next moment he was easy-going Fred again.

Fred told Sam and the others something of this. He was as surprised as anybody by his newly discovered skills. He was even more surprised to learn that everyone did not share them. Indeed, it was obvious from the reactions of those who saw him perform that his talent was rare indeed.

He did not tell the others—why, he did not know—that Dickie had given him a fee on top of the one he earned for doing his books, in return for several pieces of advice on how to improve the profit levels in his store, offered absentmindedly by Fred in the middle of his mathematical legerdemain.

'You wouldn't mind Fred being a partner?' he asked the others anxiously. They looked at him. He was a far cry from The Wreck of several months ago. His clothes were clean, his looks, manner and physique were outstanding— it was no wonder that Rosina Campbell had taken him for a lover. And, although his artlessness was changing into something more responsible, he was still full of a charm which attracted men and women alike.

What else would he discover that he could do? thought Geordie. How much more would he change? Was he even aware that he was changing?

Fred rose, announcing that he was tired and would have

an early night. They all watched him enter his tent, yawning and stretching while he did so.

Sam asked the others, who had all agreed to Fred becoming a full partner, 'How old do you reckon Fred really is?'

'How old do you think, Sam?' Geordie countered.

'I used to think that he was in his twenties, late twenties, that is,' said Sam slowly, 'but now I think that he's older.'

'Mid-thirties, wouldn't you say, Sam?' said Geordie. 'It was his manner which made you think that he was younger.'

'Yes,' said Sam. He echoed an earlier thought of Geordie's. 'What else will he find that he can do? He was helpless when we brought him here. He could barely feed or look after himself. The next thing you know,' he said with a laugh, 'is that he'll be looking after us!'

They all had a good laugh at this. Big Sister, who had been working in the hut, had come out to join them.

'I wonder where he came from,' she said slowly. 'And what he did before he became a drunk in Melbourne and then in Ballarat.' Her voice was anxious. Somehow they had all taken Fred for granted. Only Geordie had wondered seriously about Fred's past.

'I'll tell you one thing,' said Geordie. 'By his body and his general condition he's always had enough to eat, and although he's so big he'd never done any manual labour until he came here. Do you remember his hands when he began digging—what does that tell you?'

'A clerk, then?' queried Bart.

'Perhaps,' said Geordie, who had watched Fred more than the others.

A clerk, thought Kirstie, remembering the sleek young men she had seen in Melbourne. They had been so different from the outdoor labourers she was used to, and from the men in the diggings.

Was that what Fred had been?

Chapter Nine

It was Sunday in the diggings and Ballarat was quiet. There had been an open-air service beyond the creek which many had attended for something to do, rather than as a genuine act of devotion. Now, after a mid-day snack, the diggers and their women and children were enjoying being idle in a variety of ways.

Young Dan'l walked over to The More. He found Sam was away—on an illicit visit to Kate Clancy, presumably. The rest of his party were still unaware of his interest in her.

Bart and Geordie were mending tack. Kirstie was knitting a jacket for Baby Rod who was tied to the steps of the hut beside her. A tattered book, which she had been reading earlier, lay on the ground by her feet. She had grown tired of reading about impossibly noble young men and well-behaved heroines whose lives seemed to have little to do with hers.

They never said what a difficult game love really was. None of the heroes went off and took up with beautiful, if elderly, flytraps bang in front of the young women who adored them so. Well, she adored Fred, but he never looked deep into her eyes, whispering polite nothings, and she didn't think that that was what he had been doing with Rosina, either.

Pat and Davie were kicking a ball about on the parched earth, being a mild nuisance to their elders when they ran in and out of them. Allie, who had long ago found another little girl of her own age to play with, sat quietly whispering and giggling with her in the manner of little girls the world over.

Before he went to sit with Kirstie, Dan'l asked Geordie a question. 'Where's Fred, then? He's not doing his books today, surely?'

'No,' said Geordie, looking up from his work. 'He's in there, reading,' and he jerked his thumb at the tent which did duty as his home.

'Reading!' exclaimed Dan'l with some surprise, for Fred's life since he had arrived at Ballarat had been a purely physical one.

'Yes,' said Geordie briefly. He did not tell Dan'l that coincidentally with his recall of his mathematical skills Fred had suddenly picked a book from the little library of battered texts which Geordie carried around with him, and said diffidently, 'May I, Geordie?' before he began to read it.

Since then he had read through them all, and Geordie had noticed that his reading speed was as remarkable as his numbering speed, and he also frequently stopped to re-read, and to think about what he had read.

Geordie's Shakespeare appeared to be his favourite, even though it seemed to trouble him. Geordie came in one evening to find Fred lying on his mattress, his arms behind his head, the book containing the *Tragedies* open before him. He could almost feel Fred's distress.

'Anything wrong?' he asked.

Fred slowly moved to look at him. His eyes had been set on some distant scene.

'I've been reading *Hamlet*.' He paused. As usual, late at night, in the half-dark, he was not the Fred Waring of the daylight hours, something which both Fat Lil and Rosina had discovered, and Geordie was coming to know.

'Oh, Geordie, I've read it before, I know I have. I know that it means something to me, something bad and painful.'

His face twisted. He became more unFredlike than ever. 'Why can't I remember, Geordie? I only know that when I read some of the speeches they make me feel so unhappy. Unhappy beyond…' he struggled for words '…unhappy beyond the speeches themselves.'

'I don't know, Fred,' said Geordie gently. 'If I could help you, I would. The only thing that I can say is, don't fight your feelings. One day you might break through them to your past.'

'But, Geordie,' said Fred earnestly, 'why should I feel so miserable when I can't remember? Hamlet, now, he's so unhappy, and I know that I was unhappy when I read the play before I forgot who I was…who I am. And that worries me, too, because the one thing Fred has been, is happy.'

He spoke of himself as he often did, although less frequently these days, as though Fred were someone else, not the tormented man lying on the mattress.

'Oh, Geordie, it seems to me that if I had been as unhappy as Hamlet I wouldn't want to remember. But that's a wrong thought—even Fred knows that.'

'Read something else then, Fred, something which makes you happy.'

'Like *Twelfth Night*,' said Fred eagerly. 'We read that together. Viola had bluey-green eyes, too.'

'Like Kirstie?' queried Geordie watchfully.

'No, yes, oh, I don't know,' said Fred restlessly. 'Someone. Yes, I'll read it again. Not *Hamlet*, that frightens me.'

He picked up the book of *Comedies* and began to read

aloud from it in his beautiful voice, the voice which had
helped to entrance Kirstie and to which Geordie listened,
taken out of himself. He was back in a London theatre, a
pretty woman by his side, watching Macready staging the
play which Fred was reading aloud. Like Fred, he pushed
the memory away because it made him unhappy.

He told Dan'l nothing of this—only said quietly to him,
'If you want to speak to Fred, I don't think that he would
mind if you interrupted him.'

Dan'l shook his head. 'I was just wondering. I came to
see Kirstie, really.'

Geordie watched him walk away to sit by Kirstie. He's
courting her, he thought, amused, and although he knew
that Kirstie would never accept Dan'l, he also knew that
she liked to talk to him, and to listen to his tales of his
past. Unlike Desdemona, who fell in love with Othello because of his stories, Kirstie's heart was already given to
another, and both she and Dan'l knew it.

I might change her mind, though, thought Dan'l, so he
was content to sit by her and watch the slow life around
them. Emmie and Mrs Tate emerged from the Tates' tent
with mugs of hot tea for everyone. They handed them
around, so that, for once, Kirstie was waited on.

The noise of the tea-party brought Fred from the gloom
of his tent. He blinked a little in the strong light and carried
his tea over to where Kirstie and Dan'l sat and they gos-
siped happily together about the scandals of the diggings.

'Will Fentiman heard today that Rosina's show caused
great excitement in Melbourne,' said Dan'l. 'They've
lengthened her stay at the theatre. She's not taken another
lover yet—or at least, that's what they're saying.' He
avoided looking at either Fred or Kirstie when he passed
on this piece of news.

Fred was quite equable. Kirstie flushed a little, remembering the dance and how she had behaved at it.

'Not all the news is good, though,' Dan'l said. 'There's been an outbreak of fever at Dead Man's Gulch. They're a careless lot there—but, with luck, it won't spread.'

Fever and stomach troubles were endemic in the diggings. Sanitation was poor, and the food eaten by most gave them little protection against infection since much of it was tainted. So far, however, most outbreaks of fever had been contained: unspoken was the fear of a major epidemic—something which the diggings had been spared so far.

'Geordie said to keep things clean, and to boil all our water,' said Kirstie soberly, 'but he also admits that there is little we can do about bad food.'

More cheerful things occupied them after that. Lew Robinson had beaten Annie for straying again. Fred avoided Kirstie's satirical eye when Dan'l told them this. Bart called the men over for a game of cards, grumbling a little at Sam's absence.

'Dunno where he gets to these days,' he complained. 'Running a woman, I suppose.'

This surprised them all. Sam had been so steady, but it was noticeable how often Bart, who was not remarkable in the brain department, was right about such things.

Sam was indeed running a woman. He had met the Widow Clancy one evening when he had been walking home early from the Music Hall. He was feeling in need of a good night's rest, rather than engaging in drinking and jollity into the small hours.

Kate Clancy had gone dancing with a big digger, a mate of her dead husband's, who thought that taking her out for the evening entitled him to marital rights once it was over.

Her cries of protest had brought Sam running and, after giving the digger what for, he had escorted Kate home. She ran a little haberdashery, and seeing him walk by the next day she had invited him in for a cup of tea. She knew him by reputation: all the Moore party were known to be good people, and matters had gone on from there.

'I want to marry you, Kate,' he had said to her recently, 'but it's Kirstie I'm thinking of. She's looked after us all for so long, and I don't know how she'd feel about me bringing in another woman over her.

'I'm hoping that she'll marry soon, perhaps one of the men who are dangling after her—preferably young Jack Tate. He's her age and steady. The trouble is that I'm afraid that she'll have none of them, she's so taken with Fred Waring. Give me a little time, Kate, in the hope that she'll soon settle on one of them. If not, we'll marry and she'll have to get used to the idea that you'll be in charge, not her.'

Kate Clancy was a sensible woman. She agreed with him. Kirstie Moore was a bit of a firebrand, and it would be better if she married soon and left her and Sam to settle down together on their own.

She was as honest with Sam as he was with her. 'I can't promise to do for you and the rest all that Kirstie does. But I would look after you well, you may be sure of that, but I can't promise to look after half of the camp as well.'

Sam quite understood. 'That's one reason that I would like her to marry. It might make her slow down a little. I can't stop her, but a husband might.'

Kate hesitated and then asked quietly, 'What would you say if Fred Waring did offer for her after all?'

Sam looked at her. She was big, comfortable and sensible. 'Do you think that's likely, Kate? He's been after so many women, and he's never looked at her that way once.'

'Less likely things have happened, Sam. She's suddenly become a very pretty girl.'

'As Fred was when we first rescued him, no, I wouldn't be happy. But I must admit that he has changed a lot lately.

He's more sober in his ways. He's making money with his book-keeping as well as working hard for the syndicate.

'He's a bit old for her, perhaps, but he's not as old as Dan'l and much younger than Dickie—and I wouldn't have objected to her marrying either of them. But I don't see it myself, not with Fred I don't.'

Kate did not argue with him. She simply sighed a little and hoped that Kirstie would accept one of her suitors soon. She had no wish to invade another woman's territory, but neither could she wait for ever—and so she told Sam.

'If only I were as simple-minded as Fred,' said Sam when he left her, 'then decisions would be easier to make.'

But Fred wasn't simple-minded at all these days. The kaleidoscope in his head, which had shaken itself so suddenly on the night when he had recovered his ring, had not gone away. It had reappeared when he had rediscovered his talent for figuring at Hyde's Place, and had surfaced again to make him able to read Geordie's difficult books—or so the others called them. It was now being shaken, not suddenly, but gently every day, and each day brought more changes for him—some major and some minor.

When he met Annie Robinson in Regent Street one evening and she gave him one of her come-hither looks he had found her quite attractive, but he had experienced absolutely no desire to pleasure her—or himself. For the life of him he could not understand why he had been so frantic for her that he could not wait to get her decently into bed, but had had her against the wall instead.

His new-found fastidiousness had ended his affair with Lil. So far as Rosina Campbell was concerned, his adventure with her, when he had thought that his womanising days were over, had seemed something which he had long wanted to do.

He had no notion of how he could have long wanted a

woman whom he had never met before he had seen her in the diggings, but there it was, and when their affair was over he had no regrets. What's more, he also knew that if she were to return to the diggings he would not take up with her again.

As for his wild and compulsive drinking, Fred found that a complete mystery. These days he could take it or leave it. When he had drunk champagne with Rosina on their last few nights together, he had enjoyed it, but after she had gone had reverted to being temperate again. It was almost as though a different man had drunk and wenched his way around Ballarat.

He was still cheerful Fred and his outward manner had altered little, but something was making him more and more responsible. When he did the books for the various store-owners—for many now offered him work—he found himself offering them shrewd advice on how to run their businesses more effectively. The same held good with his work for the Moore syndicate, who watched him in amazement while he accumulated a store of capital from all the different ventures he was engaged in.

At first some treated him as a bit of a joke, but Dickie Vallance had soon found that it paid to take Fred's advice and began questioning him the moment he walked into his store.

Geordie Farquhar watched Fred change with carefully controlled interest. He wondered how much longer his gambling would last. It had originally been as compulsive as his drinking and womanising had been. He did not have long to wait.

Shortly after Geordie had found him reading *Hamlet* and Sam had asked Kate Clancy to marry him when the time was ripe, and the fever outbreak had begun to spread, the Yankees came over to Hyde's Place to issue a challenge to

Fred. Big Red was with them, and they had brought along a new chum: a little dark man who, they said, had the beating of Red, and they wanted to see him take Fred on. They were sure that The Doc, as they called him, could master anyone—even this fellow Waring.

Fred agreed to a match, so Hyde arranged that five of the Yankees, Fred and a digger called The Jug Head because of his big ears, should all pitch in together and play until one of them was an outright winner.

'However long it takes,' said The Doc, 'even if it runs to days—which it won't do.'

He was an unpleasant little man, Fred thought, not at all like the rest of the Yankees, especially Big Red who had become Fred's chum.

They sat down at ten o'clock that night. Fred, his skills much greater since he had rediscovered his mathematical powers, was now a far better player than when he had first encountered Big Red. He still sat there with his carefree smile and his lazy posture, but behind this easy façade his brain was as cold as ice.

Quite soon he saw something which he was sure that Big Red and his mates did not know. The Doc was a cheat and an exceedingly skilful one. So long as other players remained in the game Fred took no advantage from this, but once everyone else but The Doc dropped out Fred used his knowledge to contain, and then beat, him.

Only the watching Ned Hyde grasped what was happening—and wondered again at Fred. The stakes were high, monumentally so, for Fred was betting all his free cash. At one point The Doc pulled a pistol out of his belt and put it on the table before him. No one could fathom why he did this.

Shortly afterwards, Fred, who had recently bought himself a watch—something which he had never possessed before—solemnly pulled it out of his pocket, detached it with its chain, and put it on the table before him.

He grinned across at The Doc, and when he had won the next hand, he scooped up his winnings, picked the watch up by its chain, swung it gently, then half-sang 'Bang Bang' in The Doc's direction. No one knew what that meant, either. Only Ned Hyde laughed to himself, and tried not to catch Geordie Farquhar's eye.

If The Doc was annoyed at Fred's satire he did not betray it. He had your true poker face, but it availed him little. He was well aware towards the end of the game that Fred was using his own tricks against him, but there was nothing he could say without giving himself away.

At almost seven o'clock in the morning, with the sun streaming in through the tent door, the game finished with Fred the winner. Many of the spectators, Geordie included, had gone home once Fred's victory had become certain. Fred yawned and stretched after he had picked up his winnings. The Doc flourished his pistol and made a great play of shoving it into his belt.

Fred made an equally elaborate show of recovering his watch. He had the strangest feeling that with the last card played something had ended. He counted his winnings—bills and coin and gold dust in little leather bags—and then looked across at Hyde.

Hyde knew immediately what he wanted. 'Finish counting it, Fred, put it in my safe, and collect it later.'

Fred nodded. 'I don't want to take it home on my own.'

He yawned again. 'Oh, I'm tired, Ned. Bone weary.'

The Doc had walked away without a word, but Big Red and the rest of the Yankees came over to shake Fred by the hand. 'I'll take my revenge another day,' Big Red roared genially. 'Luck can't stay with you forever.'

Fred shook his head. 'I don't think that we shall play

again, Red,' he said quietly. 'You're a good fellow, though. I'm proud to call you friend.'

'Shrewd these days, aren't you, Fred?' said Hyde, once he and Fred were alone. 'I don't blame you for being careful.'

He led Fred into his back room and Fred watched him lock his winnings in his big safe. He could not have told Hyde how he felt. Drained was not the right word. Satisfied or fulfilled might be better, but they were not right, either.

Above all, there was the sense of something having ended.

He shook his head, said to Hyde, 'I'll be back later with the Moore chums acting as guards,' before walking through the outer room, garish and dirty in the daylight.

It was time to go home and to bed.

Kirstie was serving breakfast before she realised that Fred was not with them. They were having it around the big table in her hut for once, and he never arrived—which was something surprising, since Fred was always the first to turn up when grub was served.

She asked no questions of the others, merely snapped at Geordie when he came in late, yawning. He did not enlighten her as to why Fred was absent, and when, the meal almost over, he did not appear a red mist rose in front of her eyes.

Well! That hadn't lasted long, had it? Faithful to the memory of Rosina, was he? Not he! He was most likely off again with Fat Lil, for Kirstie was remembering the days when he had always been late for breakfast, or didn't arrive for it at all. Well, she might have expected this. If it wasn't one whore it was another!

She worked herself into such a passion of rage that when she went outside and saw him walking to the diggings, his face grey with tiredness, his felt hat on the back of his black curly head, she could hardly contain herself.

'All I can say to you, Fred Waring,' she said, addressing him when he drew level with her, 'is, if she hasn't seen fit to give you your breakfast after the pair of you have made a night of it together, don't expect anything from me.'

She was almost dancing with rage.

Fred was bewildered. 'I don't know what you're talking about, Big Sister.'

'Oh, that's a fine tale, that is, Fred Waring.' She shook her iron ladle at him. 'Reformed, reformed, you said. I've a mind to make you go without dinner as well.'

'But I'm hungry, Big Sister,' said Fred, who was too weary to make out why she was so cross with him again. 'I haven't seen Fat Lil for weeks. Except to say hello to her.'

'Hello, is it? Is that what you're calling it now? It used to be having fun.'

By now Geordie, Bart and Sam, who all knew how Fred had spent his night, were helpless with laughter. Poor Fred stared at them, injured, badly wanting his grub. Big Sister, still beside herself, rounded on them, too.

'And what's so funny, now, Geordie Farquhar? A man of your education should set an example to us all. Not go encouraging Fred to start his tricks all over again.'

'Start what?' asked Fred plaintively. He honestly had no idea why Kirstie was so cross with him.

Geordie thought that if he did not stop this soon Kirstie would either burst or assault Fred with the ladle which she had begun, almost unconsciously, to swing dangerously in front of her.

'Oh, Kirstie,' he said, wiping his eyes. 'You're being so unfair to Fred. He hasn't spent the night with Fat Lil. He's been playing poker with the Yankees at Hyde's.'

Kirstie's mouth opened—and then shut. Her face flamed

an even stronger crimson. 'Is that the truth, Geordie Farquhar? Or are you just having me on to protect him?'

'It's the truth, Big Sister,' said Fred. 'And I won, as well. I was winning when you left, Geordie, wasn't I? How did we come to be arguing about Fat Lil? She wasn't at Hyde's.'

Kirstie was not to be put down by this. Tears came into her eyes when she looked at the innocent and injured Fred, and the grinning men.

Inspiration struck. 'Well, Fred Waring, so far as I'm concerned, it's nearly as bad that you spent the night with the Yankees playing poker as being in bed with Fat Lil.'

'I know,' said Fred humbly. 'And I agree with you. I shan't do it again. I've been thinking that all the way home.'

'Oh…' This came out in one giant breath. 'Oh,' she exclaimed. 'You're impossible, all of you. Stop laughing, do.'

Big Sister had a terrible desire to hit someone, to scream, or to kiss Fred, who suddenly looked very unhappy because she was cross with him. Yes, she wanted to hit him with the ladle either for not being with Fat Lil when she thought he was, or for wasting his time playing poker when he should have been sleeping—she didn't know which.

'Oh, why do I put up with you all,' she wailed, and ran into the hut where she threw herself on her bed and began to cry, great sobs which shook her through and through.

Outside Fred looked at the trio, at Jack Tate who had come to see what all the noise was about—even Emmie and Mrs Tate were staring at him.

'What did I do?' he asked, still humble. 'I didn't do anything. Why is she so cross?'

Geordie stopped laughing long enough to clap him on the back. 'She's a woman, Fred. Isn't that enough?'

This only served to bewilder Fred the more. 'Well, Fat

Lil and Rosina never carried on like that and they were women.'

Geordie felt that he understood why Kirstie wanted to hit Fred. 'Well, they wouldn't, would they?' he said, wondering if Fred could work that out. 'Oh, go to bed, Fred. I'll bring you some breakfast.'

'Well, thanks,' said Fred. 'But I can't sleep too long. We've all to fetch my winnings from Hyde's safe.'

He looked sorrowfully towards Kirstie's hut. 'I don't understand why she doesn't like me, Geordie. The other women did.'

For some reason Fred didn't understand, Bart, Sam and Geordie all began to laugh helplessly together.

'Oh, do go and lie down,' said Geordie, still laughing.

And why he can't use the brain he undoubtedly possesses to work out what is wrong with Kirstie, I shall never know, he thought when he went to collect some food for poor starving Fred to eat.

Later they all went round to Hyde's to collect Fred's winnings. It was safer with the four of them: they were less likely to be attacked. Hyde, looking weary, but still immaculate as always, welcomed them into his back room.

Fred had changed his clothes. He was wearing new cord trousers, a pale blue shirt, new boots and a straw hat with a blue silk band. He had seldom looked more handsome, and Kirstie, watching him go from the hut window, had another good cry at the sight of him. *No one should look like that. It was more than a poor girl could stand. Particularly when she had been so unkind to him.*

Fred, though, was not thinking of Kirstie when Hyde handed over his winnings in a little canvas sack. He looked at Ned and said earnestly, 'I hardly like to tell you this, you've been such a good friend, and I hope that you'll always be one. But I shan't play cards again for money. Either here or anywhere else.'

Hyde and the others stared at him. 'Why, Fred?' Hyde said. 'You're a natural. I've never seen anyone who could play as well as you. And you're honest, which is more than I can say for many.'

'I can't explain why,' Fred said carefully. 'It's as though something came to an end last night. I've enjoyed myself, but it's over, like the drinking and the women,' he added hesitantly. He had taken off his new straw hat and was twisting it in his hand.

'It's nothing to do with you, Ned. It's something in me. I have the feeling that—' He stopped. 'I can't explain. It may be something to do with what I was before I lost my memory. You know that I have no memory of anything before I arrived in Ballarat.'

Hyde nodded. 'Yes, Fred. Geordie told me after you claimed your ring.'

'That's it, then. I don't think that I shall change my mind.'

Hyde put out his hand. 'It's been a pleasure knowing you, Fred. If you do change your mind, why, you know where my Place is.'

Geordie watched Fred shrewdly. 'Was it what Kirstie said, Fred, that made you change your mind?'

'No,' said Fred. 'It was after the game ended last night. I suddenly knew that I never wanted to do it again. That I'd enjoyed myself over the last weeks, but it was over. That in some way that I don't understand it's not for me.'

He began to look distressed, as he often did when he was questioned. 'Leave it, Geordie. I'm glad that Ned didn't argue with me. He's a good fellow, is Ned.'

None of them questioned him further. Sam began to wonder what sort of man Fred would be now that he had given up all the pleasures which had filled his days since he had arrived in the diggings.

He would not mind giving Kirstie to the sort of person Fred was turning into, so different from what he had been.

Chapter Ten

Fred continued to work on Ned Hyde's books while he built up a nice little part-time business as an accountant and business adviser which occupied the evenings which he had previously spent gambling. Big Sister, regretting her out-burst over Fred's supposed reversion to Fat Lil, spent her time making sure that he received the best of the grub, but he still looked unhappily at her even when she handed him the largest and the tastiest share of the food.

It surprised him how much he minded that she seemed not to like him. He had not worked out why the trio had been so amused at his bewilderment and, watching Dan'l come and go, Fred found that he was also unhappy at the time Dan'l spent with Big Sister—even if she gave him little encouragement.

The first night after he had stopped gambling and Big Sister had been so cross with him the tiger ran through his dreams again. This time Fred knew for sure that he had lost something precious to him forever. He had woken up sweating and shouting—something he had not done for a long time. Oddly enough, the first person he thought of when he had recovered himself a little was Big Sister. He imagined her looking reproachfully at him, her beautiful eyes huge just as she had done on the morning when she had attacked him so unfairly.

Geordie, who was tired himself after his late night at Hyde's, did not wake up to comfort him, and Fred lay there, his heart pounding, wondering why a tiger should pursue him so relentlessly. There were no tigers in Ballarat, that was for sure, nor were there any in the rest of the colony, either.

He had another half-dream when he finally drifted off to sleep. This time the tiger had appeared, then it had vanished, but in some strange way it was still present, even if unseen. He found himself looking at an old man with a kind, if sad, face who seemed to want to tell Fred something, but the dream faded before Fred could understand what he was saying.

In the morning Fred remembered the tiger and his sense of dreadful loss, but he had forgotten the old man. Fortunately, none of the images which had troubled him occurred again and Fred began to forget them.

They were all sitting round the fire one evening getting ready to play cards when Sam at last told the Syndicate that he was walking out with Kate Clancy.

'But I don't want Big Sister to know yet,' he ended.

'Why not?' asked Bart who, like Fred, needed telling, although Geordie didn't.

'Oh, I'm hoping that Kirstie will be fixed up one way or another before we wed. I'd like her to accept Jack Tate.'

For some reason this upset Fred. 'Oh, no, she's already refused Jack,' he said aggressively. He didn't like the thought of Big Sister being replaced by Kate Clancy, even though he was pleased for Sam.

Conversation ended when Bart began to deal the cards for the Syndicate's poker and beans card school—the beans stood in for money. Fred had discovered that he still liked playing cards in a friendly way: he always took care not to try too hard since he didn't like to spoil the fun for others. Geordie was the only member of the party who grasped this. It was part, Geordie thought, of the essential kindness towards others which was one of Fred's most distinguishing characteristics.

His kindness didn't make him like Jack Tate much, though, which the others thought odd, since Jack was just the sort of good mate Fred usually took to.

For his part Sam hoped that when he did marry Kate it would not spoil the essential good nature of the Syndicate. He was determined to keep Geordie, Bart and Fred as his partners since all of them, in their different ways, seemed to need his support.

Bart needed it not only because he was a little simple-minded, but because Emmie was rapidly becoming more and more lethargic, and if Kirstie married and moved away she would be unable to look after their children on her own. Geordie was a different case. In some fashion it was he who wanted to be needed, to be part of a family, helping and caring for them. It was noticeable how much he had looked after Fred in his early days, not only because he liked him, but because it gave him a purpose in life.

Geordie was an educated man, and a good man, and it was a bit of a puzzle to them all how he had come down to being a shop assistant and then a labourer in the diggings. He never spoke of his past, and the others respected that and never questioned him about it.

All in all it was not surprising that the other diggers thought of Sam's party as a good one: their essential decency shone out of them all. It was not simply their original rescue and later protection of Fred which had given them this reputation.

And what of Fred? Once he would have been Sam's

primary consideration for care, but Fred had changed and was still changing and now seemed to need less protection than either Bart or Geordie.

Geordie, who had been enquiring about the fever epidemic which was now beginning to engulf the whole camp, said before the game could begin, 'There is something which I feel bound to tell you all—the outbreak of fever is getting worse and it will not be long before it reaches us. Today, when I was out, I was stopped on Rotten Row by the wife of one of our chums. She asked me to look at her little girl who was in a bad way. She had heard that I had once done some doctoring. I examined the child and she was undoubtedly suffering from the fever and her condition was grave.

'Now, Rotten Row is not far from here, so I fear that we cannot escape it. If anyone should feel low or fevered at any time of the day or night, I beg them to tell me immediately. Delay could be fatal.'

They all fell silent. 'Pray God it misses us,' said Sam at last.

'Amen to that,' echoed Bart, who remembered the bad years in London when cholera had been rampant and the grief and misery which it had caused. The fever was not cholera, but it was bad enough.

It took them some time to recover their usual high spirits. They watched the children playing around them before sending them off to bed; the shadow which lay over them seemed intolerable.

Life went on, though, and since the epidemic grew, but did not come any nearer to the area where the Moore party lived and worked, its threat seemed to recede. Some mild excitement was caused when Bart made a strike but, alas, the vein petered out rapidly and so their dreams of wealth receded equally rapidly.

On that day Dan'l came round, sprucely turned out. He was even wearing a new stove-pipe hat and a striped black and white waistcoat, rather like the humbugs in the little sweet shop which had opened just off Bond Street to cater for the increasing number of children in the diggings. Or at least that was what Fred told them after Dan'l had gone.

Dan'l was carrying a great bunch of flowers, which he had gathered from the bush which was moving further and further away as Ballarat expanded and the crowds continued to pour in.

'He's come a-courting in earnest,' said Bart when Dan'l stopped to talk seriously to Sam before knocking on the door of Kirstie's hut.

Kirstie was busy making bread. Mrs Tate had mysteriously produced some yeast—she would not say from where—and had then announced that 'she din't know 'ow to make bread wiv it'. Inevitably the task fell to Kirstie whom Ma had taught back at the farm in the old days before gold had been found at Ballarat.

Dan'l walked in to find her punching dough vigorously.

'Oh, it's you,' she said, in a voice which was hardly a welcoming one. She had hoped that it was Fred knocking. He had taken to watching her with a wounded expression on his face which all her little kindnesses failed to remove.

Dan'l watched her throwing the dough about. He could hardly hand her the flowers whilst she was working against time so determinedly.

He showed them to her. 'They're for you,' he said, unnecessarily, 'when you've finished baking.'

Kirstie gave the dough one last murderous punch, then put it in her big bowl near the stove to prove, being careful to lay a wetted cloth over the top as Ma had taught her.

She felt sorry for Dan'l, as she had done for Jack Tate, but there was no helping it. She wiped her hands clean and took the flowers from him.

'They're beautiful,' she said. 'You're so kind, Dan'l,' which was true and there was, sadly, nothing left for her to do but hurt him.

She found a jar which had held jam, poured some of her precious water into it and arranged the flowers as slowly as she could before putting it on the table. She knew what was coming next and, sure enough, it did—she had no way of stopping him.

Dan'l held his splendid hat in his hand. He was quite a good-looking man, although his face bore the marks of his trade.

'I've been talking to Will Fentiman,' he said. 'He's asked me if I'd like to go to Bendigo and open a booth for him there. I'm too old to go battering around the ring much more, so I've said yes to his offer. I shall manage it for him, and take a share of the profits.'

He stopped speaking. Kirstie's pretty face was grave and serious. She was learning to be kind at last.

'I must go,' he said simply. 'I can't be a bruiser much longer—I don't even want to be one any more. What I'd like to say is this: will you come with me? As my wife, of course.'

He ended his plea with a nervous laugh, and then, suddenly turning bold, said, 'Oh, do say yes, my darling. You're a grand girl. A man couldn't ask for a better wife. Look at the way you work.' He waved a hand at the spotless hut, the shining pans, the washed pots and the bowl of dough which was casting its aromatic smell around the room.

'You're as pretty as a picture and I love you as well.'

Kirstie felt so sorry for him. As with Jack's proposal, she was almost tempted to accept him. She would be settled. It would be her own hut in Bendigo, not Pa's, and she would be free to live her own life, not worry all the time about the others.

But Fred's face rose before her, and she knew that it was hopeless. She could not accept Dan'l when she loved someone else, it would be neither fair nor right, and could even be a recipe for disaster. She could not, must not, agree to be his wife if she didn't love him.

'I'm so pleased for you, Dan'l.' she said and his face lit with hope. 'But I can't marry you—it wouldn't be fair to either of us. Find some nice girl when you get to Bendigo, a girl who will love you as you deserve to be loved. I hope that you will be prosperous and happy, but I can't marry you, I can't.'

He had never mentioned Fred's name to her since the early days of his courtship, but he did so now.

'It's Fred, isn't it?' he said mournfully. 'You're serious about him. You don't want to be one of his fancy women—not that he has had any fancy women since Rosina left. Oh, Kirstie my darling, if I can't have you, then I hope that one day you'll get what you want. He must be blind not to see what a treasure you are.'

Kirstie swallowed painfully. 'You're so good, Dan'l,' she said. 'You deserve better than me.'

'There isn't anyone better than you,' he said, 'I know what I'm losing. I'd hoped that you might change your mind, but I saw your face that night when he was hurt and again when you thought that he had gone back to Fat Lil.'

It was over. Kirstie had nothing left to say but, 'Oh, Dan'l, believe me when I say that I wish you well.'

Why was life so hard? Choices, Geordie had said to her, life is about choices. Well, choices were damnable things, somehow you always hurt someone when you made one.

She went to the window to watch Dan'l leave. He spoke to Sam and shook his head. She wondered what he was saying. Fred was beginning a new hole and he spoke kindly to Dan'l too, and she gulped back a sob when they shook hands.

Dan'l said goodbye to them all. He was off to Bendigo in the morning. If Kirstie had accepted him he would have delayed leaving until they were married, but now he had nothing to keep him in Ballarat. He was the first loss in their little group, but she also knew that he had to take the chance Will Fentiman had offered him—it might not come again.

Fred said to Geordie that night when they were alone in their tent, 'Dan'l said that he wished me well in everything and that I ought to look a little harder at what was in front of me. What do you think he meant by that?'

Geordie often answered a question with another question.

'What do *you* think he meant by it, Fred?'

'I don't know. Something about book-keeping, perhaps?'

'I don't think so.' Geordie hesitated. 'I think that one day you might come to understand what he meant, Fred. If you're lucky, that is.' He would not say anything further.

Fred went back to the book he was reading. These days he always read before he went to sleep.

It was a copy of Byron's *Don Juan*, a long story in verse which made Fred laugh out loud, even though he did not share the poet's attitude to women. He should have met Big Sister, he thought once, rejecting the poet's shameless dismissal of them. He didn't think that he had read the poem before he had lost his memory, but he couldn't be sure.

Geordie, who had gone to Hyde's Place for the evening, returned to find Fred asleep, the book open before him. He picked it up and read a few stanzas. 'Love's riotous,' Byron had written satirically, 'but marriage must have quiet/And being consumptive live on a milk diet.' Geordie shook his head at this, laughing a little wryly, wondering what Fred had made of it. Unlike Fred, his own sleep was long in coming, and he thought that Kirstie's also might be troubled after Dan'l's failed declaration. The next morning, when he saw the blue shadows under her eyes he was sure that he had been right.

Fred damaged his wrist that afternoon. He struck rock and his pick had rebounded. After he had hauled himself out of the hole and Geordie had examined him, Geordie advised him to finish for the day.

'You won't lose much,' he said. 'The evening gun will be going off soon. Let it rest and then you might be fit again tomorrow.'

Passing Big Sister's hut—her headquarters, as Geordie had facetiously nicknamed it—Fred heard muffled sobbing coming through the partly open door. This was strange. Big Sister always offered the world a cheerful, if rather snappy, face.

Fred hesitated, then decided to try to find out what was wrong. He knocked at the door but there was no answer, so he pushed it a little further open and peered in.

Big Sister was sitting on the long trunk which had come from the Moore farm, and was crying bitterly. Great sobs were tearing her apart and shaking her whole body. She was so abandoned in her grief that it frightened him.

Fred moved forward hesitantly. It was wrong to see her like this. She was the Moore party's mainstay, and what would they do if she failed them?

She heard him, and looked up. Her face was blotched and ravaged, all her delicate prettiness had disappeared.

'What is it, Big Sister?' asked Fred urgently. 'What's the matter? Is it Dan'l going that's upset you so?'

'No,' she sobbed. 'It's not Dan'l. Oh, Fred, I've lost my heart!'

Fred scarcely knew what to say. 'Lost your heart, Kirstie?' faltered out of him. He was so agitated and distressed for her that he used her real name without thinking.

'Yes, Fred. My little pendant heart. The one Ma gave

me. It was all I had left of her. It was only a tin thing I
know…' She broke down again and her sobbing redoubled
its force.

Fred only knew that this had to be stopped somehow
before she made herself ill. It hurt him to see her so dis-
traught. Even his breathing was affected.

He sat down beside her. 'Tell me about it, Kirstie. How
did you lose it?'

His voice was so kind and gentle that Kirstie found that
her grief was increased, not lessened, but from somewhere
she managed to dredge up some self-control.

'It was on a bit of ribbon around my neck. I wore it
under my dress. I know that I had it on this afternoon before
I went down to the creek to wash out the clay from Pa's
claim, but when I got back here I found that it was gone.
I went back to the creek to look for it—it must have fallen
off there—but it was hopeless. I couldn't find it. I shall
never find it,' and she began to cry again.

Kirstie scarcely knew why she was so terribly distressed.
Whether she was crying for the heart which Ma had given
her—bought from a pedlar—as a reward for being such a
good hard-working girl, or whether it was her own heart,
lost to Fred, for which she was grieving, didn't seemed to
matter. In her sad state the one reason was as good as the
other.

Fred's own feelings were the strangest mixture of regret,
pity, and something which he hardly recognised as love. It
had nothing to do with having fun, and yet seemed to be
connected with it. In any case poor Kirstie needed to be
comforted, and comfort was what he would give her.

He put his arms around her, pulled her to him and began
rocking her as though she were small Rod.

'There, there,' he said. He had an insane desire to say,
'Kiss it better,' the words he had used to tease her over
Annie, but because of that he couldn't bring himself to utter

them. Besides, they didn't seem quite right. Why, he wasn't sure.

Gradually Kirstie's sobbing lessened when she realised that Fred's arms were around her at last, even if only in the sort of comfort which he would have offered to the little ones. Fred, however, had discovered that holding and comforting Kirstie was not at all the same thing as comforting the little ones. She was so warm and soft, not at all like the spiky girl he was used to, the girl who had nagged and teased him, the girl who had waved her iron ladle at him.

She was a pleasure to comfort, and yes, to love, and holding her so affectionately seemed both right and true— as though he had come home. So right and true, indeed, that he suddenly lifted her head gently, put his big hand under her chin and tipped her poor red and swollen face towards him.

The disfigurement from her crying did not seem to matter at all. He concentrated instead on her beautiful, drowned bluey-green eyes, and stroked her soft hair. For the first time he regretted his fun with the women, thinking despairingly that a kiss from him would be sure to be misunderstood.

'Fred?' said Kirstie in a wondering voice. His lips were almost touching her cheek, and for a moment it seemed that all her dreams were coming true at last. Indeed, who knew what might have happened, now that Fred had found his courage and Kirstie had lost hers, had not the door flown open and Pat burst in shouting.

'Oh, Big Sister, I've cut my knee. Pa says, will you look after it for me.'

Fred and Kirstie sprang apart. She was Big Sister again, always ready to care for those about her, never to be comforted herself, and Fred was—well, just Fred—still lost in the dream of life which had replaced his real one.

Later, when Kirstie had dressed Pat's knee, prepared the food, and washed the dishes, she wondered what might have happened if Pat had not interrupted them. Well, at least she had had Fred's arms around her for once, even if only in friendship.

Fred didn't know what he felt. Only that he had seen Kirstie for the first time, and not Big Sister, the sexless virago who ran the Moore claim. She was a pretty young woman, and he had no right to push himself at someone who had shown again and again that she did not care for him. It would have been very wrong to have taken advantage of her grief to… He stopped thinking of what might have happened.

Fred was still blind, but he was on the verge of being about to see.

Chapter Eleven

The temperature climbed rapidly that summer and the fever responded by becoming more and more virulent. Finally it infected the whole of the diggings.

Geordie was puzzled by it. He had thought at first that it was like a fever which he had seen in England which started slowly and then became virulent only in its later stages. This fever, though, came on rapidly, and then was slow to leave the victim. Sometimes the patient died quite suddenly when apparently well on the road to recovery. There were few doctors in the diggings and so he was constantly being called upon for help and advice.

One sunny afternoon Pat, usually so lively and naughty, was strangely quiet. He had been his noisy self at breakfast, but later on Kirstie found him stretched out on the ground near her hut, his eyes glazed and his face blotchy.

Fear clutched at her heart. He and Davie had been playing with a lad whose family had been struck down recently. Given the nature of the diggings, it was impossible to avoid all contact with infection, since so many were afflicted.

'Pat, what's the matter?' She knelt down beside him and put her cool hand on his forehead. It was burning hot.

'Oh, Big Sister,' he moaned. 'I feel so ill. I think I must

have caught the fever.' He suddenly began to vomit and Kirstie held his poorly head for him until he had gasped to a finish. His face had turned an ashy white. Putting him down, she ran for Geordie, who was working some little distance away.

Geordie knew at once that something was really wrong for Kirstie was neither voluble nor noisy. She simply said, 'Come quickly, Geordie, I think Pat's caught the fever.'

The others heard and stopped work to watch Geordie pull himself out of his hole and follow Kirstie to where Pat lay, breathing noisily, his eyes closed.

'He seemed quite well at breakfast,' Kirstie said, sitting him up against her while Geordie examined him, his face grave. 'But look at him now.'

'Yes,' Geordie said at last. 'It's like that, it comes quickly and goes slowly.' With gentle hands he unbuttoned Pat's shirt and felt his chest and stomach. 'Best get him to bed. Help me with him, Kirstie, the sooner he's there the better.'

They half-walked, half-carried Pat between them to his tent, undressed him and laid him on his mattress.

'More work for you, I fear,' Geordie said, looking at Kirstie's anguished face. 'The other women must help you—for a change. I'll set up a roster so that he's not left on his own.'

He began to organise affairs rapidly, fetching a pail for Pat to vomit into, and extra sheets and blankets. 'You mustn't let him become cold,' he said.

'Cold?' echoed Kirstie doubtfully, thinking of the heat of the day outside the tent and the fug inside it.

'Yes, cold. The fever's treacherous. Every now and then he'll begin to shiver violently and throw his clothes off. That's when you must watch him.'

Sam came in, to look at Pat lying there so still and silent, so different from his normal lively self.

'Where's Davie?' Geordie asked. 'Does anyone know?' for the two boys were usually inseparable.

'I'll look for him,' offered Kirstie, rising from Pat's side.

'No,' said Geordie. 'You can't do everything. Send Allie. It'll do her good to be responsible for a change. Save your own strength for the nursing she won't be able to do.'

Allie's face when she came back told all.

'Davie's ill, too. He went down to the creek to help the Tates and he suddenly began to be sick. Jack's going to carry him back when they think that he's fit to be moved. They said that he was in a bad way. He looks awful—worse even than Pat.'

Emmie Jackson, who had been indifferent while the commotion went on around her, making no effort to help, suddenly began to wail helplessly on hearing this news. Kirstie felt an unChristian desire to smack her. Whoever rose to the occasion, it wasn't going to be Emmie.

All work stopped on the claim. Fred volunteered to fetch Davie home while Bart tried to comfort Emmie. The children, including their friends from other claims, stood around, their faces uncomprehending.

'Keep them away from Pat and Davie,' advised Geordie. 'I don't know how the fever spreads, but better safe than sorry. Has anyone any idea where Pat and Davie have been playing lately?'

Kirstie spread her hands helplessly. 'Oh, you know as well as I do, Geordie, that they're here, there and everywhere. If it isn't one place it's another. They've been playing with kids whose families have the fever, that I do know.'

Fred came back with his small burden. Davie was even more stricken than Pat. He lay in Fred's arms barely conscious. Geordie looked at him and sucked in his breath a little. Emmie began to have hysterics. It was evident that she was still determined to be one of life's passengers. She sank to the ground and began to rock herself.

'Make up a bed for him beside Pat,' said Geordie gently to Kirstie. 'Sit down, Fred. Hold him until the bed's ready.'

Once Davie was safely in bed, Geordie examined him carefully before leaving Kirstie to watch over both boys so that he might warn the Moore party that worse might befall them and prepare them to cope with it.

'Time for a council of war,' he told them, moving them away from the stricken Emmie who had been joined by Mrs Tate, who was making vain attempts to comfort her.

'I have to tell you,' he said, 'that it won't stop with the two lads. It never does. But at the minute it will make nursing easier to have them together. Bart, you must try to make Emmie help with the nursing, even if she only does a little. Kirstie can't be left to do everything, she'll go down herself.'

'I could move in with Bart,' said Sam. 'We can use my tent for the sick, if that would help, and the men must take turns with the nursing, too. We can't leave it all to the women.' He, too, feared that the entire burden of caring for the sick would fall on Kirstie.

Since they were all in agreement, Sam carried his bedding and few possessions to the Jacksons. Emmie had stopped crying, and Bart was trying to persuade her that for once she must rouse herself and take her share of the extra work. This merely served to start her wailing again.

Mrs Tate, whom misfortune seemed to have stiffened, said briskly, 'We could all do wiv a nice cup of tea,' and went off to make one. She persuaded Emmie to come and help her and even succeeded in getting her to hand the mugs around when it had been brewed.

'You're a good friend, Nellie Tate,' said Bart, gratefully drinking his tea. 'Many would have stayed away when the fever struck.'

'That's what friends are for,' she said. 'You've all been very kind to us. You helped us when Ginger hurt his arm, even fed us when we ran out of money. I haven't forgotten that. It wouldn't be right to abandon you now.'

'How bad are the boys?' whispered Fred to Geordie, before starting work again.

'Bad enough, Fred, bad enough.'

Geordie was right. The fever did not spare them. On a brilliant starlit night, three weeks later, he came out of the Jacksons' tent. The moon was high and the air was warm. One might even say it was a perfect night for lovers. Few in the diggings had time, or inclination, to admire it. He walked over to Kirstie's hut, stayed there some little time and then made for the tent he shared with Fred.

Fred lay dozing, fully dressed, on top of his mattress, exhausted after the weeks of nursing and night watches. They had long given up trying to keep all the sick in one tent once most of the party and their friends succumbed to the fever.

Geordie sighed and yawned before going over to Fred to shake him gently awake. Fred sat up, alarmed. 'What is it, Geordie?' he exclaimed. 'What's happened?'

He stopped at the expression on Geordie's face.

'No…' he said slowly. 'It's Emmie, isn't it?'

'Yes,' said Geordie, violently. 'She went half an hour ago. Died without so much as a word. Goddamn it, Fred, she had no need to die. She wasn't as ill as Pat or Davie, and they're slowly mending. What did I do wrong? Or was she determined to go?'

His distress was manifest in the language which he used, for Geordie rarely swore.

'It's not your fault, Geordie,' Fred said, trying to comfort him. 'God knows, you did all you could. You've not spared yourself since Pat fell ill. How are the others?'

Geordie turned away from him, trying to hide his tears. 'Better, I think. Sam and Bart seem to be holding their own although what Bart will say when I tell him about Emmie...' He stopped again and put his face in his hands.

Fred was no longer careless Fred. He had gone for ever. These days he was aware of nuances of human behaviour which would once have passed him by: responsibility had claimed him for its own.

'There's something else wrong, isn't there. Geordie? It's not just Emmie, is it? Tell me what it is.'

'It's why I woke you, Fred, when you need to sleep. It's Kirstie. She's been ill all day without telling anyone because of Emmie's needs. She's got the fever, Fred. I've put her to bed in the hut, and if you don't nurse her there's no one left who can—all the women are sick. Mrs Tate fell ill yesterday, and I must stay with Sam and Bart and Ginger Tate—they're at the crucial stage where they will either survive, or die. It's as stark as that.'

Fred was already moving about the tent, collecting a few possessions.

'Don't worry, Geordie. I'll go at once.' His face was a mask of grief. 'Of course, she said nothing—that's her way, isn't it? She knew you had your hands full with Emmie and didn't want to increase your burden.'

'Yes,' said Geordie. 'I have always been frightened that she'd drop dead before she gave way. I'll come with you. She—and you—may need my help before I go to the others.'

Kirstie had been struck down nearly as heavily as Davie and was already only half-conscious. Fred lifted her off her bed which lay on the floor and held her while Geordie put the mattress and bedding on to the long trunk so that it would be easier for him to nurse her. She looked dimly at Fred when he laid her on it. She had managed to undress herself and put her nightgown on before finally giving way to the fever.

For a moment she recognised him. 'Fred?' she whispered, and then she was lost again.

'She's already had one severe bout of vomiting,' said Geordie. 'She might start again at any time. You know what to do.'

Fred nodded. Yes, he knew what to do. He had already done it many times, but he had never thought that he might have to do it for Kirstie.

'She'll not be too ill, will she, Geordie?'

He knew that the question was a silly one as soon as he had asked it. Geordie could give him no assurances. Emmie had not looked as though she were going to die. It was Davie whose condition had worried them, but Emmie had died and Davie had survived.

Fred did not know what he and their party would have done without Geordie. For some reason both of them had escaped the fever, and they were nursing their own Syndicate, as well as the Tates, all three of whom had gone down together, and whose partners had fled the claim.

Fred's changing self had been strongly affected by his nursing of the fever victims, even before Kirstie had been struck down. He had tried to remain cheerful, but the old carefree, childlike, irresponsible Fred finally vanished in the epidemic.

Fred hardly felt him go.

In the long days and nights during which he nursed Kirstie he learned much more about himself. Even after embracing her on the afternoon she had lost her tin heart, he had always thought of her as a young girl, not really a woman at all, despite her many suitors. So, when he looked tenderly after her, sponging her down, seeing her nightgown clinging to her body during the sweats of the fever, having to strip her to put on one which was clean and dry, he was astonished to discover how lovely her body was, how perfect her little breasts.

Why, she's just like…, he thought, but the name, almost on his tongue, escaped him. I must have known a woman like Kirstie once. I wonder who she was and when I did? I wonder where she is now?

I must not frighten her was another thought. I must remember that to her I am only Fred, who likes having fun, and even if she doesn't recognise me at present, because she is delirious, that doesn't matter. He handled her with reverent care so that, if she ever remembered this time, she would know of his respect for her modesty.

At first Kirstie was quiet in her delirium, staring at him with lost eyes. Then she began to talk, and would not stop. She talked of Ma and the farm, and her little brothers and sisters who had died young. She told Fred, looking blindly at him, of her worries about Pa, and of how she hoped that he would find a good woman.

Then, at the last, she talked of Fred, of how she grieved over his drunken irresponsibility in the early days, and of how she worried over the fun he had with women, particularly Fat Lil, but, most of all, with Rosina.

'He'll never settle down, never,' she wept, and then sat up, saying woefully, 'and he'll never look at me. I'm a little girl to him, Big Sister. Oh, I hate that name, I do, I do!'

Her weeping became so strong that Fred held her to him and stroked her hair as though she were small Rod or Emmie's now motherless baby.

What he felt for her was quite different from what he had felt for the women whom he had pleasured so happily. Not completely different, but there was also present a desire to care for her and to protect her as well as to love her, which had been missing with them.

What surprised him was that he must have felt like this

for a long time without knowing it. He remembered all the occasions when he had taken the children from her so that she might rest, how he had carried her basket, heavy with shopping, had helped her to wash the pots, had hung out the washing for her—to Sam's amusement—had brought her ribbons from the little fair, and how he had nursed a sore heart these last few weeks because he had thought that she did not like him.

All for Big Sister, who was Kirstie, who must not die, now that he had found her after all these careless months. Kirstie, who had rejected her good suitors for him when he had been feckless Fred Waring. He also knew, at last, what Dan'l was telling him on the day he had left for Ballarat and the answer to Geordie's last question.

Geordie came in soon after and looked at him with sad eyes when Kirstie, who had fallen quiet, suddenly renewed her lamentations over Fred, not angrily, but in a lost voice. 'Oh, no,' she ended. 'He'll never, never look at me, now that I've lost my heart.'

Fred stood up abruptly, his face working and went outside where Geordie found him, shortly afterwards, leaning against the wall of Kirstie's hut, his head propped on his hand.

'Don't fret,' said Geordie kindly. 'There's still hope if the fever breaks.'

'If, if, if,' exclaimed Fred despairingly. 'Damn all ifs, Geordie, you don't know any more than I do. Oh, God, how could I have been so blind, so unknowing of my true love.'

'We're all blind,' said Geordie gently. 'We're born blind. Sometimes we see the light, not often, and not for long. You've found your light, I think.'

Fred did not hear him. He was listening to a new and dreadful voice which said to him, You've lost one love, now you're going to lose another! What did that mean?

What love had he lost, and when and why? No, he would not believe the voice, he would try to hope.

Geordie touched his arm and they went back into the hut together. Kirstie was now the worst affected. All the others were slowly recovering.

'We must never leave her on her own,' Geordie said.

Fred held Kirstie's hand and Geordie dozed on the floor. He, like Fred, was dog-weary and could have slept on a rail. Fred was half-asleep himself. Kirstie's hand was still in his when, towards dawn, she spoke suddenly in a normal voice, saying 'Fred?'

His eyes flew open.

Kirstie spoke again. 'Fred, what are you doing here?'

'Kirstie!' he exclaimed, looking at her. Her body was running in water, but her eyes were clear, and her hand was cool.

'Kirstie! You called me Kirstie.'

'Oh, my dear,' said Fred, almost reverently. 'You are back with us again.'

'I haven't been away, Fred,' she answered, her face puzzled. She heard Geordie stir and groan on the floor, and at the same time grasped her condition. 'I've had the fever? Is that why you're both here?'

'Oh, yes, Kirstie. You've been dreadfully ill, so ill that we feared for you.'

He was so relieved that he gathered her to him, just as he had done on the night when she had found him shouting in his sleep. Only this time he was conscious and knew her, and the love he was offering was for her, not for someone in a dream.

Geordie stretched and woke and came over. 'The fever's broken,' he said professionally. 'She needs to be dried— and quickly. She mustn't become cold now. She needs a clean nightgown, and clean sheets and blankets.'

He helped Fred to change her, and to roll her in a dry blanket before they laid her on the floor while they remade the bed.

Kirstie looked at them wide-eyed. She felt all skin and bone.

'You've been nursing me, Fred?'

'Yes, Kirstie. Oh, you were so ill, and there was no one left but me to look after you. The Tates have been dreadfully ill, too.'

'Oh, Fred!' She sat up, her eyes wild. 'Pa and the children! How are they? And poor Emmie. She died, didn't she? That was the last thing I remember. How are they all?'

Geordie came over to her. 'They're well now, even the Tates. You were the worst affected. It was all that work which I told you not to do which weakened you,' but his voice was kind and Kirstie knew that he was not really scolding her.

'Your bed's ready, now. Come on, Fred. Put the patient back in.'

Fred lifted her up and tucked the covers round her.

'It had to be me who looked after you,' he said earnestly. 'You do understand that.'

'And a right good nurse he made,' said Geordie, smiling. 'You couldn't have asked for a better one. Try to sleep, Kirstie. Now the fever's gone, sleeping will help you to recover.'

She smiled back at him, astonished at how weak she felt. She had been so surprised just now to wake up to find Fred sitting by her. An even bigger surprise had been the smile on his face when she had spoken to him, not a smile for anyone else, but one for her. Then he and Geordie had changed and cared for her, and that should have been distressing and upsetting, but it wasn't because they were so kind.

She went to sleep after thinking that, and when she woke

up again Geordie had gone and Fred was sitting beside her, reading.

'Fred,' she said. He looked up and his face shone with pleasure, and again the pleasure was for her. It was not Fred's smile, given to everyone. He put his book down and came back with a tin cup full of lemonade.

'Kate showed me how to make this, just before she was taken ill, the day after you were. Geordie said that you were to drink it. It will do you good.'

He sat by her on the bed, helped her to sit up, and then put an arm around her to support her while she drank. It almost made being ill worthwhile to have Fred's arms around her at last. She thought that Fred kissed the top of her head while she was drinking the lemonade, but that couldn't be true, surely.

All the same she turned her shining eyes on him, and did not know that Fred had to stop himself from kissing her properly because she was still ill, and he and Geordie had agreed that she must be carefully treated. It would not do for her to have a relapse in her weakened state, Geordie had said.

Kirstie lay back and watched Fred moving about, tidying things up before beginning to prepare a meal for the invalids. It occurred to her that he was much quieter than she remembered him being, and she knew, looking at his absorbed face while he worked, that this was not solely due to his worrying about her and the other sufferers.

His work over, he carried the food out before returning to sit by her bed to eat his own grub. Once he had finished he washed the pots before fetching a worn pack of cards out of his jacket pocket and returning to sit by her again.

'Do you feel strong enough to play snap, or shall I show you some card tricks? The Patriarch taught me them when I was a boy.'

There he was again! The Patriarch—he had idly men-

tioned him once or twice recently when he hadn't been
thinking. Geordie had questioned him occasionally, saying,
'The Patriarch—who was he, Fred? Can you remember?
He's popped up in your conversation lately. He sounds an
interesting man.'

Of course, he couldn't remember—or, more truthfully,
the last time Geordie had asked him he had been on the
verge of saying, 'The Patriarch? Why, he was…' and the
name had been on the tip of his tongue, but had eluded
him.

He shook his head. Kirstie was saying, 'Card tricks,
please, Fred,' so he forgot about The Patriarch and concentrated on amusing her. She watched his clever hands while
he did waterfall shuffles before playing Find the Lady with
her, and she laughed weakly because she never managed
to find her, however hard she tried.

Fred also began a line of comic patter—to confuse her—
she thought, which made her laugh and then choke because
she was so weak. He made a distressful noise, put down
the cards and held her gently, patting her back to stop the
choking. Before she could stop herself, Kirstie put her arms
around his neck and kissed him on the cheek.

'Oh, Fred,' she exclaimed, and began to pull away,
blushing.

'My dear,' he said lovingly and then kissed her very
lightly on the lips, reminding her of that night, soon after
he had joined them, when she had found him having a
nightmare, and he had kissed her, not knowing who she
was—and again, on the afternoon when she had lost her tin
heart.

Eyes wide and her mouth trembling, she murmured,
'You mustn't be sorry for me, Fred, just because I'm ill.'

'I'm not sorry for you, Kirstie. I think I love you, truly
love you. No, that's wrong, I *know* I love you. I think that
I've loved you for a long time, but I've been so blind all

these months. It wasn't until I thought that I was going to lose you to the fever that I understood my own feelings.'

Her pale face paled even further. 'No, Fred, you mustn't tease me.'

'I'm not teasing you, Kirstie, and it's not just having fun that I'm talking about, as it was with Fat Lil and Rosie, although I want that with you, too. I must have loved you for a long time, but I was so busy enjoying myself, and somehow it seemed wrong to think of you that way. Why, I don't know.

'Then, when you were so ill and like to die, I thought of all the wasted months, and, oh, my darling, I mustn't tire you with my importunity but, believe me, I meant every word I have just said.'

He picked up her hand and kissed it. 'Someone must look after you, you've spent too much time looking after and caring for the others. Let me be the one to do that.'

Kirstie lay back on her pillows. She must have died and gone to heaven. It could not be true that Fred was looking at her, his eyes full of love, and saying such things.

'I thought that it was Rosina Campbell whom you loved. I hated her the most for that. The others didn't matter, they were nothing. Even Fat Lil—they were just play. Even I could see that, but Rosina...'

'Rosie?' He looked at her, his face suddenly serious. 'You mustn't mind about Rosie. I might have loved her once, long ago, when we were both younger—and different.'

Fred didn't know where the last two words had come from. He continued, still earnest. 'Poor Rosie—she's afraid and alone, Kirstie. She's lost all the glory which she used to have. I think that in the end we comforted one another because in our different ways we were both lost. So don't be jealous of her. The only thing is that you're so young, and I'm too old for you. I don't know exactly how old I am, but you ought to marry someone nearer to your own age, not a battered ruin like me.'

Marry! A battered ruin, thought Kirstie faintly. He's so handsome, how can he believe that? But marry? Marry Fred? Yes, it was as she had thought, she must have died and gone to heaven where all one's wishes were granted.

She stroked his hands, scarred by the months of work with pick and shovel. 'Marry you? Do you really mean that, Fred?'

'You must know that I do. You're not the sort just to have fun with. You're serious and you take things hard. Yes, I mean it. I want to look after you, like you looked after poor Fred before he found himself again.'

He gazed tenderly at her, then fell on his knees beside the bed. 'Will you marry me, Kirstie?'

She began to cry, great, gasping sobs, so strong that he pulled her to him again and began to comfort her. 'Oh, Kirstie, I'm sorry. Don't mind me. I shouldn't have said this to you while you were still weak, but I'm frightened that if I don't say it now I might never be brave enough to ask you at all. I have so little to offer you. I didn't intend to distress you.'

'You're not distressing me,' she managed between sobs. 'I'm crying because I'm so happy, Fred. Of course I'll marry you.'

They sat together, arms around one another, both feeling as though they were about to burst with joy. Geordie came in and found them, his sad face a little lighter when he saw rowdy Fred, quiet at last, beached in some haven which he had never thought to reach.

They did not spring apart or look guilty. Fred laid Kirstie lovingly down, and said to Geordie, 'When Kirstie is well again, we are to marry. I must ask Sam's permission, but I have enough now to keep a wife.'

Geordie put his hand out to shake Fred's, and then kissed Kirstie on the cheek.

'I never thought that you'd come to your senses, Fred. You've chosen a good girl for a wife, a girl who loves you. You keep him up to scratch, Kirstie. Make sure that he doesn't stray again once you're hitched.'

He thought that Fred, whoever he was, had sown his wild oats in the last few months and was now more than ready to settle down. Were they the wild oats which he had never sown in his old life, he wondered, and what would happen if Fred ever recovered his memory?

He looked at the radiant Kirstie and at Fred's quiet happy face. Worry about that, he told himself, if it ever happens. He, Geordie Farqhuar, would not play God, he had tried that once, and look where it had got him! An exile in a tent in the diggings at Ballarat, far from all he knew and loved, including the land he had left.

He watched the lovers who could suddenly not have enough of one another and wanted to see the world through each other's eyes. He watched Fred adjust the shawl around Kirstie's shoulders, and Kirstie kiss the hand that cared for her.

[illegible faded text from previous page showing through]

Chapter Twelve

Fred asked Sam for Kirstie's hand in marriage. He knew—how?—that it was the right thing to do. Sam looked at Fred and thought that he was very happy to see him marry Big Sister. He wouldn't have been happy to give her to the Fred whom they had rescued from the nick, but the new Fred with his confident air, proud of himself in a shy way, taking more than his share of work and responsibility, was a different matter.

He was happy because now he could make Kate Clancy his wife. Kate had come round to help to nurse the Moores, and then had fallen ill herself. Fortunately she had only been lightly affected and he knew that she would be ready to marry him once Kirstie was settled with Fred.

Kirstie realised later that because she had become so involved with her own feelings for Fred she had failed to notice how much Pa had changed. For one thing, he had spruced himself up after years of slopping about in his oldest clothes.

'I was worried,' Sam said to Kirstie when he told her that Kate had accepted him, and of how he had originally been reluctant to marry her, and she him, because of how Big Sister might feel after all these years of looking after them, if he suddenly brought a new woman in to take her place.

It was typical of Sam's kind-heartedness that he had even considered such a thing and his pleasure that he could go ahead and marry good-humoured Kate was touching. He refused the suggestion of a double wedding, and said that Fred and Big Sister ought to have the fun of their own wedding day.

Geordie quietly suggested to Sam that now Kirstie was to marry Fred the title of Big Sister ought to be forgotten.

Kirstie recovered quite quickly from her illness. She thought, and who was to say that she was wrong, that knowing that Fred loved her was the best medicine she could have had. Her face glowed and shone with happiness, and having Fred to herself, and not continually having to share him with others, was as nice as she had always thought that it would be.

Geordie called them the lovebirds, and he did not say it in mockery. When Fred said to him once that he thought that he might be a little old for Kirstie, it was the only thing which worried him, Geordie said gently, 'Don't refuse happiness where you find it, Fred. In my experience age doesn't matter at all. And it's not as though you're really an old man. I should guess that you are somewhere in the late thirties at the most.'

Fred forgot about his age after that and concentrated on making Kirstie happy and preparing for the day which would give him the right to have fun with her—for even the new Fred found this description of the marriage bed to be a true and meaningful one. Oh, there would be responsibilities as well, but they would be built on the joy that he was sure they would share.

He made certain that Kirstie rested as much as possible while she was convalescent. In the afternoons while they waited to marry she sat out in the sun.

'No running around straight away,' he said, severely for him. 'Allie is getting a big girl now, and was really helpful before the fever struck her down. You weren't as old as Allie, Sam says, when you started looking after them all when your Ma became poorly.'

Well, that was true enough, Kirstie thought, and it had been wrong of her to treat Allie as the baby she had been when Ma was taken ill.

It was pleasant lying there, watching other people work, and seeing the life of the diggings. She became aware of things which she had never noticed before. She saw, as though for the first time, that before the gold fever had arrived this land had been beautiful in its wildness, but that the diggings had made it ugly. On the other hand, living here was more interesting and exciting than it had been at the farm—and it was the diggings which had brought her Fred.

He and Sam were working on the new claim which they had been granted on licence by the Commissioner, having exhausted their previous patch. So far, although the Moore party had never made a really big strike, they had always found more than enough gold to cover their living expenses and put a bit by as well.

Bart had made a few good strikes in the past, but the shock of Emmie's death had made him apathetic and he now worked sporadically, although recently he had shown signs of recovery.

The others were kind and understanding and Sam, Geordie and Fred agreed that Bart must be allowed his grieving. Only the prospect of Kirstie and Fred's coming marriage could bring a watery smile to his face.

Occasionally Fred looked over to where Kirstie sat and winked at her. She began to drift off into sleep, happy and fulfilled, dreaming about Fred and the future.

Her doze was interrupted by an almost simultaneous

shout from Sam and Fred. Bart and Geordie hauled themselves out of their hole and ran over to where they both stood, filthy and grinning triumphantly. After all the months of back-breaking work they had struck it rich together—Fred particularly so.

All work stopped while the group reorganised themselves in order to haul out what had been found before taking it down to the creek to wash out the gold. The Tates came round, pleased for them, and their shouts brought still others, generous in their joy at a strike, whoever had made it.

Kirstie insisted on getting up and helping them. It's only right, she said, that after all these months of piggling out what the men had found, when it was only a little, she should see what a real strike looked like and help with it.

Fred came over to her and put his arms around her.

'Oh, Kirstie, loving you has brought me luck at last,' he whispered into her ear, for the strike proved really big, and they would be getting married on something, rather than nothing, supplemented by Fred's part-time book-keeping.

Celebrate they did. They sat around the fire after their evening meal, sharing it with the Tates and some of their neighbours who brought over banjos, bottles and a cake—a rare treat in the diggings. They talked and sang together. Fred had his arm around Kirstie and sang as enthusiastically as any, not knowing whether the true gold was the yellow mineral he had wrenched from the ground or, as he suspected, the pretty girl beside him. At least she need no longer work as hard as she had done now that she was to marry him and he had made a real strike.

The children ran about them, no one reprimanding them for noise and horseplay on this happy day. In the middle of it Fred remembered that he had said that he would do Ran Struan's books for him that night. He kissed Kirstie and told her to be good before he left them, saying cheerfully, 'I promised Ran and I must keep my word.'

'There's a good mate,' said Sam, half-fuddled for once, but pleased that his future son-in-law showed a proper responsibility towards life—it boded well for Kirstie's future.

Geordie watched him go. Tall and straight and purposeful, no longer the jolly, irresponsible half-man, half-child, who had always spoken of himself as Fred in the third person, and had lived for the day. It was not only finding Kirstie which had changed him—the old Fred had ignored Kirstie as a woman—it had taken the new Fred to see what she was: a selfless, loving partner for him in his new life.

Fred whistled through his teeth while doing Ran's books in the small room behind his chemist's shop. On his arrival Struan had raised his brows and said, 'I never thought that you'd come tonight, Fred,' for the news of the Moores' major strike had already reached him.

'I promised I would, didn't I,' said Fred, not raising his eyes from the column of figures which he was adding up so speedily. For once, out of friendship, he accepted the glass of spirits which Ran offered to him after he had finished work, grimacing a little while he drank it.

'I hear that you're getting married soon,' said Struan chattily.

'Yes,' said Fred. He was brief these days.

'It'll be easier for you now you've made a strike,' said Struan. 'You've a good woman there, Fred.'

'I know,' said Fred, rejecting the offer of another glass. 'I've had enough tonight, Struan.'

'No more Fat Lils, then,' said Struan, winking at him. Fred did not take offence.

'Gave up Fat Lils before I offered for Kirstie,' he said gravely.

They were still sitting around the fire when he had walked home through the dark. The singing had died down and the drinking had ended. Kirstie was waiting for him. A lone banjo player serenaded them with a plaintive air.

'Not very long now,' he said, sitting down beside her and kissing her in the scented hollow of her neck. Every time he touched her shivers of joy ran up and down Kirstie's body. Even a light kiss on the top of her head made her senses reel because it was Fred who was saluting her. It was surely time, she thought, that she had real fun with him. Like to die when I do if this is how I feel before we get to that!

The diggings were determined that Fred and Kirstie should have a great send-off, particularly after the strike. There was to be nothing hole in the corner about the wedding, even if Parson Harry's credentials to marry them might not be all that certain. Everyone used him, and provided that he had been sobered up he could be relied upon to do a dignified job.

Kate Clancy, looking forward to her own wedding, made Kirstie a wedding gown, and a circlet of pink rosebuds to wear in her hair. It was surprising what you could find in the diggings' makeshift stores if you looked hard enough for it. Kate even found light shoes, fine lace for the dress, and long gloves which Kirstie had never worn before.

All the chums in the Moore Syndicate helped to dress Fred on the day, and Geordie supported him on his walk to the improvised altar. Even Fat Lil and Ned Hyde grew sentimental about it, although Fat Lil did make some rather dubious jokes about what the women in the diggings would do for entertainment now that Fred Waring had turned respectable. All the same, it was typical of the folk in the diggings that, raunchy though they were, something like Fred and Kirstie getting hitched touched their battered hearts.

Sam's prediction of a bang-up wedding came true. Without spending too much of his new-found wealth, he threw a big party in the Dance Hall, taking it over for the afternoon. All the new mates the Moores had made since coming to the diggings attended, including some like Fat Lil whom Kirstie privately thought were not all that matey. Nevertheless, she tried to be as gracious as possible when Fat Lil insisted on kissing the bride before she and Fred left for her hut which was now to be their home. Sam was building a kitchen addition to his tent for Kate.

Kirstie thought Fred looked more handsome than ever in his wedding gear. He was wearing a respectable black suit and a white silk shirt which had been lent to him by Ned Hyde. Fred thought that Kirstie had never looked lovelier than she did in the dress which Kate had made for her, so that altogether both parties were thoroughly satisfied with themselves and each other.

'The prettiest pair the diggings has ever seen,' sobbed Fat Lil. 'It quite makes up for losing him.'

Afterwards no one was quite sure who had actually invited her to the wedding, but since she thoroughly enjoyed herself along with everyone else, no one thought it worthwhile to make a thing of it. Somehow the party ran over into the Dance Hall's normal public time, but the proprietor seemed not to mind in the general happiness of the day.

Walking back to the hut with his wife, alone at last, Fred thought that what was more important to him than his bride's new-found beauty was her essential goodness, which shone through her every action. Best of all, after the long excitement of the wedding, was to carry her into the hut to find that the children had filled it with flowers.

He sat her on the bed, put back her veil, let down her beautiful ash-blonde hair and began to teach her to have fun with him. Stars shining in her eyes, she looked up at him when they were finally in bed together, and said softly,

'I'm not frightened, Fred, not like some brides. I know that you will be patient and show me what to do.'

Fred nearly choked on hearing this artless confession. He stroked her gently, trying not to frighten her. She was no Fat Lil nor a long-married woman and he must go easily with her. At some point in their early loving he had a dim memory of having done something like this before, but forgot it in the pleasure of showing Kirstie how to enjoy herself with him.

Like to die, indeed, thought Kirstie later, lying in Fred's arms after her gentle initiation into the arts of love, for yes, Fred was as kind in that as he was in everything. Now I truly understand why women love men and have their babies, and she drifted into sleep, her head on Fred's broad chest where she had sometimes imagined it in the hopeless days before he had known that she was there, and that she loved him.

Fred woke in the night, not to have his usual nightmare of loss and fear with the tiger coming after him, but to discover that he had found someone to replace what he had lost. Or, at least, that was what he was thinking when he hauled himself out of the mists of sleep—but this insight disappeared in the light of day as night thoughts often do.

He was unaware that Geordie, watching him, wondered how long it would be before Fred found himself now that he had found happiness.

Pa's wedding followed next, and the burden Kirstie had carried for so long was lifted from her shoulders and now it was only Fred and the little hut which they shared for which she had to care

The fever had left Kirstie weaker than she had been and she was happy in her new idleness, although when she began to recover she became more like her old forceful and busy self. Losing the underlying worries caused by looking after so many, and which had made her short and snappy, meant that she achieved a new placidity.

There was time for her to sit in the sun and read and knit without the endless chores of everyday life pursuing her. Fred's big strike was not followed by others equally big, but he was digging out enough gold to mean that they were more than comfortable.

Besides that she had Kate, now Kate Moore, for a friend, another woman to talk to and one who could advise her. She wasn't Ma, but she was someone on whom she could lean a little when she was tired.

Fred watched over her with pride as well as love. One day, soon after they were married, he came in with a large parcel, which he handed to her, saying, 'This is for you. Guess what's in it.'

She looked up at him in wonder.

'A present? For me, Fred?' Big Sister had rarely received presents. They were always for others—apart from the ribbons which Fred had occasionally bought her.

'Who else?' he said, dropping a kiss on the top of her head and enjoying the sight of her wondering, excited face when she opened the parcel to find inside it a pretty dress, a fine petticoat and a shawl.

Her face flushed with pleasure, Kirstie held the clothes up against her to find that they were a perfect fit.

'Oh, Fred, they're beautiful. Oh, you're so kind to me— and how did the sempstress know my size?' she asked, quite overwhelmed.

'That was easy,' he told her. 'Kate had your measurements from when she made your wedding dress. Put them on tonight and we'll go to the Dance Hall and show the world what a beauty Mrs Fred Waring has become.'

'Oh, Fred,' she exclaimed, laying the dress carefully down on their bed before throwing her arms around him and kissing him. 'You mustn't tease me. I know I'm not a beauty.'

'Then you know wrong,' he said, picking her up and whirling her around the room. 'And when we get there you're going to enjoy yourself for once instead of watching others do so—and you'll not only be the prettiest girl in the room, but you'll also be wearing the most beautiful clothes.'

'That I will,' she said reverently, picking up the dress and holding its delicate silken smoothness against her own soft cheek after Fred had put her down again. 'I've never had anything as fine as this before, never.'

'Ah, but then you were only Big Sister, but now you're Kirstie Waring, Fred Waring's wife, and you deserve the best I can give you.'

Fred had a dim memory of having said something similar before, long ago in his lost past—but, as such stray memories usually did, it disappeared almost immediately.

They went to the Dance Hall that night and her bitter memories of Fred enjoying himself with Rosina Campbell and her own bad behaviour no longer haunted Kirstie, and, as the nights of having fun with Fred followed the days when she could take her ease, she gained a new softness of face and body. Happiness claimed her for its own. Marriage to Fred was all and more than she had hoped it might be.

The whole party still ate together in the open on fine evenings when the day's work was done. Kate and Kirstie prepared and served the meal for them all. Afterwards the Tates came over to sit with them, laughing and talking— the relief of being alive now that the fever had fled the diggings was still with them.

Fred asked Geordie why the pair of them had been

spared, even though they had spent their time nursing so many.

'I don't know,' Geordie admitted. 'We know so little really. Doctors are like men struggling in the dark, looking for something with a candle which keeps going out, but it's not the fashion to say so. We pretend that we know so much, but it's not true. We have no notion of how fever spreads, or whether all fevers are the same. This one, now, was different from the fevers I treated back home.'

More and more he was finding that he could talk to Fred as an intellectual equal. The Fred who had lived only for the body and the day was gone. His marriage to Kirstie had steadied him even further. He read more in the evenings. He looked for second-hand books which sometimes turned up in troughs in the stores. He was beginning to find that the manual labour of the diggings made too few demands on his re-awakening mind.

Fred did not need to tell Geordie this: he could see it for himself.

Now he said slowly to Geordie, 'Perhaps one day we might know more. Observation, if it were careful and thorough, might help.'

'Yes,' Geordie agreed, before they joined in the general conversation again. Bart, who was beginning to recover from the shock of Emmie's death, was laughing about Annie Robinson.

The Robinsons had not fallen victims to the fever epidemic, and in the middle of it Annie had given birth to a half-Chinese baby boy.

'But there was only one Chinese family in the diggings, then,' said Ginger Tate, amused.

'Right,' said Bart, 'and the odd thing is that no one has ever seen Annie with a Chinese. She told Lew that she'd never been with one and couldn't explain how the baby had come to be—well, what it is. Lew's half-crazy. He says that as soon as Annie recovers from the birth—she's been very ill—he's going to beat her senseless.'

'Oh, but what about the poor baby?' asked Kirstie sorrowfully.

'Well, as to that Annie says that she's going to keep it, whatever Lew says. She threatens to leave him if he tries to make her give it up. She's always wanted a baby and Lew has never given her one.'

'It's not really funny, is it,' commented Kate soberly when the men had done laughing at this tale of woe, as Bart called it. She was sitting by Sam and keeping watch over small Rod and Emmie's motherless child.

'No, not really,' said Geordie, who, like Fred, had not joined in the laughter.

Fred, indeed, was the only quiet person. He was relieved that Annie's baby was patently not his, but it could easily have been. Careless Fred of the old days had never troubled himself about such things, but sitting there, beside Kirstie, his hand in hers, the new Fred looked back at his behaviour in wonder. It was as though cause and effect had not existed for him, and they seemed so plain to him now that it was hard for him to imagine the world which he had once lived in.

The kaleidoscope had shifted again.

Kirstie sensed his painful thoughts and pressed his hand gently. 'Don't worry, Fred,' she said.

He knew what she meant. He was grateful for her support and pleased as well. Kirstie had changed, too. Happiness had made her kinder and more understanding.

Jack Tate, sitting opposite to them, watched them with regret. He had found another sweetheart, but she was not Kirstie. He could not prevent himself from having a fling at Fred, sitting there as though butter wouldn't melt in his mouth, happily married to the girl whom Jack had wanted.

'Oh,' he said, the sneer plain in his voice, 'we all know what Annie is like, don't we, Fred?'

Fred looked across at his tormentor. 'Yes,' he said, 'but what about Lew and the girl at Fat Lil's? Annie has had a lot to put up with, too.'

'And knew how to console herself,' said Jack with an unkind laugh.

Geordie, seeing from Kirstie's face that she was about to be as fierce in defending Fred as she once was in attacking him, changed the subject rapidly.

'Have you heard the latest news?' he said. 'There's been a shoot-out at The Silver Dollar, the den where the Yankees play poker. That cardsharp whom Fred played, the one they called The Doc, was caught cheating. He was drawn on by The Jug Head—remember him, Fred?—in the middle of the game. He was caught short despite having his pistol on the table.'

'What happened then?' asked Sam, fascinated.

'The Jug Head winged him, and when the police arrived everyone swore black and blue that The Doc had shot himself accidentally—even The Doc agreed with them.'

'Did you notice him cheating, Fred?' asked Bart.

'Yes,' said Fred. 'It was very obvious to me that he was a cheat. It was one reason I gave up playing cards, but not the main one.' He did not elaborate further.

That night when he and Kirstie prepared for bed he picked her up and sat her on his knee. He put his arms around her, and hid his face in her neck.

'Kirstie,' he said, his voice muffled and sad, 'you don't mind too much about me and Annie, I hope. That was the old Fred. I'm sorry now for the way I behaved then. I don't even understand why I did.'

'Oh, Fred,' she said. 'I minded at the time, dreadfully. But it was before you married me. You wouldn't go after her, or other women now, would you? Jack wasn't fair to bring it up after so long.'

'But he had a point,' said Fred gravely, and then said no more. He concentrated instead on trying to show his wife how much he loved and treasured her, and in the doing they forgot both Jack and Annie.

Later that night, though, Fred had his worst dream yet. It began happily enough. He was walking to the creek in the brilliant sun with Kirstie on his arm. Everything he saw was so sharp and bright that it wasn't really like a dream at all. Halfway to the creek he turned to Kirstie to kiss her—but it was not Kirstie he saw, but another girl.

Oh, her eyes were bluey-green like Kirstie's, but her hair was red and her expression was soft and sad. Her clothes were different too: they were fine and elegant, not at all like Kirstie's. She put out her hand to take his and spoke to him, calling him by name—but the name was not Fred's.

The sun went in. It grew dark. The girl suddenly disappeared and now he had neither her nor Kirstie. He was quite alone on a vast plain where he groped around, calling the girl by a name which he could not remember when he awoke.

In the dream he walked on, although he knew that there was something dreadful waiting for him, and that the something was the tiger. It was not coming for him as it usually did, but was quite still, caught in mid-spring. He looked at it, wondering why it did not run at him but hung in the air before him, motionless.

The sun came out again and the old man with the sad face was there. He was standing before the tiger, and he was telling Fred something which he did not wish to hear—that it was the red-headed girl whom he had lost and that losing her had almost destroyed him.

Worst of all was the fear that he might lose Kirstie as

well, and he began to call her name as loudly as he could to bring her back again, for he was not even sure that he was dreaming.

His voice grew so loud that it woke him up. He found himself sitting up in bed, running in sweat, with Kirstie holding him, her eyes wild, trying to comfort him. She could feel Fred's heart thumping and he was shaking and shivering even more than he had done on the night when she had found him having a nightmare in the open.

'Oh, Fred, what is it? What's wrong?'

'I thought that I'd lost you,' he panted. 'I remember now. I loved a girl once. A girl with red hair and eyes like yours. Oh, Kirstie, I lost her, I lost her forever and then I dreamed that I'd lost you, too.'

The dream was fading and Fred tried to do an impossible thing: both to remember it and to forget it.

'The tiger was there,' he said wretchedly, 'and something else.' The memory fled before him. 'I've dreamed so often that I'd lost something and I now know that it was the girl. She spoke to me this time, and oh, Kirstie, I think that Geordie is right. He says that I don't want to remember who I was because the memory is too painful for me. It's something to do with the girl, Kirstie. But the tiger—that's a mystery.'

For some reason he didn't understand, he didn't tell her of the old man who frightened him nearly as much as the tiger, for all the kindness on his face.

Kirstie stroked and kissed him, saying, 'I'm with you, Fred, hold on to me,' which he did. Gradually he calmed down clinging to her as though she might disappear if he let go of her.

It was my name he called, Kirstie thought when at last he fell quiet. I am the one he needs now, not someone else, even if he once loved another girl who looked a little like me. She comforted Fred until he slept again, remaining awake herself in case the dream returned—but it did not, and towards dawn she, too, slept.

Fred was quiet at first the following morning, and Kirstie, giving him his breakfast, was as kind and loving as she could be. He recovered a little after he had eaten, for Fred still loved his grub as much as he had always done. He might be quieter than he was, but he had not lost his zest for life, and by the time that he was ready to begin digging he was as lively as he had ever been.

Kirstie watched him start work after he had exchanged a few words with Geordie, and began her day's tasks with a lighter heart after he had waved to her before helping Geordie put in place the windlass which they needed now that they had dug a deeper hole than ever before.

Halfway through the morning Kirstie and Kate took out mugs of tea for them all, and they stood about, laughing and talking, Fred no less than the others. Jack Tate came over from the Tate's claim, carrying his tea, and their combined laughter and banter rang out on the warm air. They were so occupied that none of them noticed Lew Robinson coming towards them, an ugly expression on his face.

He stood, his hands on his hips, glaring at them all. 'So, there you all are,' he bellowed, 'and the blasted bridegroom himself. Fancy yourself, don't you, Fred Waring?'

Fred, startled, turned to face him. 'Lew?' he asked unnecessarily.

'Yes, Lew. Annie's husband—or didn't you know? I beat the names of all her fancy men out of Annie last night, and guess whose name was on the list? But you don't need to guess, do you, Fred?'

Kirstie said, 'Leave it, Lew. It won't help you or Annie.'

'Leave it!' roared Lew, lowering his head and walking up to where Fred stood, an agonised expression on his face. 'He didn't leave my Annie alone, did he? Did you, Fred?

I'm going to kill you, Fred, you and the rest of her fancy men. But you're the first.'

He ignored Geordie and Sam who advanced on him. 'It's nowt to do with you, Geordie Farquhar, nor you, Sam Moore, this is between me and Fred. Put 'em up, Fred. Put up your dukes, let's see what your fancy skills are really worth.'

'Oh, Lew,' said Fred sorrowfully. 'You're right to be angry with me.' He then added the fatal words, 'But it was only once, you know.'

'Only once!' screamed Lew. 'Only once! Damn you, Fred Waring, is that all my Annie was worth to you that you could only trouble with her once? Oh, blast you to hell, damn you!'

Before Fred or anyone else could prevent him, from somewhere he found a swingeing blow which struck Fred high on his left temple. It was so effective that, to the accompaniment of Kirstie's scream, Fred fell like a stone, Geordie catching him before he reached the ground.

And, as he fell, the tiger, which had chased Fred for months, caught him and ate him...

Chapter Thirteen

Rosina Campbell toured the Bendigo gold field after her triumphant appearance at the theatre in Melbourne. So triumphant that the management engaged her for another run after she returned from Bendigo, allowing her a short holiday before she started it.

She was staying in some splendour at The Criterion Hotel. She had not yet found another protector, and while she stayed in the colony she never took another lover after Fred. It was only too plain that she was wanted as a trophy rather than as the genuine partner which she had been with Fred.

His nicknaming her Rosie, she realised afterwards, had been his way of separating her off from Rosina Campbell, courtesan and high-class whore. She had simply been someone who shared his fun privately and joyfully. She had been told of his refusal to discuss her with Hyde or with anyone else. Her informant had found this amusing: she found it touching.

On her return from a matinée at the theatre, early in the evening, she found The Criterion lobby in an unwonted state of agitation about a new visitor. For once the staff were being attentive, and the manager had appeared to do the honours.

It was all for a tall, mild-looking old man, silver-haired and handsome in an odd way. He raised one sardonic eyebrow at the fuss—but he obviously expected it. His glance passed briefly over Rosina. She felt summed-up, absorbed and noted. She knew a man of power when she saw him, and this old man was a man of power, even if he did live in this Godforsaken corner of the globe.

Later, seated at the common dining-table, for even Rosina could not command more in a Melbourne dominated by the exigencies of the gold rush, she saw him enter with the manager still in attendance. He ushered him reverently to the seat opposite to hers, without apology, although it was usually left empty.

She had already asked who he was to be told, most respectfully, that he was old Tom Dilhorne, reputedly the richest man in the colony.

Thomas Dilhorne's father, one supposed, but they bore no resemblance to one another. They were so unlike, indeed, that looking at the subtle face opposite to her, with the pull of his attraction still strong in old age, she wondered how he could have fathered a creature so coldly opposite to him.

She felt compelled to speak to him, to discover whether in conversation he shared the proud arrogance of his son. On taking his seat he had half-bowed to her, and she had acknowledged him almost without thinking.

'You are welcome, sir. My name is Rosina Campbell, as I suppose you know.'

He nodded. 'No need for pretence, madam. The manager has informed me. I am honoured to meet you. I am Tom Dilhorne, as I expect you know, too.'

His voice surprised her by its pure articulation. He possessed neither an upper-class drawl nor the colonial bray to which she had become accustomed. There was a pause while they were served. He spoke to her again.

'I understand that you have been touring the gold field: a strange experience for you, surely.'

She was plain with him. 'Oh, men are men everywhere, you know. In the diggings and in palaces, too. Only the trappings are different.'

He smiled—and she caught her breath. If only she had known him when he had been young. There was nothing, she thought, nothing of Thomas Dilhorne in him. But Fred? Now that might be another matter.

'Indeed, you have the right of it,' he told her. 'How few of us realise that. You are fortunate, indeed.'

It was not what she might have expected him to say. Fortunate? When she had come down to this? But he was not speaking of money or power, but of something else. The something which had enabled her to enjoy poor Fred, and which was now enabling her to endure her fate with fortitude.

'Forgive me for speaking of him,' she said, impulsive for once. 'But I believe that it was your son whom I met when I first came to Melbourne, many months ago now.'

A pang crossed his face briefly and was gone.

'You met Thomas?'

'Yes,' and then, almost without thinking, she said what she suddenly knew to be true and must be said to his father. 'A most unhappy man, I fear.'

Tom Dilhorne bent his head for a moment before looking her full in the face.

'Yes, I fear so. He lost his wife in the most tragic circumstances.' He paused before adding stoically, 'Now we have lost him. His death has been assumed, and I am here to close the matter.'

Rosina could not prevent herself from saying, 'Dead? But how?'

'He disappeared here, in Melbourne, many months ago, shortly before he was due to return home. It is to be assumed that he was assaulted, although no body has been found, but his personal valuables have turned up in a pawn shop, presumably left there by the thieves who attacked him.'

He paused again. 'His mother is desolate.'

And you, too, thought Rosina, and you, too.

'How useless to say that I am sorry, but I must say it.'

'Yes, and I thank you.'

Should she tell him of Fred and his likeness to Thomas Dilhorne? But Fred could not conceivably have been Thomas. He had repeatedly denied having known her before they had met in Ballarat. He had been most plainly a digger by his manner and by his body. She remembered his superbly muscular physique and his calloused, workman's hands. It would be foolish to raise the old man's hopes for his lost son on the basis of something of which she had become less and less sure: that Fred Waring and Thomas Dilhorne were one and the same man.

Had anyone told her of Fred's lost memory she might have had fewer doubts that he really was Thomas, but Rosina had never fraternised with the commonalty of the diggings, and by the time that she had arrived at Ballarat Fred's lost memory was no longer the source of gossip that it had once been.

Tom Dilhorne, that man of uncommon intuition, noticed her hesitation after his last simple word, and wondered at it. The moment passed when the waiter serving their part of the table spoke to him and to Rosina, and the chance was lost. After he had departed, their talk moved on to other things.

Rosina decided to tell him nothing of Thomas's savagery with her. It would pain the old man, she knew, for here was a man who—unlike his son—never wore his heart on any sleeve. Rosina knew that she was signalling to him that he attracted her and that he was well aware of what she was doing.

'Your son does not resemble you,' she said abruptly.

'Thomas? No.' He sighed. 'His twin, now, my other son, Alan, does: we are very alike in looks and character. All that Thomas and I shared was our devotion to our wives.'

Warned off, Rosina thought, amused. They sat silent for a time after that, each thinking of the lost past, and when they began talking again it was of inconsequentialities. She wished once more that she had met him earlier, when they were both younger, and it was only later, after she had reached her room, that it occurred to her that she had had the same thought over Fred.

Old Tom watched her leave. So Thomas had met her and the meeting had evidently not been to her taste. Her silence was evidence of that—and her knowledge of his unhappiness.

He sighed. It was useless to repine, to hope that Thomas might have found something in her to comfort him, or that he might have comforted her. For the shooting star's path was plainly downwards. After the diggings, what would be left for Rosina Campbell who had once ruled a kingdom?

And for him, Tom Dilhorne, what was left? To find how Thomas might have died, and never to know why. Or never to find him at all. Never to find him healed, but to live with the memory of that last intolerable scene at breakfast, and his son's reproaches.

I should have been kinder to him, he thought. I had hoped to be kind, but my last manipulation has cost me my son, and I shall not manipulate again, but accept.

To lose him like this, though, is hard to accept.

Fred was gone. The tiger had eaten him. The pain of it was so strong that it brought him to his knees, crying aloud inarticulate words which made no sense. He was in the dark, on the ground, being beaten, and then someone took him by the hair and poured a scalding liquid down his throat, so that he cried out aloud again.

And then he was in strong sunlight in a place he did not know, surrounded by people he had never seen before. He was still on the ground, and they were staring at him, as distressed as he was. There was a pretty girl with Bethia's eyes kneeling beside him, trying to comfort him.

But Bethia, oh, where was she?—and he cried out again at the memory of her loss, and a little sallow man with a sad face, came forward and said, 'Lie still, Fred, let Kirstie take your hand and we'll help you to the hut.'

Why were they calling him Fred? Who was the man? Who was Kirstie? He knew neither of them.

There were other people there whom he didn't know. They were all wearing rough clothes in this strange wild place he had somehow arrived in. What was he doing here? His clothes were rough, too, and his hands! Oh, God, what had he done to his hands? He stared at them—they were the hands of a workman, brown and scarred, the nails broken.

'Where is this place?' he said, looking around him. 'Who are all of you?'

'Fred,' said the pretty girl, her face troubled and grieving. 'Oh, Fred, what's the matter?'

He knew that he was Thomas Dilhorne—so why was she calling him Fred?

To think was so difficult that the pain re-appeared. It increased until it whirled him away, and then the tiger was at him again, and this time it ate Thomas, too, and the pain which he had previously thought unendurable became worse still.

So unendurable that everyone and everything disappeared into the dark where the tiger spat Thomas and Fred out. They were one again and no one could tell where the one began and the other ended.

He was whole and healed, but kneeling on the ground weeping. He still did not know where he was until he looked at the ash-blonde girl with Bethia's eyes and knew that she was Kirstie and his wife and that he loved her. He had Thomas's memories, and Fred's, too: the kaleidoscope had shifted for the last time.

It was too much for him to bear. Geordie Farquhar saw his face change. He was the only one who understood what was happening to Fred, who put his hand out blindly, saying, 'Help me, Geordie, help me,' before falling forward unconscious.

'Carry him to the hut,' Geordie said to Sam and Bart, who stood there bewildered.

Lew was horrified. Despite his threats, he had never really meant to kill Fred, only to hurt him, to make him pay a little for having Annie, and then for insulting her. After all, his blow had been a light one, and although Fred had dropped heavily, Geordie had broken his fall so that he had not even caught his head on the ground.

And when he had recovered consciousness Fred had crawled about, moaning, saying unintelligible things about tigers and strangers. He had not known any of them, not even Kirstie, until he had collapsed again, without warning this time.

He hovered about, worried, while the Moores carried Fred to his hut, until Geordie came out, looking grave.

'Go home, Lew,' he said, but not unkindly. 'Fred's had a shock. Nothing to do with you really. The blow might have started it, it's true, but it wasn't your fault.'

'I didn't really hit him very hard,' said Lew despairingly. 'I never meant to hurt him quite so badly. I just wanted to punish him for having fun with Annie.'

'I know,' said Geordie. 'Go home now, and try not to punish Annie any more. You're not blameless yourself.'

'Go home to what?' asked Lew. 'You know what I'll find there.'

He walked away, his head hanging. He had had his revenge, and he didn't like it now that he had achieved it.

Geordie cleared everyone out of Fred's hut, including Kirstie—particularly Kirstie. Who knew what the man who had been Fred might say? Kirstie did not deserve to be hurt. He persuaded her that Fred would be better alone with him until he had recovered from the shock which his returning memory had inflicted on him.

Kate Moore came over and took Kirstie to the tent which she shared with Sam, and gave her tea and sympathy. She trusted Geordie, they all did, Kirstie most of all. She thought of him as a true friend. One who had helped her to accept the new life of the diggings, who had educated her, and comforted her through the pain which loving Fred had caused her in the past.

Geordie knew this and sometimes thought bitterly of why he was here at all, and whether any of them would trust him if they knew the truth about him. He pushed that thought away and sat beside Fred, who lay on the bed on which he had nursed Kirstie, his face turned away from Geordie and anyone who might enter while he came to terms with himself, and what had happened to him.

He knew where the tiger had come from. He remembered the screen in the sunlight behind his father when he had railed at him—and he thought that he deserved to be haunted and pursued by it as some payment for his self-righteousness. He remembered his cruel words to his father with such scalding shame that he could hardly lie still on hearing them again in his head. For he knew who the old man with the sad, kind face was, and that the riotous living of his early days in the diggings had taught him that his father had been trying to help him, and his response had been…had been…

He rolled restlessly on the bed and tried not to think of how harshly Thomas Dilhorne had spoken to the parents who loved him. He knew, too, what he had lost, and that he would never find her again. Worse than that, he knew that he had been unable to let her go, and had behaved after a fashion which would have pained and distressed Bethia, had she known of it, not only to Rosina in Melbourne, but to others too numerous to mention.

The new man, who was neither Thomas, nor Fred, but in some strange way was both, cringed with shame when he remembered how much he had resented Lachlan because his mother had died bearing him.

He remembered also the sandy-haired giant, his twin brother, Alan, who had slipped in and out of his memory in Ballarat. The brother who had so often told him to loosen up and whom he had dearly loved—but had also bitterly resented for his enormous zest for life which he, Thomas, could not share.

Except that he had shared it to the full when he had been Fred…

He relived his meeting with Rosina Campbell in The Criterion Hotel in Melbourne as though it had happened to him yesterday—which in some odd sense it had. He remembered his last words to her—'It is not my intention to engage in unseemly romping—with you, or anyone else.'

'Unseemly romping!' So that was what Rosina had been taunting him with when she had seen Fred's extraordinary likeness to Thomas Dilhorne. His lack of reaction to her gibe must have been proof for her that he and Thomas, for all the likeness between them, were two different men. What, he wondered, had she made of Fred who had bedded her so lustily? And what did he make of himself for doing with her so joyfully what he had obviously longed to do as Thomas, but had refused to acknowledge to himself?

It was over and done with, he had sowed his wild oats, belatedly perhaps, and he knew that he would never be unfaithful to Kirstie. He also knew that as Fred he had made Rosie happy: happier, she had told him once, than she had been for years. Fate, however, had made him pay almost immediately for his past brutality to her in the hotel, and he could not deny that his punishment had been earned. He tried to remember how it was that he had come to lose his memory…

Despite his successful dealing with the entrepreneurs in Melbourne over the matter of the railway, he had been deeply unhappy. He had known that he was not liked because he would not join in the roistering which they had expected of him because he was Alan's brother and old Tom's son.

On what should have been his last evening there he had left the official celebratory dinner with Mrs Theresa Spurling, the swashbuckling widow of one of the original proposers of the railway. She had offered him a lift back to his hotel in her new and splendid carriage.

At least that was how it had begun. They had not gone very far when she had said archly, 'The evening is yet young, Mr Dilhorne. Why not come home with me and end it with a dish of chocolate? I usually take one before retiring, a companion would be pleasant.'

She was plumply pretty and no rival for Rosina Campbell in either looks or charm, but she was making her interest in him as plain as Rosina had done. The invitation was ambiguous and discreet enough not to offend. His father had said—damn his father—see life a bit. Thomas supposed that bedding the inviting Mrs Spurling could be called life.

At first everything went reasonably well. They conversed about nothing while they waited for the chocolate to appear.

It had become depressingly obvious that this was not the first time that Theresa Spurling had entertained a gentleman after taking chocolate with him. Something further was definitely expected of him. Thomas decided to supply it.

Was this seeing life? If it were, then seeing life was remarkably banal. It grew even more so later when they retired to the sofa to enjoy themselves. It was fake Louis Seize and, whatever position he took up on it, was extremely uncomfortable—which didn't help matters at all.

Things went from bad to worse. The something further wasn't being conspicuous by its success—far from it. His mind or his body, he wasn't sure which, didn't seem to be up to its self-imposed task, however hard he tried.

Whatever else she was, Theresa Spurling was both kind and perceptive. After some abortive attempts by Thomas at what his mind persisted in calling unseemly romping in a ghastly memory of his conversation with Rosina Campbell—and if she had wanted revenge on him she had certainly got it—it became apparent that Mr Thomas Dilhorne was capable of neither desire nor performance.

Mrs Theresa Spurling was doomed to retire to bed unsatisfied.

'No,' she said gently, pushing him away at last. 'Your heart's not in it.'

'No,' he began, furiously embarrassed. 'I'm sorry. I didn't mean to deceive you.'

He sat up and, avoiding her eyes, began to fasten his clothing again.

'No need to be sorry,' she told him. 'I understand that you lost your wife in tragic circumstances. I expect that you find life difficult.' Her kindness made the whole wretched business worse, not better.

'Yes,' he said. He could think of nothing else to say.

'Let me order the carriage to take you back to the hotel.'

'No,' he said, not wanting to be beholden to her in any

way after his humiliation. 'I'll walk. It's not far. I'd rather walk.'

And that was true. He strolled through the busy town. It was lit up and roaring as though it were day. Not far from the hotel he passed The Black Cat, the gambling den which the others had wanted him to visit on the previous night.

He walked by, hesitated, and then walked back. His father's advice had proved damned useless in one area, how about trying it in another? Grandfather Fred Waring had been a compulsive womaniser, drinker and gambler—did his grandson, who so resembled him in looks, possess no leanings in those directions?

He walked down the steps and into The Black Cat...

Now, remembering something of what had happened next, Thomas/Fred shivered.

The Black Cat had been blue with smoke and packed with gamblers, most of them diggers, throwing away their hard-won gold, or trying to turn small winnings in the open into bigger ones at the card tables.

He was not surprised to discover that he disliked the place intensely and was not at all attracted to the notion of spending any time there—whatever his stupid father might think. Fun, he remembered thinking disparagingly, where's the fun in this? He was careful not to drink and also careful to avoid any camaraderie with the dirty ruffians around him when he began to play cards.

He had been pleased to discover that his skills had not left him and more than one man there gave this well-dressed, handsome nob with the cold face and obvious card sense, resentful sideways glares when he relieved them of their money.

One party of diggers found him particularly obnoxious. They laughed and sniggered behind their hands at him. The words, 'By Gow, he's a regular Miss Molly—he needs teaching a lesson,' floated over to him, but he took no notice of such uncouth goings-on.

Their leader, a large ruffian, finally sat down opposite to him, and said in a pseudo-matey voice, 'You want to be careful, chum. You won't find your kind of fun here—and you might get more than you bargain for.'

The whiskey reek was foul upon him. Thomas raised his eyes and gave the man his haughty stare.

'I've come to play cards,' he returned coldly. 'I neither wish to talk nor to find fun,' and he turned away from the man to concentrate on his cards.

'Cheer up, mate,' jeered the brute coarsely. 'You look like a preacher who'd thought he'd gone to Heaven and found himself in Hell. Tell you what, mate, I'll buy you a drink. Loosen you up a little. You look as though you need it.'

He had said as dismissively as he could, 'Thank you, no. I don't drink.'

'What! Prefers boys to girls, I'll be bound, don't drink, don't smoke, plays cards like a damned accountant. How *do* you get your jollies, chum?'

Thomas remembered only too well that he had turned a furious face on his tormentor when coarse laughter, provoked by his taunts, rang round the packed room.

'Not by talking to such as you,' he retorted before he could stop himself from saying anything so unwise.

The big man's eyes narrowed. 'I'll not soil myself, mate, by arguing with you. But you *will* drink with me before you leave—or it'll be the worse for you.'

'I said before that I don't drink,' replied Thomas desperately. He was not his heavyweight twin who would have sailed into a fight with these oafs and taken the room with him, but he was no coward, either.

The ruffian ignored him. He picked up the bottle on the

table before him, and then tried to pass it to Thomas, who was still angrily refusing him.

'Hold him for me, mates,' said the digger to his companions, 'while I get it down his throat—teach him how to be a real man.'

Thomas rose and stepped back to avoid being manhandled. He was suddenly aware that not a soul in the den was on his side. Unashamed glee at seeing a nob humiliated shone on every face.

The diggers' advance on him was checked by the arrival of the owner of the gaming den, who shouldered his way through the watching crowd to spoil the fun.

'Break it up, mates. I want no trouble here.'

He turned to Thomas. 'If you know what's good for you, mate, you'll leave. My customers don't like their offers of a free drink being refused quite so rudely. We're all chums together these days. We've no time for toffee-nosed mollies.'

'So I gather,' said Thomas, seething inwardly. 'And seeing that you're prepared to allow your clients to be humiliated, I'll leave with pleasure.' His progress to the door was followed by derisive laughter.

He was so outraged that he failed to grasp what danger he might be in on his way back to the hotel. It was, after all, only a short distance down an alley before he reached its flamboyant entrance. He forgot or, in his arrogance, he ignored, the temper of the men he had left behind him.

The big digger had turned to the proprietor. 'Spoiled our fun, you did,' he said, and then looked meaningfully at his mates. 'There's an arrogant swine out there who needs teaching a lesson. If we can't give him one here, one outside might be even better.

Thomas was halfway down the alley when they attacked him. He had no chance to defend himself. He had no memory of anything after the first blow which felled and stunned him. He dropped to the ground where their boots completed what the home-made cosh had begun.

They propped him up against the wall and stripped him. First his gold watch and his ruby stick-pin were taken, and then the ring which Bethia had given him before they were married—which, months later, he had seen on the finger of the big digger in Hyde's Place. His fine coat, his shirt, boots and trousers followed suit until he lay, half-naked in the dirt of the alley—his clothes were nearly as big a prize as his jewellery.

'Doesn't drink, he says,' laughed the digger, kicking the semi-conscious figure on the ground again. 'We'll see about that.'

He grasped Thomas by the hair, put the bottle of spirits he was carrying to his mouth, and when his victim moaned and tried to reject it, he held his nose until the contents of the bottle were inside him.

'Let's see what he thinks about drink, now,' he added, aiming a final blow at Thomas's head, a blow which not only deprived him of consciousness, but was to affect him crucially for months to come. As a result of it memory-less Fred Waring was born.

At the time all that it did was to complete the transformation of a serious and elegant gentleman into a grotesque parody of himself—drunken, half-naked, his face and body bruised and swollen, left for the watch to find him some hours later and drag him to the nick, believing him to be one of the vagrants who slept in the streets.

Before that the moon came out and shone down on him. The pain and grief of the last eighteen months, as well as his pride and dignity, had been stripped from him. Oblivion claimed him. He had half-hoped for it more than once. Now he was in its grip.

And when he entered it again the world had changed completely.

Thomas remembered, but only vaguely, the humiliations he had endured before Fred came fully to life. The prolonged drunken bout which had been begun by those in the alley who had poured the spirits down his throat continued for weeks—he was never sure quite how long. Weeks during which he had lived and suffered in the streets and gutters of Melbourne and Ballarat, enduring constant humiliation.

When the Moores had rescued him he had begun his compulsive womanising, as though he was making up for the months of abstinence and proud denials of his needs. He remembered again his anger with his father and knew why he had been so angry. He knew that he had thrust away his own humanity and his needs, and had seen them as demeaning, which was why he had been so cruel to those around him.

He knew too that Geordie had been right. He had not wanted to remember Thomas Dilhorne, had chosen for a time to be a child again before he had been reborn as Fred and then he had wanted to remain careless, happy Fred and forget Thomas Dilhorne, that cold, proud man. More than that, in some way he had needed to be brought down, to be purged, and to live among the lowly whom he had despised.

Always in his thoughts he came back to Kirstie, and in the end he had found her and, in finding her, had found himself. The hard life of the diggings had been a kind of redemption for a man who had driven himself mad with his pride of self. He knew, too, that his feelings that Kirstie was untouchable were because she reminded him too much of Bethia, whose memory must not be besmirched.

Except that, in the end, in knowing Kirstie and loving her, the joy which he had once shared with Bethia was sealed and renewed, and that once the essential core of him recognised that, he was ready to be Thomas again. Only this time he was a Thomas who knew humility because he had been a derelict in the streets, had been baptised back into humanity by Sam, Bart and Geordie, had celebrated life with Fat Lil and Rosina, had suffered and had transcended suffering.

Only after that could his mental and physical torment end and he could be once more the man whom Bethia had known and loved.

Geordie made no effort to speak to him. Fred, whoever he was, must come to terms with himself, if he could. Once he went out and came back with a great tumbler of spirits. Fred lay passive when he returned. His agonised writhing had stopped.

'Fred,' he said. The figure on the bed did not stir, so Geordie touched his shoulder gently. Fred looked up at him, his face grey, only his eyes alive.

'I know that you don't drink spirits now,' he said, 'but take this, Fred, and try to sleep. Don't torment yourself further.'

'How?' began Fred.

'Don't speak now. Tomorrow, perhaps. Now drink it—and sleep.'

Fred took the spirits and drank them down before handing the tumbler back to Geordie. Geordie took Fred's wrists, and fixed his eyes on Fred as he had done when he had stopped Fred drinking.

'Sleep, now,' he said again.

Obediently, Fred lay back, his own eyes still fixed on Geordie, and fell at once into a deep sleep. A dreamless sleep, with no loss, no tiger and no old man to disturb it—they were all gone forever. He slept as though he were a child again.

'Leave him,' said Geordie again to a frantic Kirstie when he entered Sam Moore's tent. 'He needs to be alone. He's not seriously hurt, but he's suffered a dreadful shock and now he's sleeping. When he wakes up I'll look at him again.'

'Oh, Geordie,' Kirstie half-sobbed. 'Fred cared for me when I needed it, why can't I care for him? And sleeping? It's only noon.'

He took her hand and looked deep into her eyes as he had done with Fred.

'Trust me,' he said, remembering again that he had said these words before, and hoped that this time he would not be wrong. Kirstie calmed down at last and began to cry, not frantically, but gently.

'I do trust you, Geordie, but I'm frightened. Now that he has his memory back, will he want me? Will he know me? He seemed not to know me after Lew hit him.'

'No need to be frightened,' Geordie said. 'Fred knows us all now. He remembers who he was, but he also remembers that he was Fred.'

'Just let me see him, Geordie. I promise to be good and not disturb him.'

He nodded and led her into the hut so that she could see Fred sleeping peacefully as he had rarely done before. She sat with him for a little before Geordie took her away, and Kate, kind and motherly, gave her a bed for the night, since Fred slept on. They all told her not to worry and in the end Kirstie also fell asleep, exhausted by the day's revelations.

Chapter Fourteen

Thomas was propped up on pillows, not moving, when Geordie came in the next morning, a bitter-sweet taste in his mouth. It was a compound of the pleasure and love of Kirstie present, and the pleasure and love of Bethia past, and now he could face his loss of her, and not let his burning resentment of it destroy both him and his life.

'Kirstie?' he said eagerly to Geordie. 'I need to see her. She'll be worrying about me.'

'Later,' said Geordie. 'Yes, she's worried, but we need to talk first now that you've recovered.'

Thomas nodded. 'If you say so.'

He had trusted Geordie when he was Fred, and he trusted him even more now that he was Thomas and could read Geordie in a way which Fred could not.

Geordie looked closely at him. What was plain to him was what he had seen once or twice before: whoever Fred Waring was in the present, in his unknown past he had been a man of power, no clerk, no underling.

'Well, then,' he said. 'Remembered who we are, have we?'

Thomas smiled, a trifle ruefully. He gave Geordie, not

his slow Fred smile, but some memory of it, not such a smile as the old Thomas Dilhorne would ever have given.

'Yes,' he said simply, and said no more.

'Well, T.D. It is T.D., isn't it? Thomas, Tom or Theo?'

Thomas looked surprised. 'Yes, Thomas. How did you know?'

'The ring, remember? And then you've called yourself Tom or Thomas once or twice lately when you weren't thinking. You even wrote Thomas down last week when you were signing Hyde's books for him, before crossing it out. After Lew hit you it was plain that your memory had returned and that you had no idea of where you were. Then I saw your face change when you suddenly remembered that you had been Fred.'

'I see,' said Thomas.

He was quiet and controlled and offered little when he spoke, thought Geordie, amused. It was difficult, talking to him, to recall the open frankness of Fred.

'Yes, I've remembered,' he said. 'Everything. I am both Thomas and Fred, and it's a strange feeling. They were very different men.'

'As I thought,' commented Geordie. 'And the D? What does the D stand for?'

Thomas's rueful smile returned. 'Well, that's a lot harder, Geordie. Difficult is what it stands for, in fact.'

'Difficult?' Geordie was watchful. 'Why difficult, Thomas? Don't you want your name back?'

It was Thomas's turn to scrutinise Geordie's face carefully. He considered a moment, shrugged his shoulders and decided to tell him the truth. He was sadly aware that the old Fred would have blurted everything out in one overpowering outburst of information. But if he was not entirely the old Fred, neither was he entirely the old Thomas.

'For a time yesterday, after I first remembered who I had been before I lost my memory in Melbourne, I wanted to stay Fred. I must confess that to you, because I owe you my confidence for all that you did for me when I *was* Fred. But now I have come to terms with who I am. The difficulty may not lie with me, but with others.'

He was so changed in his measured and careful speech, and the habit of authority which had returned to him as though he had never lost it, that Geordie was fascinated.

'Now, you do intrigue me, Fred…I mean, Thomas,' he said at last.

'Yes, well, my name is Dilhorne, Thomas Dilhorne.'

He lay back on his pillows and waited for Geordie's inevitable reaction.

'Dilhorne?' said Geordie queryingly, and then, his face breaking up. 'Not one of *the* Dilhornes, the colony's richest magnates? The son, are you the son?'

Thomas, wryly amused at Geordie's amusement, smiled ruefully at him. 'I'm afraid so, Geordie. Complicated, isn't it?'

'Complicated!' Geordie began to laugh, almost hysterically. 'Complicated.' He choked. 'Oh, my God, Fred—I mean, Thomas. There's you, belonging to the richest family in the colony, filthy with it, digging like a lunatic, labouring for months to make your fortune, and that's not the half of it.'

Thomas watched him warily, smiling a little himself. 'Well, what is the other half of it, Geordie?'

Geordie exploded again before wiping his eyes. 'Oh, God, Fred, Thomas, I heard the nobs talking about you in the shop, just before I left Melbourne. They came in out of the rain one morning. ''Young Thomas Dilhorne,'' they said. ''He's not like his father was,'' they said. ''He doesn't drink, doesn't gamble, doesn't wench, and can't be bribed or bought. He's a damned arrogant, stiff-necked prig looking down his nose at everybody.'' It doesn't sound much like Fred Waring, does it?'

Thomas blushed a little. 'No, Geordie, it doesn't, I must admit. On the other hand, though, it must have been what the prig really wanted to do—drink, wench and gamble, I mean.'

'So that's what you were running from,' said Geordie, more sober now. 'The man who was Thomas Dilhorne, the man you were.'

'Partly,' said Thomas, 'but not only that, I think.'

'And Kirstie, Thomas? What about Kirstie? I'm thinking of B.K., Thomas, who gave you her love, as well as her ring. What about her? I wouldn't want Kirstie to be hurt.'

Thomas's face twisted in pain. 'So that's why you didn't let her in. It was B.K. you were worried about.'

He fell silent. 'I might have trusted you to protect Kirstie, and of course, you were right to do so. But there's no need for you to worry about B.K., Geordie. She was my wife, Bethia, Bethia Kerr. We were married for ten years and then she died, having our first long-wanted child. No one can hurt Bethia now, Geordie, nor can she hurt Kirstie. Kirstie is my true wife, and I think that Thomas loves her more deeply than Fred did because he understands her worth more.'

'I'm sorry, Thomas,' said Geordie gently. 'I didn't mean to hurt you, but I had to know.'

'You've no need to reproach yourself, Geordie. You were right to think of Kirstie—you weren't to know about Bethia.'

'So that was your other reason, Thomas—for becoming Fred, I mean.'

'Losing Bethia like that? Yes, she was my childhood sweetheart. I think that I went a little mad when she died. You see, I had led such a good life, a virtuous life, and my reward was to lose my dearest love. I wanted to hurt people—as I had been hurt—and, oh, my God, Geordie, how many months has it been since I was attacked in Melbourne? Time meant nothing to Fred, you know.

'My father and mother must believe me dead, and, God forgive me, I parted from them in such anger, that their last memories of me must be bitter ones. I was so cold to my mother even though she looked after my little boy—and me—so lovingly. And all without so much as a word of thanks from me.'

He covered his face with his hands. 'Oh, Geordie, I was shameful. I could hardly bear to look at poor little Lachlan, or my parents, or anyone. I hated everybody, even the memory of my twin brother Alan who lives in England now.'

He raised his tormented face, wet with the tears he had shed, to look at Geordie.

'I hated him because he looks like The Patriarch, my father, and I look like my worthless grandfather, Fred Waring—my mother's father. It was strange, was it not, that I should call myself after my drunken grandfather, Fred? Mother says that I greatly resemble her brother Rowland who was killed in the Peninsular War—and my second name *is* Frederick.'

'Not strange at all,' said Geordie. 'I've seen cases like yours before, Thomas, back in—back when—no matter. Men who had a blow and changed, sometimes for good and sometimes not. The blow was the least of it for you, I think. You didn't like Thomas Dilhorne much so it gave you an excuse to get rid of him. Human beings are kittle-kattle, Thomas, and that's the truth.'

'Yes,' said Thomas. 'And it was that first blow, back in Melbourne, and the drink they poured down my throat which set me off on the drunken spree which I was still in when Sam rescued me from the police and the nick. I remember that I first called myself Fred Waring in the magistrate's court and I remained Fred until yesterday when another blow brought Thomas back to life. And now I don't know who I am. I was once Young Tom and hated that, and then I was Thomas and I apparently disliked him even more—and then I was Fred.'

'Everyone liked Fred,' said Geordie reminiscently.

'But I'm not Fred, either, although in many ways I shall be sorry to lose him. Whoever I am, I'm Kirstie's husband, and my parents' son and Lachlan's father, and they ought to know that I'm not dead—and how do I tell Kirstie who and what she has married?'

'Not poor Fred, but a man of power and wealth who is used to wielding both,' said Geordie.

'Exactly.'

He was so different from Fred and yet so much of Fred was still in him, it was unbelievable. You could sense the cold power which Thomas Dilhorne possessed, but the love and sweetness of Fred was there, too, and overlaid it. And authority. The authority which he had occasionally shown as Fred, which had caused Hyde to comment more than once that sometimes Fred spoke as though he were used to giving orders.

He said now, diffidently, but surely, 'I don't want this known, Geordie. You'll not talk, I'm sure. I'm still Fred Waring to the Moore party and I want to remain so for the time being—until I know what to do. I'm not certain what effect my revealing that I'm Thomas Dilhorne will have on everyone.'

He hesitated. 'I was liked for myself as Fred, you know, not because I was a rich man who could dispense favours.'

'I understand,' said Geordie, 'and I agree with you. I'll keep your secret—but don't take too long before you tell Kirstie.'

'I shan't, and you may trust me to tell her at the right time. You see, I want my last hours in Ballarat to be happy ones. I owe you all so much—I might have been dead from drink by now, if you hadn't rescued me from the nick.'

Geordie shook his head. 'I think not. You would have come out of it, I'm sure, but it might have been hard and long for you on your own. I admit that we made it easier for you.'

'My debt can never be repaid,' said Thomas simply. 'It is not something which has to do with money.'

Geordie looked at him, thought of Fred as he had been on the day when Sam had brought him home and silently agreed with him. 'And now I think that you ought to see Kirstie.'

'Yes,' agreed Thomas. 'I must tell her something of the truth.'

He lay back again after Geordie had gone, and watched the door for Kirstie, his dear love. She stole in hesitantly, only for her face to light up when she saw him reclining there, apparently well.

'Oh, Fred!' she exclaimed, coming over to the bed, and kissing him. 'I was so worried. I thought that you might be really ill and that Geordie wasn't telling me. I should have known that he wouldn't deceive me.'

He held her to him, and then lifted the bedclothes so that she could slip in beside him.

'I know that it's daytime,' he whispered in her ear, 'but nobody is going to disturb us this morning. Geordie will keep them away. We need to be alone together.'

They lay there, arms around one another. Kirstie was only too happy to be with him again, her head on his chest.

'My dear,' he said. 'I have something to tell you. I have remembered who I am.'

At that she turned wide eyes on him, so full of doubt and fear that he kissed her on the cheek.

'There's no need to worry, my darling Kirstie. We are well and truly married. I have no other ties.'

She could not have described the relief which ran through her. 'Oh, Fred,' she said, 'I can't say that I wasn't worried, particularly when Geordie wouldn't let me see you.'

'He was protecting you, my darling. I have a father and a mother in Sydney who will think that I am dead since I gather it is many months since I disappeared in Melbourne and became Fred. We must go home at once. They do not deserve to mourn me any longer than is necessary.' He did not mention Lachlan—time enough to tell her later. As for Thomas Dilhorne, how could he tell her of him? Sooner or later she must learn the truth, and Sam and the rest, too. But, oh, he wanted to be Fred a little while longer, even if he were a changed Fred, which he knew by Geordie's manner that he was.

'Sydney?' said Kirstie, almost as though he were speaking of faraway England.

'Yes, Sydney. I have a home there for you to look after. It overlooks the Harbour. You'll like it.'

She turned her head to look into his eyes. 'You're not a poor man, then?'

'No, I'm not poor. I was attacked in Melbourne by thieves. I was there on business. I lost my memory and came to the diggings by accident.'

'Pa thought that you must have been a clerk—or something like that. He was right, then.'

'Yes, and we must go to Melbourne at once. Not tomorrow, but the day after if we can book seats on the coach.'

Kirstie could see that he had changed—but he was still Fred when he smiled at her. He took her face in his hands. 'It will be a new life for you, my darling—not at all what we expected when we married. It will mean leaving Pa and the others, but you will like my mother—and my father, too.'

He took her fully in his arms and kissed her passionately. 'We lost a night together, my love, and I intend to make up for that at once,' and he began to make love to her with all the gentle passion which Fred had always shown her—so he had not changed in that.

Afterwards Kirstie was to think that it was a symbol of their new life together, to be so lavish with precious time that they could leave the claims of work and duty and pleasure themselves so happily that she fell briefly asleep at a time when she would normally have been running round preparing a mid-day meal and concentrating on the many tasks of the day.

Fred had his arm around Kirstie. They were standing by the coach which was being loaded for its journey to Melbourne. He was well aware that Kirstie was half-excited, half-frightened before they set out on this journey into a new world. Like Pat when he knew that they were going to the diggings, she had not realised the full enormity of what was about to happen to her.

She was going to leave Pa and the kids behind, and all the friends they had made, and travel with Fred, first to Melbourne, and then to Sydney. She was going to abandon everything she had known during the whole of her short life.

Thomas had paid his farewells to Ballarat on the previous day. Like Young Dan'l he had made his rounds, kissing Fat Lil outside her tent, shaking Ned Hyde, Dickie Vallance and the others by the hand.

Even Jack Tate had come over to say goodbye. He looked sadly at Kirstie and wished them well. 'I hope that you'll be happy with Fred,' were his last words to her.

Thomas had still not told them who he really was. They assumed, as Kirstie did, that he was taking her to some little house in Sydney's growing suburbs, not the large and beautiful mansion that he had shared with Bethia. He was still Fred Waring, even if he was a different man from the one he had been for nearly a year.

He had sat round the fire with them for the last time on the previous evening. He had handed to Sam, Bart and Geordie a quarter each of the gold and the money which he had saved over the months of his diggings. Bart and Sam stared at him when he passed the small canvas bags over to them.

'No,' said Sam, shaking his head. 'I can't take this, Fred, you'll need it.'

Thomas shook his head. 'I have a home and a job waiting for me in Sydney, Sam. I want you to have it.'

'But it's yours,' said Bart, bewildered by such largesse, small though it seemed to Thomas.

'Yes,' agreed Thomas. 'It's mine to give to you. It's little enough thanks for what you all did for me. You baptised me in Jordan water,' he said, pointing to the creek. 'I'd have been lying in the street, still The Wreck, otherwise.'

'We didn't do it to save you,' said Sam honestly. 'We needed a hand.'

'That's not the point,' said Thomas, hugging Kirstie to him. 'You did it, and you cared for me afterwards. You fed and clothed me until I was of some help to you.'

'But you need it, son, you and Kirstie.'

The 'son' nearly unmanned Thomas. It reminded him of his own father.

'Trust me, Sam,' he said gently. 'Kirstie will be safe with me, I promise you. She'll not want.'

Which was the understatement of the year, thought the listening Geordie, remembering all that he had heard of the Dilhornes' wealth!

'No buts,' said Thomas. 'You've given me your riches,' and he hugged Kirstie to him again. He was not quite as demonstrative as Fred had been, but the old Thomas would have raised his arrogant brows at the new one's public displays of love and affection, so freely given to those around him.

Sam looked steadily at his son-in-law. He had indeed changed. The cold authority which Geordie had seen was visible to Sam, too, however gently Thomas spoke. He knew men who were masters of others and Thomas showed the signs of being one of them most plainly. He was obviously used to being obeyed, but his affection for them all was quite plain, too, and tempered his manner.

Geordie had told Sam that Kirstie would be safe and secure with Fred, even if he had not told him of Fred's true identity, and Sam trusted Geordie enough to accept his word.

'Well…' said Sam hesitantly. He was not entirely sure that Fred ought to be giving away so much.

'Very well,' said Thomas, who obviously considered the matter settled. He looked about him. It had grown dark while they talked. Earlier Bart had fetched out the cards and they had played together for the last time, Kirstie looking over Fred's shoulder at his hand. They were always a pair these days and could scarcely bear to be parted.

Now that the little game had ended and the gold had been passed over, Thomas was free to admire the lights of Ballarat, to enjoy the distant music, and to remember the days and nights of Fred's stay in Purgatory, the fun and the comradeship.

He was returning to the world of duties and responsibilities, and for a moment he wished to be Fred again, but there were his parents and Lachlan whom he now wanted most earnestly to see and to cherish. Lachlan, Bethia's last gift to him, who deserved to have his father again. Lachlan, whom he had never treasured as he should have done.

These memories of love—and duty—meant that Fred finally slipped away, leaving behind only the best part of him, to prevent Thomas from ever reverting to what he had been. He tightened his grasp around Kirstie's shoulders and hoped that she would enjoy her life as rich Mrs Thomas Dilhorne as much as she might have enjoyed being poor Fred Waring's wife.

The trunk containing their few poor possessions was finally hoisted on to the coach. Kirstie and he embraced Bart, Sam and Geordie, for they—as well as many of their friends in the diggings—had come to see them off. He had given Geordie a letter for Sam telling him the truth about Thomas Dilhorne, the truth which Kirstie did not yet know, but which he would tell her in Melbourne.

He was determined to be Fred as long as he was in Ballarat—Thomas Dilhorne and his splendours had no place there.

His last private words to Geordie had been to offer to send him, through Dilhorne's, wherever he might want to go, or to find him work more suited to his talents.

'For the moment my place is here,' Geordie had told him. 'I have reached a haven where I am a little at peace.'

'But you must not lose touch with me, nor I with you,' Thomas said. 'Nor Sam and the others, either. They are my family, too, and when we are finally settled in Sydney Kirstie and I will come back, if only for a short stay. I trust you, Geordie. You know where to find me, should you need me.'

He had given Geordie, as well as Sam, the addresses where Thomas Dilhorne was known.

'You might not if—' began Geordie.

Thomas stopped him. 'I don't want to hear, Geordie,' he said firmly. 'I know what you are, not what you were—and that is all that matters. The friend I never had before I became Fred. The truest friend a man could have.'

Now, fully loaded and all the passengers aboard, the

coach drove off. The Moore party, Ballarat and the diggings were behind them. Kirstie suppressed her tears and sat, her hand in Fred's, enveloped in his love while they were driven into the future.

Chapter Fifteen

Had it not been for the dreadful mission on which he was engaged, Tom Dilhorne might have enjoyed his time in Melbourne. He discovered that old age had not dimmed his entrepreneurial skills and his devious intellect and enormous personal charm, which had always attracted both men and women, were as potent in action as they had ever been.

He knew that if he had not stressed his devotion to his absent wife Rosina Campbell would have been only too ready to console him for his loss of Thomas—finding for herself a rich, elderly protector into the bargain. He was always aware of the signals, however faint, which men and women gave off, and age had increased this ability, not lessened it.

Redmayne and Herbert, the main sponsors of the new railway, found old Tom Dilhorne all and more that legend had said he was, but human with it. Redmayne, indeed, said to his wife, 'How in God's name did he acquire such a prig for a son? Shame the poor devil's lost, though. He didn't deserve that.'

Tom met Theresa Spurling in his odyssey round a Melbourne indifferent to everything but the gold rush. The police had assumed his son's death as a matter of course. The lack of a body was a little puzzling, but what of that? Men disappeared all the time, and the recovery of Thomas's valuables from the pawn shop certainly meant that he had been attacked and robbed, so it was most likely, as Tom had sadly told Hester before he left home, that Thomas had been killed because dead men tell no tales.

Mrs Spurling received him in the room in which she had entertained Thomas—if entertained was the correct word to describe his encounter with her. Like everyone in Melbourne, she found the father very different from the son. She left him in no doubt that her evening with Thomas had been an innocent one, and like Rosina she informed him that Thomas had been a most unhappy man. She could throw no light on what might have happened to him.

'I blame myself,' she said, 'for not insisting that he used my carriage—but he was determined to walk.'

'A strong-minded man, my son,' said Tom gently. 'Do not reproach yourself. You could not have known what would happen.'

Like every other enquiry he had made, this one resulted in yet another dead end. He walked back to The Criterion Hotel by the route which Thomas had taken, passing The Black Cat, which was now open all day and all night in order to relieve excited diggers of their new wealth. On impulse he walked down the steps into the dark and smoky room to see if anyone there, after all these months, might remember having seen his son.

It was, as he suspected, yet another dead end, and in any case he could not imagine any circumstances in which Thomas might have visited it. He had most likely been attacked at random in a street or alley. Reluctantly he decided that there was little point in further exploration: Thomas was gone, and that was that. The only thing to do was to finish Dilhornes' business in Melbourne and go home to Hester.

Redmayne had suggested that he ought to arrange for bills to be posted offering a reward for information about his son, to be circulated in the gold fields in Bendigo and Ballarat as well as Melbourne—something which might offer Hester a little hope.

Consequently, on the following morning, he decided to visit both the printers and the police to make the necessary arrangements. Dressed *à point*, for even misery could not destroy the habits of many years, he walked slowly down the hotel's stairs into the lobby.

It was, for once, empty, except for a girl standing beside a big, curly-headed man in the clothing of the diggings. Their backs were towards him.

The girl heard him coming and looked up at him. She was in her very early twenties, strikingly pretty, with ash-blonde hair and deep bluey-green eyes, like those of his late daughter-in-law. Her clothes were simple, serviceable and clean. They consisted of a blue and white print dress, a knitted shawl of the same colours, a straw bonnet trimmed with pink cotton roses, and strong, heavy, black laced-up boots.

Her companion, who had been talking to the clerk, turned towards her, and bending down, kissed her on the cheek. She, equally enthusiastically, kissed him back.

Tom would have thoroughly enjoyed this sentimental little scene had not the big digger looked up at him so that Tom saw his bronzed face for the first time. Unbelievably the digger was his son, Thomas, with an expression of happiness on his face such as his father had not seen for years. It was replaced by a smile of such pleasure that Tom could scarcely credit it.

His own sensations were first those of enormous relief—to be replaced by an equally enormous anger at his new-found son for having caused such misery and havoc by his sudden and inconsiderate disappearance. To say nothing, also, for having the bad taste to stand there, with such an artless and insouciant smile on his face, his arm around the pretty girl beside him, as though it were only five days ago that he had raged from his home to disappear into nowhere.

His face grim, he walked down the stairs towards them.

Thomas and Kirstie had arrived in Melbourne in the late evening. They were tired after their long journey and had been warned by the other passengers that their chances of a bed for the night were not good.

Once off the coach Thomas made for the inn in whose yard their journey had ended. It was full, however, and the proprietor shrugged his shoulders, and said that even the annex, a converted barn with a common room housing makeshift mattresses, was also full.

Kirstie, dog-weary, still frail after the fever, gave a great sigh. The excitement and strains of the last few days, as well as the journey, had taken its toll of her reserves of strength, low since her illness.

Thomas squeezed her hand, and said to the proprietor, 'My wife has recently been ill and needs to rest. Is there nowhere where we might lay our heads? Anything would be better than the streets.'

He gazed at them, a little intrigued. The pair of them were obviously beyond the common run: the girl was so pretty and the big digger was something more than the usual brutes who besieged him for help. When Thomas added desperately, 'I'm prepared to pay you well,' he rubbed his chin and said, to Kirstie's great relief, 'I might be able to oblige you, but the accommodation will be rough.'

'If it's better than the street,' said Thomas, 'we'll take it.'

It *was* better than the street, but only just. It was a loft above a barn full of stale hay in which they were invited to spend the night. The old Thomas Dilhorne would have given short shrift to the mere notion of inhabiting such a place. The new one, however, after looking at his tired wife, agreed to pay for it a sum which would have brought him a luxury bedroom in a good hotel before the gold rush had arrived.

They hauled their small trunk up with them, and Thomas took out of it a clean shirt for him to put his head on and a petticoat for Kirstie to do the same. When they finally lay side by side, holding hands, he thought ruefully that Kirstie could have no inkling of whom she had married, given that this was the best that he could find for them.

Kirstie knew only one thing. She was with Fred who loved her and whose care for her had managed to find them a place for the night when anyone else might have given up. And since her life had been so hard and austere, her demands from it were so much less than Thomas's.

For sheer excitement neither of them could sleep at first. They made love in which passion and relief were mixed, and Kirstie at last fell asleep in Fred's arms. Propped up against the wall he watched tenderly over her until kind sleep finally claimed him too.

They went down to breakfast to find that the only food on offer was tea, or coffee, and rolls, and the price for them was exorbitant. Nevertheless Kirstie looked about her eagerly: everything she saw interested her, it was all so new and strange.

'We'll go to The Criterion Hotel,' Fred told her, 'and try to find rooms there. I left my luggage in store with them before I was attacked. With luck, they may still have it.'

They walked through the crowded streets, indistinguishable from the diggers and their women who thronged about them. The Criterion was a splendid place: it seemed like a palace to Kirstie, and was nothing like any hotel which she would ever have thought herself likely to enter.

'Are you sure that we shall be welcome here?' she asked, timid for once, overawed by such grandeur.

'As I recall,' said Fred, 'anyone is welcome who has enough money to pay whatever is asked of them, regardless of what they look like these days, and I have plenty, both in my pocket and once I make myself known again.'

There was a clerk on duty in the lobby who stared at them, but not unkindly, and Fred began by telling him his real name. It was the first time Kirstie had heard it. She was surprised to hear him say that he was Thomas Dilhorne who had left luggage here nearly a year ago, and had not reclaimed it. Did they still have it, and could he and his wife reserve a room?

The clerk disappeared and Fred turned to speak to Kirstie. 'Thomas Dilhorne is my real name, Kirstie. I should have told you before, but I wanted to be Fred as long as possible. I left a letter for Sam telling him who I am and giving him our address in Sydney. I told Geordie soon after I first recalled who I was.'

He saw immediately that his name meant nothing to her, and was glad of that, even though it meant that he would have more explaining to do in the future.

'Thomas?' she said, 'Not Fred.' She could not think of him as Thomas. To cover her confusion she looked about her, interested.

A tall, silver-haired old man with a strange, but handsome, face was coming down the main staircase, and he was undoubtedly finding the pair of them of the greatest interest. She was still looking up at him when Fred turned and kissed her on the cheek. She kissed him back—and, as she did so, Fred saw the old man.

A smile of the purest pleasure, a real Fred smile, lit up his face. He strode towards the old man who had reached the bottom of the stairs and was advancing on them, his expression quizzical, one eyebrow raised ironically. She lost sight of his face when Fred threw his arms around the old man's neck, embracing him, before standing back to take her hand.

The old man's expression never changed. 'Well, well,' he said, his drawl ironical. 'At last, Thomas, we find you, not dead, but risen. What have we here? It is to be hoped that there is an explanation.'

Kirstie stared at the old man whose own steady gaze took her in and summed her up. There was something of surprise on his face now, as well as amusement.

'Fred,' she asked. 'Who is this man? Is he your father?'

If he were, he was nothing like Fred in his appearance or in his manner.

'Fred?' The man's voice was questioning, ironic.

'I can explain,' said Fred quickly.

'It is to be hoped,' said the old man again.

'Yes. He is my father,' Fred told Kirstie who was looking at him for some sort of explanation.

'Your father! He frightens me.'

'He frightens everyone,' said Fred briefly. 'Father, I have so much to tell you. I am sure that you will be wondering…'

'Yes,' said the old man. 'We are agreed on that.'

Fred moved his hands helplessly. 'Before I say anything else I must inform you that this lady is Kirsteen Moore, my wife. We were married a month ago. Kirstie, this is my father, Mr Tom Dilhorne.'

'Indeed, then I must welcome Mrs Thomas Dilhorne.' He gave her a formal bow and for the first time he smiled. Oh, but he was attractive, still frightening, but attractive— and yes, Fred…Thomas, was not a bit like him.

Thomas, indeed, was suddenly almost Fred again, the

words spilling out of him, 'Oh, my story is such a strange one that I scarcely know how to begin…'

The old man put up his hand. She must try to think of him as Fred, no, Thomas's, pa.

'Not here,' he said. 'We cannot talk here.'

The habit of command was in his voice. He was obviously used to being obeyed. Fred immediately obeyed him and fell silent. Fred's pa spoke again and what he said surprised her. He spoke of nothing to do with herself or Fred, of why and how they came to be here, but with grave courtesy he addressed her and her alone.

'Have you eaten lately, Kirsteen?'

What a strange question to ask of her in the middle of this strange meeting. But, of course, he was right. She had eaten little since leaving Ballarat the previous day and part of her light-headed feeling was a combination of the strain of the long journey, their poor night's sleep in the hayloft, and hunger.

'No, we have had very little food since we left Ballarat yesterday.'

'Ballarat, hmph? I thought not,' said Fred's pa. 'Food isn't important to Thomas, here.'

Now this was grossly unfair to poor Fred. 'Oh, no,' she said, as spiritedly as though she were the old Kirstie giving everyone what for and keeping them in order. 'It wasn't Fred's fault. He loves his grub, does Fred. Everyone knows that.'

'He does?' said Fred's pa, his eyebrows rising, his eyes on the blush which spread over Thomas's face. 'I'm pleased to hear it.'

He turned to the clerk who had been watching them, his mouth open. 'Food, then,' he said to him shortly. 'In my room as soon as possible—and plenty of it—we must keep Fred happy. Wine, too, coffee afterwards, and tea,' he said, looking at Kirstie. 'You would like tea?'

'I've never drunk coffee. I think that I'd like to try it.'

That seemed to please Fred's pa. Kirstie couldn't think why. 'Excellent,' he said.

The clerk intervened. 'Food? In your room…? It's not the habit of the management to serve food in guests' rooms.'

'It is if I ask for it,' said Fred's pa serenely. 'Food is always served in my rooms when I order it in hotels which I own.'

The clerk's surprise was as great as Kirstie's.

'You own, Mr Dilhorne?'

'Ask the manager. Food, then?'

Fred's pa obviously made a habit of being short and making arrogant clerks jump about. He turned back again, 'Oh, and the best you can find,' he added. 'Expense no object.'

Then to Thomas and Kirstie, he said, still short, 'Upstairs now. We have a lot to discuss that's best not done in public.'

Kirstie was interested to note that Fred—would she ever be able to think of him as Thomas?—obeyed his pa's orders as rapidly as the clerk was doing. She took his hand before they went upstairs, Fred's pa leading. Thomas looked at his father's straight back. He suddenly felt a surge of affection for him which was almost overwhelming.

How typical of him, he thought, not to be surprised, to take everything in his stride when he found his son, name changed, appearance changed, a new young wife on his arm, and then to exhibit nothing but grave interest, before talking of food as though it were the most important thing in the world! And it was true, his own hunger was fierce; he had grown used to enjoying his food and eating plenty of it.

He remembered that his mother had once told him that

the only time she had seen his father disconcerted was when she had first presented his twin sons to him.

'Mother!' he said urgently to his father. 'How is she? And Lachlan?'

'I thought that you'd never ask,' said Fred's pa gently. 'Very worried when we found that you were missing. She sent me after you. Lachlan was well when I left Sydney. He's changed, of course, since you last saw him.'

Thomas suddenly saw that behind his father's erect stance and iron self-control he was tired and old. He thought—for the first time—I shall not always have him, and I have always taken him for granted.

'A strong woman, my wife,' said Fred's pa to Kirstie. 'Pretty, too. You're like her in many ways—ready to defend Thomas from me, weren't you?'

Kirstie nodded. She was beginning to lose her fear of him a little. When they reached his room she found that it might more properly be described as rooms. In this town, where even a bed for the night was hard to find, Tom Dilhorne had a bedroom and a small living room with a table and armchairs.

He did not press either of them to talk, or to explain anything immediately. He simply saw them sat down before sitting down himself, saying, 'Food first, serious talking afterwards. I gather that you drove in from the gold field.'

Improbably they made small talk. Afterwards Kirstie was to realise how much this had put her at ease and taken Fred off the defensive, so that he sat there, quiet, tiredness written on his face, something his father had plainly seen.

Tom was thinking sadly, even while he put his new daughter-in-law at ease, that he might renounce manipulation and deviousness, but they had no intention of renouncing him.

A servant appeared and laid a white damask cloth on the table. Trays of food were brought in and wine and a large

basket of fruit. They seemed to know what Fred's pa
wanted. Clean white damask napkins were handed round
and knives, forks, spoons and plates. Kirstie watched what
Fred and Fred's pa did with all this magnificence, and then
imitated them. She saw approval in the old man's eyes. He
noted her behaviour—he apparently noted everything.

The food was good and she liked the wine. Fred's pa
handed her a glass of it first and watched her drink it.

'Had any before?'

'No.' Kirstie found herself as short as he was.

'You'll like it. Don't drink too much, though. Not good
for you.'

Fred ate his grub as he had always done. He wolfed
down plenty of it with massive enjoyment of its quality and
delicacy. If he saw his father's ironic eye on him he gave
no sign of it, kissing Kirstie's hand when the meal was
over. His father offered him the bottle of wine questioningly, and he said with a smile, 'Yes, you pour,' before
taking the glass and drinking from it appreciatively.

His father, watching him, merely said, 'You've changed
your mind, then?'

Fred flushed a little and nodded agreement. 'Yes, but I
take very little alcohol these days,' then flushed again because he could grasp the double meaning in what he had
said.

Kirstie put out a hand to pat Fred's proudly. She thought
Fred's pa ought to know the truth about his son.

'He gave up drinking spirits quite a long time ago. He
only takes a little wine occasionally now.'

'Gave up drinking spirits, did he?' said Fred's pa
gravely. 'I'm pleased to hear that, Thomas. I shouldn't like
to think of you drinking spirits.'

For some reason Fred went quite scarlet when Fred's pa
said this, but neither he nor Fred's pa explained why Fred's

pa had looked so amused at what she had said. She thought that explanations would never come.

Finally the servants came and removed their empty dishes and what was left of the food. Fred's pa gave them a message for the clerk about reserving a room for herself and Fred. 'Mr and Mrs Thomas Dilhorne,' he called them. She had never thought to sound so grand.

It was gradually becoming apparent that Fred's pa was a very rich man. She might have guessed that once she had seen his beautiful clothes and the way in which he expected everyone to do as they were told, without argument. Something else struck her. Fred must also be rich. She found the mere idea overpowering and tried not to think about it.

Fred must have seen something written on her face because he put his arm around her. It was his turn to reassure her; having done so, he faced his pa. She realised, quite suddenly, that Fred was afraid of him, and she wondered if either of them knew that. But, of course, Fred's pa knew, he seemed to know everything, and that was why his look at Fred was occasionally a sad one.

Kirstie was not aware that her knowledge of human beings was as surprising in its way as Fred's pa's was, and that Fred's pa had already begun to think that his son's choice of a new wife was not merely the result of his falling in love with a pretty face, but was an attraction for someone who possessed longer-lasting attributes.

'You see, Father,' said Fred, 'you know nothing of the truth of my disappearance and Kirstie doesn't know the full truth of it either, and God knows, it's hard enough to believe. It's a long story, too, but I'll try to keep it down to the essentials.'

He knew that he was talking like the hard businessman he had once been, but he needed to keep the narration of his strange odyssey as emotionless as possible if he were to get through it without breaking down. He looked away from them both while he told them what must have happened to him on the night after he had left Theresa Spurling's home, and of how, as a result of the blows and the forced drinking, he had lost his memory and had ended up living in the streets and gutters of Melbourne as a drunken derelict.

'Not that I can recall very much about that time: it's as though it happened to someone else. I'm not even sure how I reached Ballarat. I only know that I was taken there by a derelict nicknamed Corny—I never did know his real name—but then, I didn't really know anything. He disappeared soon after we arrived in the diggings. And then Kirstie's father, Sam Moore and the rest of his Syndicate rescued me from the nick where I had been taken for begging in what passed for a street in Ballarat.

'After that I worked as a digger for their little Syndicate until I began to earn money of my own and bought into it. I only recovered my memory three days ago, and I've been two men ever since: Thomas Dilhorne and the Fred Waring I've called myself for many months. Fred had forgotten Thomas and everything to do with him.'

He saw his father's amusement at the name he had adopted.

'Yes, Grandfather Fred,' he admitted wryly. 'God knows why that was all I could remember of my old life—a man who had died before I was born, a man whose dissolute life I had always shuddered at. And Kirstie married Fred, not Thomas. Sometimes that worries me, but she's always been so brave that I know that she'll be brave about this too. My only hope is that the Thomas Dilhorne I used to be has disappeared along with Fred. I find myself to be the oddest mixture of the two of them—the best parts, I trust.'

For the moment he passed lightly over his life as a digger, only saying that he had lived like one, enjoying a digger's pleasures. Old Tom had already taken note of his

son's ruined hands and his strongly muscled body—
Thomas was no longer a sedentary businessman.

Thomas dwelt on the goodness of those who had rescued
him and in doing so had brought him back to life again.

'Among them my dearest Kirstie,' he said, hugging and
kissing her again. 'And then I fell in love with her, but
because I was poor simple Fred I didn't fully understand
what was happening to me. It was only when I nursed her
through the fever which struck the diggings that I knew
that my life would be incomplete without her. I think that,
in their different ways, both Thomas and Fred were learning to be human again. When I did recover my memory,
quite accidentally, I thought of you and Mother and Lachlan, and that you must suppose me to be dead since I had
disappeared so long ago.'

His father nodded. 'Yes, I understand why you called
yourself Fred and, yes, we thought you dead. Your assail-
ants pawned your valuables. I have them here.'

Thomas put out his hand. 'All but Bethia's ring—the one
which she gave me when we were betrothed. I forgot everything else, but when I saw it on the thief's finger I knew
that it was mine and that it was precious, although I didn't
know why.'

He stopped, slowly drew off the ring and held it in his
palm. 'You are my wife now, Kirstie,' he said slowly.
'Much though I loved Bethia, she has gone, and I must lay
both her and her ring to rest.'

He picked it up from his palm and kissed it before putting it into his pocket. He did not see his father's approving
face, only Kirstie's and the blazing love on it.

'Lachlan,' she said suddenly. 'Who is Lachlan?'

'Lachlan is my little boy. He must be nearly three years
old now. Bethia died soon after he was born... We had
waited so long for a child and then— I lost her.'

He could speak of her now, and though the grief for her

untimely death was still there, it no longer drove him mad to think of her.

'Oh, Fred, I'm so sorry. No wonder you wanted to forget,' she said impulsively, surprising Fred's pa with her perceptiveness. She turned to him. 'He didn't tell you how he got his memory back. That was the strangest thing of all. It was Lew Robinson who made him remember when he hit him because Fred had had an affair with his wife Annie when he was still so wild about the women when he first came to us. Only he wasn't the father of Annie's baby, because it was half-Chinese.'

Thomas saw his father's knowing eye on him. 'I can understand Lew being unhappy about that,' said Fred's pa gravely.

'Yes,' agreed Kirstie, 'but he shouldn't have taken it out on Fred. He wasn't the only man Annie misbehaved with, and by then Fred had given up running after women for good.'

This artless confidence had Thomas closing his eyes, flushing scarlet again, and wondering what his father was beginning to make of his headlong career in the diggings. Before he could say anything Kirstie roared cheerfully on, trying to persuade his father that his unruly son was a reformed character.

'He changed a lot while he was Fred,' she said earnestly. 'But he still remained happy and carefree. No one was as happy as Fred.'

'One would hardly have said that of Thomas,' murmured his father, trying to avoid his son's embarrassed eye.

'I suppose that I was behaving more like Alan,' said Thomas slowly. 'I always envied him for being so easy. He used to tease me because I was stiff and proper. Loosen up, he used to say, when we were boys, and dance around me as though we were in the ring. I kept remembering that when I was Fred, but not who had said it.'

'But he's not, you know,' said Fred's pa. 'Alan's not easy. You're more alike than you think.'

Thomas put this away to think about later. 'When my memory returned we came here as soon as we could. I'd made a big strike when I was Fred. I thought then that it was riches. But now…' and he shrugged. 'I couldn't tell the Syndicate that. I never told them who I really was. I only left a letter for Sam, Kirstie's pa, telling him the truth, and that Kirstie would be safe and well with me.'

'Oh, but it was riches,' said Kirstie to Fred's pa. 'We all did well that day, but Fred did the best, Pa said, because he worked so hard. Pa said he had a real head on his shoulders when he settled down and began to keep the shop-keepers' books for them.'

'One point of agreement between your father and me, then,' said Fred's pa. 'It is only fair to tell you that Thomas, Fred, is a very rich man, and if he says that to him what he gained in the gold field wasn't riches, then…' He left her to work this out: which she did, rapidly.

'Rich,' she said, rising from her chair, her voice hollow. 'Of course. You must be those Dilhornes. Oh, Fred, I'm not fit to be your wife.'

Her eyes filled with tears. She choked and got no further.

Thomas went over to her and held her in his strong arms. How much he has changed, thought his father, remembering his son's untouchable coldness to everyone and everything after Bethia's death. Thomas's next words confirmed this thought.

'Oh, Kirstie, it is I who am not fit to be your husband.' He stroked her hair and kissed her cheek before gently persuading her to sit down again. His care and love for her were touching.

'You are still my wife, and you are more precious to me now than you were then. You must believe that.'

Her smile was watery, but it was a smile. She offered it

to Fred's pa, too. He sat there watching them, approval of
Fred written on his face. There was no doubt about that.

'You might like to change your clothes, Thomas,' he
said. 'Not that I dislike them, mind. In fact, they suit you
very well. But sooner or later you must be Thomas Dilhorne again and the sooner the easier.'

'You know?' asked Thomas, startled.

'That you hanker after Fred? Yes. It was simpler for you,
I can see that quite well. Life's not meant to be simple,
though. They have your trunks in store, I believe. They
didn't know what to do with them when you failed to turn
up to claim them. While you see about them, I can get to
know Kirstie and she can get used to me.'

Kirstie didn't want Fred to go. She was still a little frightened of his pa, even though she could see Fred in him, and
him in Fred. He had a look in his eye which reminded her
of Fred at his wildest. She wondered what he had been like
when he was young.

Thomas rose reluctantly. 'I don't like to leave her. She's
had a hard time lately.'

'I shan't eat her,' said Fred's pa, and *that look* was in
his eye again.

Thomas left them. He turned at the door to blow her a
kiss. He was wearing the red guernsey which she had knitted for him and his best dark blue corduroys. She supposed
that, if he were rich, guernseys and corduroys were hardly
suitable.

Fred's pa was watching her. 'You love him very much,
don't you?'

'Yes,' she said, colouring a little. 'Very much. He's so
kind. Now, and when he was Fred. At first, when Pa sprang
him from the nick he looked awful, but when we cleaned
him up in the creek—and then, later, when all the women
were wild for him, he looked…'

Kirstie stopped suddenly. The expression on Fred's pa's

face was exactly like that of Fred's when he was at his naughtiest. 'Fred was so like you,' she exclaimed. 'Not in looks, he's so handsome.'

She flushed again. 'I don't mean that you're not…' She broke down and began to laugh helplessly.

'I know what you mean, daughter-in-law. Don't be distressed.' The amusement on his face made it younger. 'Pa rescued him from the gaol, you said.'

'Yes, you see before that he would keep getting drunk, but Geordie, Geordie Farquhar, who used to be a doctor back home in England, helped him to get over that, but then he went in for women and gambling instead. He was so good at cards that they said that he could have earned a living at Hyde's Place. And then, he changed again, quite suddenly. I'm sure that you'll be pleased to know that Fred—'

She looked at Fred's pa, who said kindly, 'Yes, you may call him Fred.'

'That Fred has reformed so much. It will be a relief to you to learn that, as it was to Pa and me after him being so wild, sparring at Fentiman's booth, and joining in all that horseplay with Young Dan'l and chasing after Fat Lil and Rosina Campbell and the others.

'I really thought,' she said earnestly, 'that he would never settle down. But then he discovered that he was good at figures and started to do everyone's books for them. You'll be pleased about that, I think. He became less talkative, too. He was very chatty earlier on.'

'Talkative, chatty, and wild about women, was he? Drinking and gambling, too.'

For some odd reason, instead of this sad recital of sin and shame distressing Fred's pa, it seemed that it pleased and amused him instead!

'Took up with Fat Lil, did he? The local madam, one supposes. Did he satisfy her, d'you think?'

'You're as bad as he is,' said Kirstie, reprovingly, and when he smiled at her, she said, 'You're teasing me, aren't you?'

'Yes, daughter-in-law. Men are inclined to take up with Fat Lils and Rosinas, you know.'

'Yes, I do know that. I haven't lived among men all my life without knowing what they get up to. Particularly in the diggings where they can do as they please. I shouldn't have married him if I hadn't thought that he would settle down. His ma will be pleased to learn that he has, I expect.'

'Surprised, I should say,' murmured Fred's pa to whom these revelations had come as something of a delight. What had his staid and sober eldest son got up to once he had rid himself of the constraints of being Thomas Dilhorne!

'I hope that he'll still be happy now that he's Thomas again,' sighed Kirstie. 'No one was as happy and jolly as Fred.'

Fred's pa's eyebrows rose so high they almost disappeared. 'Now that, I own, does surprise me. I would never have described Thomas as jolly.'

'He was good, though,' said Kirstie defending him again. 'For all that, Fred was good. Even Geordie agreed with me when I told him that. He never hurt anybody. You're not good,' she said, a trifle anxiously. She didn't want to cross Fred's pa.

'No,' he agreed, not offended in the least, thank goodness, for the words had shot out of her before she could stop herself from saying them. 'It's clever of you to see that. I'm not good at all. Thomas is—that's his problem.'

Kirstie nodded thoughtfully. 'I don't mean that you're wicked. You...you...know about people. I shouldn't be telling you all this, but I am. I couldn't lie to you,' she added suddenly.

'I find people do tell me things,' agreed Fred's pa, struck again by his daughter-in-law's perceptiveness.

'No doubt,' said Kirstie repressively, 'and that is one reason why Fred…Thomas is afraid of you.'

'Yes,' said Fred's pa a little sadly, 'but not so much as he was, I think. Being Fred has helped him.'

'And now I am a rich man's wife, which frightens me. Geordie, Geordie Farquhar, said once that life is all about choices, and that when we choose we don't always know where our choices will take us. I thought that I was choosing poor Fred, not rich Thomas,' she said slowly.

'But you will be as successful a wife for rich Thomas, as for poor Fred, I think.'

'I don't know. It's so different, and there's so much to learn. You talk about eating food, not grub, and you say other things differently…' Her voice trailed off.

'Daughter-in-law,' said Fred's pa in a kind voice, quite different from the gently teasing one which he had been using to make her feel at ease, 'I was once so poor that I had nothing, and I lived on the streets of London without a home, and now I am so rich that I cannot count my wealth, and I am Tom Dilhorne still. So long as you are true to yourself, all else is nothing.'

'I can talk to you, Fred's pa,' she said, 'like I could talk to Geordie and to no one else—besides Fred, of course, which should have told me that Fred was different.'

She was remembering that when she had tried to tell the others her inward thoughts they had stared at her uncomprehendingly, so she had stopped. Only Ma had understood.

They sat happily together, talking of life both in and out of the diggings. She told him of Sam and Kate, Bart, Geordie and the kids whom she had had to leave behind her.

'My life now is with Fred, no, Thomas,' she corrected herself. 'My future must be with him.'

The old man thought that his son had brought a treasure

home with him, and the treasure was not the gold in his pocket. It was a treasure which he welcomed and when Thomas returned it was to find his father and his wife laughing together, and at ease.

Chapter Sixteen

Rosina Campbell was on her way to The Criterion Hotel, escorted by an admirer who wanted to be her protector, although she had refused him several times because he thought that he could buy her favours on the cheap. She had tried to shake him off, but he would have none of it. She could only compare him unfavourably with Fred Waring, the lover from whom she had demanded nothing but the joy of being with him.

'May I escort you upstairs?' he asked when they reached the entrance.

'Certainly not,' she returned, comparing him again with Fred, when she had finally driven the importunate fool away before he could so much as enter the hotel lobby.

As though thinking about Fred had conjured him up, she suddenly saw him in his digger's clothes, standing in the reception, his arm around the chit. She was about to advance on them when old Tom Dilhorne came down the stairs. She had a splendid view of the embrace with which Fred greeted him and a thousand thoughts swirled through her mind before she retreated into the shadows so that they could not see her.

A candid admirer had once told her that she was no lady,

but had then added more kindly, 'But you have the instincts of a gentleman.' Alone with Fred and the chit, Rosina would have advanced on them but, seeing the old man whom she had admired, and who had lost his son, but had apparently found him again, she had no wish to spoil his pleasure.

So, Fred Waring had been Thomas Dilhorne, after all. He had denied it so firmly that he had convinced her that he was telling the truth. She would dearly love to know the reason for such a determined masquerade. And the chit? Was she his mistress, or what? Good taste might demand that she keep away from them and never know the truth.

She went up to her room and rested on her bed, consumed with curiosity. Later, changed and dressed to kill, she decided to go downstairs and take a walk before returning to the theatre for the afternoon performance. It was a fortunate decision. Thomas Dilhorne, now dressed *à point*, although his clothes scarcely fitted him, she noticed, stood talking to the clerk.

She advanced on him and struck a pose, her parasol at the end of one extended arm, her tiny muff at the other.

'Mr Thomas Dilhorne, I take it? Or are we plain Fred Waring today? And where is our appendage? I hardly know what name to give her.'

Thomas turned and had the grace to blush. 'Rosie, I never thought to see you here.'

'No, indeed.' She was satiric. 'And what about all those protestations? No, I've never met you before. Oh, no, my name is Fred Waring. Don't call me Tom, Rosie, it isn't flattering.'

Thomas cast an agonised glance at the fascinated clerk. 'Please, Rosie. Don't make a scene here. For my father's sake, if no one else's.'

That disarmed her. She dropped her pose and moved

away, out of earshot. 'Rosie, is it?' she said between her teeth. 'What a practised liar you are—and hypocrite, too.'

'Please listen to me,' he said desperately. 'Believe me, back in Ballarat, I had no idea that I had ever met you before. I was the victim of a brutal attack here, in Melbourne, and recovered as Fred Waring in Ballarat with no memory of having been Thomas, or of having met you. I must apologise for that, even though I was, in essence, innocent of wrongdoing. On the other hand, I must also apologise for my appalling boorishness—I mean when I spoke to you here all those months ago—although it seems like yesterday to me now.'

She stared at him. 'Am I expected to believe this farrago?'

'No farrago, Rosie, it's the truth. Geordie Farquhar and the others could bear witness to it. My memory only returned three days ago.'

There was a chair nearby and she sank into it.

'And you have come back to Melbourne, with Big Sister, I believe you called her.'

'My wife, Kirstie, you mean. Yes.'

'So, I was right about that. She wanted you, and she got you. Well, at least that remarkable old man, your father, will be pleased to have you back. He was desolate, he cares for you so much.'

She was struck by his expression when she said this. 'Didn't you know that, Thomas Dilhorne? You really know very little about anything. I think that I greatly preferred poor Fred, even if he did end up marrying the…Kirsteen. He, at least, knew what he wanted, in bed and out of it. But, Thomas Dilhorne, there was very little to be said for him.'

'I deserve all that,' said Thomas, helplessly. 'I'm sorry, Rosie, for everything.'

'I'm not,' she said vigorously. 'I really enjoyed myself

with Fred. I knew that it couldn't last, I knew it then, and I know it even more now. Let me wish you luck, my dear,' and she leaned forward and kissed him on the cheek. 'And your wife, too. But you've a handful there, my friend. She'll keep you young and lively, I can tell.'

'Stop Thomas Dilhorne from being too much of a prig, you mean.'

'Oh, yes, indeed.'

She rose. 'They will be waiting for you, upstairs, I suppose. I must not keep you.'

'And you,' he said. 'I must wish you lucky, poor Fred would have wanted me to do that. His heart was in the right place.'

'Lucky!' Her laugh was harsh. 'What is lucky, Thomas? I was once like Kirsteen. But I never found a Thomas or a Fred to care for me. Think of me occasionally.'

It was his turn to kiss her cheek, and then she disengaged herself. She dropped him a great curtsy, saying, 'You will be off to Sydney soon, will you not? Goodbye and *bon voyage*, Thomas Dilhorne and may life be kinder to you than it has been to me,' and in a swirl of skirts and scent she walked out of his life.

He returned to find his wife and his father talking as though they had known one another for years. He should not have been surprised by that: he should know his father by now, and that he would see what was in Kirstie and draw her out.

She was laughing and he knew, ruefully, that by now his father would have learned the details of his headlong career in the diggings. But his father loved him, or so Rosina had said—for to know such things was her stock-in-trade—and he was sure that his father would understand and not condemn what he had done when he was heedless Fred, that he had not felt able to do when he was self-righteous Thomas.

Kirstie looked at him and her eyes widened. He was so strange and beautiful and smooth in his fine clothes and his perfectly polished boots. She had seen men like him in Melbourne—if only from a distance—but she had never thought to speak with one, let alone marry him.

Thomas ran his hand around his neckcloth.

'Damned uncomfortable, these clothes,' he said disgustedly. 'What's more, they don't fit me now. I've put muscle on as a result of all that digging.'

He saw his father's amusement when he swore. Thomas never swore. His speech had always been irreproachable.

He sat down, stretching his legs in front of him. 'And these boots, so stiff and tight,' he moaned. He had grown used to the loose and informal clothes of the diggings.

'Oh, Fred, they're beautiful—and you're beautiful, too.'

'Not so beautiful as you are.' He leaned forward and kissed the tip of her nose. Yet another spontaneous gesture with which to surprise his father.

Kirstie kissed him back, their pleasure in each other mutual.

Fred's pa said, with the courtesy which seemed so natural to him, 'Would you be offended, daughter-in-law, if Fred and I spoke alone together for a short time? I have asked the hotel to give you rooms near mine. Fred could take you there, and you might like to rest a little. We shall not be long.'

Kirstie rose, bent down, and kissed the old man's brown cheek. 'I like you, Fred's pa. Even if you still frighten me a little. Of course I shall not be offended.'

She knew, without being told, that he had dismissed Fred to be alone with her, and that he was now arranging matters so that he could speak privately with Fred.

Fred took her to their rooms. They were larger than Fred's pa's. There was a huge bed in the bedroom and a table, armchairs and a sofa in the living room. Someone had brought in flowers, a basket of fruit, and a large pitcher of lemonade and glasses. Their battered little trunk sat forlornly in one corner beside Fred's large and magnificent ones.

She was suddenly awed by all these symbols of her new life and clung to him: everything was so different both from the diggings and the loft where they had spent the night.

Fred knew without being told that she was troubled.

'I'm sorry,' he whispered. 'This must all be such a shock to you. But there was nothing I could do about it. In many ways it would have been easier if I had remained Fred and we had made our lives in the diggings.'

She pushed him away a little, saying, 'Oh, no, Fred, you couldn't have done that! Think of your poor father and mother and your little boy.'

'Yes, you'll like Lachlan, I think. He's such a dear little chap.'

'Yet you forgot him, and everything else. Even *him*.' By him, she meant his father. 'I would never have thought that you could have forgotten him.'

Thomas said slowly. 'I think that I was not only trying to forget myself, but my father as well, because I always felt that I was never quite the son he had wanted. Now, I can see that I was wrong, but then…' He shook his head.

'He told me that he would see that Pa knew that we were safe, and that if Pa and Geordie and the others ever needed any help, he would look after them. He's also going to arrange for a messenger to go to Sydney straight away to tell your poor mother that you have been found, safe and well. He won't tell her about me—he thinks that it will be a pleasant surprise for her when we arrive. Oh, and he thinks that we ought to rest here for a few days before we all go home.'

Thomas's smile was a broad one. 'He looks after everything, doesn't he? It's nice to think that the old devil hasn't lost his touch and is still capable of plotting and scheming.'

But there was no malice in his voice when he said this, as there once might have been, only admiration.

His wife, recognising this, smiled and kissed him good-bye. 'Hurry back, before I eat all the fruit and drink all the lemonade.'

Her parting kiss warming his cheek, Thomas returned to be greeted by his father in his usual dry way which cloaked his deep affection for those about him.

'My dear Fred—I almost think that I prefer to call you Fred—your wife has been telling me how pleased I ought to be that your deplorable penchant for women, drink and gambling has been overcome by a strength of character previously lacking in you.'

Thomas coloured faintly. 'Yes, I must admit that for a time I sowed all the wild oats which I had scrupulously avoided planting in youth.'

'Fun, was it?' asked his father.

Thomas's eyes lit up. 'As I remember it, enormously so—for a short time, anyway. Then it began to pall.'

'It usually does in men of sense. I blame myself a little. Your life has been remarkably short of irresponsibility. You were such an earnest, hardworking child, and then you became an earnest, hardworking man. Bethia's death hit you hard. Your standards were impossibly high, you know. How does it feel to be a sinner?'

'Remarkably better than failing to be a saint. Oh, God, these boots!' He pulled them off, throwing them into the corner, wiggling his toes and stretching his legs.

'That was Fred, I'm afraid. I don't think that I'm ever going to lose him completely.'

'I don't think that Fred ought to be lost,' said his father gravely. 'I doubt whether you would have made such a good choice of a second wife when you were Thomas.'

'I knew you would like her,' said Thomas eagerly. 'Poor stupid Fred almost threw her away. He was nearly as blind as Thomas. She's the biggest prize I brought from the diggings.'

His father nodded in agreement.

'The other prize was the friends I left behind there. I must try to help them—particularly Geordie—without demeaning them, but that's for the future.'

'I suppose you'll be opening up the villa again—now that you've acquired a wife.'

'Oh, yes. The sooner Kirstie has her own home to run the happier she'll be, and the sooner she'll settle down into her new life.'

For the first time he was speaking to his father as to a friend and a companion, without the fear that he might not be the son his father had wanted, and without the rage and pain which had nearly destroyed his life.

Tom Dilhorne surveyed his son, seeing him for the first time in years as a man fulfilled, not tormented with the belief that he was unable to live up to some standard of conduct impossible to achieve, and railing at a fate which he felt had betrayed him.

That son was gone and he, Tom, must learn to live with the new man who had taken his place. He did not think that it was going to be difficult to live with Fred.

Kirstie was sound asleep on the big bed when Thomas returned to their rooms. The kaleidoscope was shifting for Thomas as it had done for Fred. He was now able to read his father correctly and in so doing had come to understand that his early life as Fred in the diggings had justified his father's reading of him before that last dreadful morning.

He sat down by the bed and watched over her. Presently she stirred, put out her hand and said, questioningly, 'Fred?' When he took her hand she sat up, looked wonderingly about her, and said, 'Oh, Fred, I thought that it was all a dream. But it isn't, is it?'

'No.' His voice was gentle. 'I have so much to tell you. You called me Fred, without thinking, and my father thinks I ought to keep that name. Not only to make life easier for you, but because it will mean that I have overcome the sad past.'

He bent his head, put her hand to his lips where she felt his hot tears falling on it. 'Bear with me a little, my heart's darling.'

Proud Thomas Dilhorne—who was now to be Fred—was at last shedding tears for his lost Bethia. The tears he had never been able to shed before: shedding them in the presence of his young wife whose loving kindness was so great that, pulling her hand away, she put her arms around him to comfort him.

'Oh, Fred, what is it, what's wrong?'

'Nothing, my darling. I was crying for the lost past. I was never able to do so before. But it's gone, and I must let it go. We have each other now, and there will be Lachlan when we reach Sydney, and I hope that we shall have children of our own. Never again shall I seek to control my life as I did before I became Fred. We must accept whatever comes to us and try to make the best of it. I know that you are worried because I am most enormously rich, but you must not let that trouble you overmuch. My mother was an even poorer girl than you were when she married my father and they have been very happy together. It will be a new and different life from the one which you thought that you were going to have when you married Fred. You must help me with the responsibilities which I shall inherit, for my father is growing old and, knowing how you managed affairs in the diggings, I have no doubt that you will use those same talents to good effect in Sydney.'

When he had told her of Bethia Kirstie had comforted

him wordlessly, but when she answered him, it was to console him for his loss of her.

'Oh, I'm so sorry, Fred, so sorry. How dreadful it must have been for you. I have only to think of losing you to know how painful it must have been to lose her.'

'Yes, but it's in the past. I hated my father for saying that, but I see now that he was only trying to help me. I can't wait to take you home where there's a whole new world waiting for you, my darling, and a new life to be lived. You won't be like I was and reject the future, will you?'

'No,' she said slowly. 'I can't help being a little frightened though. I'm not a lady.'

'No, Kirstie, that's not true. You're my wife, and the dearest lady of all. Look!'

He put his hand into his pocket and drew out a small screw of white tissue paper. 'I was saving this for our first anniversary, our first six months together, but I think that you deserve it now. Just after we were married I had it made from the gold I found in my first big strike.'

Fred handed the paper to her, and Kirstie unwrapped it slowly, her shining eyes moving from it to his expectant, watching face before she held up what she had found inside it. It was a gold chain of the finest workmanship with a pendant heart hanging from it. The heart was really a locket, which, when it was opened, revealed the following words inscribed inside it.

For my heart's darling, Fred.

'That's what you are, Kirstie,' he whispered into her ear as he hung the beautiful thing around her neck.

'My heart of gold, Kirstie, my selfless heart of gold.'

* * * * *

MILLS & BOON®

Makes any time special™

Copyright © Harlequin Enterprises Limited 1997
All rights reserved

Mills & Boon publish 29 new titles every month. Select from...

Modern Romance™   Tender Romance™

Sensual Romance™

Medical Romance™   Historical Romance™

MAT2

FREE!

2 Books
and a surprise gift!

We would like to take this opportunity to thank you for reading this Mills & Boon® book by offering you the chance to take TWO more specially selected titles from the Historical Romance™ series absolutely FREE! We're also making this offer to introduce you to the benefits of the Reader Service™ —

★ FREE home delivery
★ FREE gifts and competitions
★ FREE monthly Newsletter
★ Books available before they're in the shops
★ Exclusive Reader Service discounts

Accepting these FREE books and gift places you under no obligation to buy; you may cancel at any time, even after receiving your free shipment. Simply complete your details below and return the entire page to the address below. *You don't even need a stamp!*

YES! Please send me 2 free Historical Romance books and a surprise gift. I understand that unless you hear from me, I will receive 4 superb new titles every month for just £2.99 each, postage and packing free. I am under no obligation to purchase any books and may cancel my subscription at any time. The free books and gift will be mine to keep in any case.

H0ZEB

Ms/Mrs/Miss/Mr ....Initials....................................
BLOCK CAPITALS PLEASE

Surname..

Address..

....

....Postcode ....

Send this whole page to:
UK: The Reader Service, FREEPOST CN81, Croydon, CR9 3WZ
EIRE: The Reader Service, PO Box 4546, Kilcock, County Kildare (stamp required)

Offer not valid to current Reader Service subscribers to this series. We reserve the right to refuse an application and applicants must be aged 18 years or over. Only one application per household. Terms and prices subject to change without notice. Offer expires 31st May 2001. As a result of this application, you may receive further offers from Harlequin Mills & Boon Limited and other carefully selected companies. If you would prefer not to share in this opportunity please write to The Data Manager at the address above.

Mills & Boon® is a registered trademark owned by Harlequin Mills & Boon Limited.
Historical Romance™ is being used as a trademark.